CW00447415

To/ Karen,

Fangs for your support
and friendship.

Hugs,

Tessa Valis

— x —

Neen.

Eyes Open by T.Valis

Copyright © 2016 by T.Valis

ISBN: 978-1533389244

Dedication: There are many people I need to thank here. Family and friends for their support on my journey to write this (Gael, Claire and Lins to name a few). My husband Bill and my kids Gabe and Rosey for giving me the time and space to actually get my head down. Thank you to the wonderful authors who I've read and have let me be a part of their world, your work inspired me to keep chasing my dream and trusting my journey.

I also wish to thank Joanne for her support and working on her book blog, loves you hun.

Thank you to Atlanta and "Christian" for all the additional help and support they've given me to make this whole thing become a real book. Paro, I love you for introducing us.

Thank you to Amy Halter for also giving my book the once over and helping me out.

Thank you to Stacey Broadbent for helping me by finding all my typos and for being a great support.

Thank you to all of my ARC readers.

Also a massive thanks to everyone who has had faith in me and no matter how negative I've been, have constantly encouraged me to keep going. Because of all of you, this is now a reality and it's proving to be one heck of a journey.

My beautiful book cover was made by Dokeshi's Book Services. I adore it.

Contents

Prologue

It all started one balmy evening. I'm not sure what inspired it, the realisation just came to me in a moment of sheer clarity. One person can make a difference, no matter how small, a visible difference can be made. Now, this brings into play the sides of good and evil. That difference can be life changing and it is up to that individual if the change is going to be positive or negative. It all comes down to that split second decision in the moment and then the path is chosen, the fork forever lost in the veils of time, the act set in motion. Although in some theories this event can be revisited via time travel the consequences and results will never be the same, something is always subtly similar.

What is evident in all life is that there are many forces at play in the universe and all in a multitude of shades of grey. Very few forces that exist can be categorised as good or evil as most and many can play both sides of that field. Pain can be a route to a stronger sense of self and achieving goals you never knew you could. It can provide a twisted form of pleasure when properly applied and without it we wouldn't know the relief of the lack of it, or what true joy is. With no reference point you can never truly confess to understanding and experiencing something. Likewise pleasure and joy can become a vice. You become greedy, wanting to experience it more and more frequently to a higher and higher level. You can become all consumed and obsessed by it. The pursuit of one's own pleasure can lead to the pain and suffering of others or worse if it is allowed to reach a vice like level. It also means that the higher you are the further you have to fall and the aspect of pain brings you crashing to a halt as you lose everything you'd strived so hard to accomplish.

So with this in mind, everything we do, say, think and feel must be micromanaged on some hidden level. People are shades, none are one thing nor another and many take delight in changing sides' dependant on their own mood. This ever changing field of play is what makes the weave of life so interesting. Everyone, no matter how small they think their part is, makes massive changes on the chess board of life. The school yard bully takes delight in torturing another child. The bully may go on to continue their ways or they might discover humility in later life and make amends for the sins of the past. The bullied child may go on to live in fear and have no life or they could use that inner strength as a fuel to propel themselves further in life so that they are never found in that weakened position again.

In this world of opposites where love can lead to hate and hate can lead to love, sometimes the sheer confusion of life can drive a person mad. Occasionally it is that madness that can keep people sane. Chaos leads to a need for order and an oppressive government descends the whole of society into chaos of anarchy and rebellion. Occasionally, leading to rebirth.

It was this realisation on that evening that, I believe, lead me to Carter Brams.

Chapter 1

I looked into my cold cup of tea and gently blew on the surface watching the skin that had formed on top of the liquid as it slowly drifted like the wake of some invisible tiny ship in my tea cup.

"Crap" I thought. "Have I been waiting here that long?"

I turned to look about me at the other tables in the coffee shop. Sure enough all of the bodies at the tables were unfamiliar and different. Not one person remained from the time I'd entered the establishment. I looked behind the counter and it seemed that even the staff had changed shift in my absence of awareness. The sweet young barista who had been coming over to check if I needed anything else on an almost hourly basis was no longer behind the counter and instead there was a tall, muscular looking young man. Mid 20's I'd have guessed. I slid my glasses back up my nose as I closed over my book and could now read the name on his lapel badge. Marcus.

Marcus obviously wasn't a "people person" as he ushered another employee from the back to clear the tables and check on the other customers. A sickly looking teenager was thrust out from behind the counter wearing a coffee stained apron. He was limply holding a tray in one hand while he brushed back his long floppy blonde fringe with the other. His name badge was only just visible in the folds of the apron, which looked about 2 sizes too big and was pinned crookedly on. Dean.

Dean awkwardly busied himself in the café, clearing tables and checking on the other customers at the other tables. He didn't come near my table until he had dealt with literally every other table in the place. I was just placing my glasses back into their caramel brown case as he nervously approached me.

"Is everything ok." he asked with a slight squeak in his voice. Obviously he was slightly younger than I had previously thought. Work experience perhaps? Or possibly it had just been a rough shift.

I looked up at him from under my eyelashes hoping that the blue of my eyes was noticeable. Their striking colour in the right lighting had on occasion granted me wonders.

"Yes thank you. My tea would appear to be otherwise though" I commented nudging the cup so the surface skin rippled and moved.

For a moment Dean just stared blankly at me. I was pretty sure I'd just spoken in English, but perhaps not. On occasion my mouth and brain do not agree and what I think I said were not actually the words uttered by my mouth. Suddenly Dean snapped to life, a slight spark in his eyes.

"Oh no, that's terrible! Would you like another cup? There's nothing worse than when a good cuppa goes cold."

That was the start of my path with Dean, which had an interesting development, but we can get to that later.

I ordered a pot of tea in the hope that a teapot would increase the chances of my beverage staying warmer for longer. Dutifully Dean tottered back off to the kitchen, with his tray load of cups and saucers, to collect it for me. As he disappeared behind the counter and out of my sight completely I heard the slight ding of the doorbell behind me as a new patron entered the shop. I turned to my left to be greeted with the sight I had waited so long in this establishment to see. Casually the new patron sauntered up to the counter where Marcus dutifully snapped to attention to serve his new customer.

I wasn't stalking this person, although having spent several hours waiting to see him in his alleged "regular" coffee spot you'd have been forgiven for thinking that. Finally I could see what all the fuss was about. For weeks a few of my friends had been insisting on their online blogs that they'd seen a man who made the statue of David look fugly. I found this claim so ridiculous that I had to prove to myself they were insane. So today, on my afternoon off, I decided to grab a book and sit in this little coffee shop, aptly named the Coffee House, and satisfy my curiosity. With the amount of hype around this guy I was almost certain I'd be disappointed. With few exceptions the hype is never worth the end result.

In this case however I had been very wrong. The man standing at the counter had almost every serving girl behind the counter peeking out from the kitchen area. Even some of the male staff were staring in awe. It wasn't his looks that were getting to me though, despite the fact he stood over 6 and a half foot tall, had strikingly masculine features and some of the longest, well-conditioned hair I've ever seen on a man. It was the feeling, or vibe if you will, that I was sensing. Something about him seemed to draw your attention no matter what you did. If you looked away you got that "hairs on the back of your neck" feeling like someone was watching you. I tried to look out of the window to avoid staring like everyone else but something kept drawing my gaze back to him, not that he wasn't pleasant to look at. He was tall, dark haired with a braided pony tail that extended most of the way down his back. He was wearing faded jeans and a well-worn looking brown suede jacket but somehow had this air of sophistication about him. Now I've read a few romance/erotic novels in my time and this man was no Mr Romance but yet, there was still something about him.

I was snapped out of my trance by Dean who dutifully had brought me my fresh pot of tea.

"There we go Ms, a fresh brew to keep the chill out. The wind has picked up out there now." he said shyly motioning to the window. He was right in his observations. Many people were being buffeted about the street outside as the wind had picked up and droplets of rain were now appearing on the Coffee House windows.

I turned back and looked at Dean with a warm smile. I thought I saw him blush slightly.

"Thank you Dean. You're a star."

"No problem Ms, all part of the job." he smiled and puffed his chest slightly as he was filled with pride at the job well done. Finally, I thought, someone who cares about customer service over profit!

"Please, call me Kira" I smiled "I think I will be frequenting this place a lot more often."

His grin grew and the blush in his cheeks deepened.

"Anything else I can get you?" he offered.

"Actually" I started, I looked up at him shyly through my eyelashes as I gently bit my lower lip to get his full attention "I would love a caramel slice if there are any left?"

"I think the case is empty but I know where there are extra slices through the back." he exclaimed before bouncing off towards the kitchen like a gazelle.

I smiled to myself. I shouldn't really flirt with anyone, I don't have the looks for it and definitely not the confidence, but just sometimes I like to chance my luck, especially where cake might be involved. That was when I noticed that Mr tall dark and pony tailed had taken a table not far from mine with his coffee and what looked like a slice of cheesecake. *Hmmm*, I thought to myself, *I don't remember seeing cheesecake in the case either*. Then again, this was his regular spot, perhaps he knew something I didn't.

I watched as he confidently got up out of his seat for a moment and paced quietly over to the large black bookcase on the wall about 10 feet from where I was sitting. I gingerly poured myself a fresh cup of tea, painfully aware that I was all the while watching him from the corner of my eye.

He stood for a moment with one arm folded across his chest, the other hand gently stroking the slight stubble on his masculine, square chin as he perused the contents of the book case. He hesitated a few times, gently raking his hand across the top of his head, messing the braid a little, before taking a small paperback from the shelf. I couldn't see the title as he tucked the book under his arm. Just as he turned on his heels to return to his table, his smart black boots squeaking on the varnished wooden floor slightly, Dean returned and proudly presented my caramel slice with a napkin and cake fork.

"There we are Ms.......Kira. It's the last one from the back. I bribed Sophie for it." he beamed.

"Who's Sophie and what did you bribe her with?" I asked in a hushed voice, my eyebrow raised slightly in interest. I could feel the cheeky smirk playing at the corner of my lips.

Before I could get an answer Dean scuttled off as if he'd seen a ghost. His eye line had been just beyond my shoulder before he pulled his startled rabbit act. A small shiver worked its way down my spine.

I felt the electricity in the air before I felt the large hand touch my shoulder. A deep, rich voice echoed softly in my left ear as a voice asked "Where did you manage to get a caramel slice?"

I turned sharply with surprise and came nose to nose with the most chocolate brown eyes I'd ever seen. Abruptly I adjusted my position removing my nose from his. My mind was scattered for a moment as I thought of all the smutty comments and compliments my friends had blogged about this man and now I was seeing it first-hand. Logical scoffed from her corner of my mind, flipping the pages of her book to return to the correct page. *Typical pretty boy player.* Dreamy was tilting her head slightly, her eyes half closed and glazed with fascination. I could feel her trying to reach out towards him from inside my mind. Her curiosity mingling with my own. Quickly my synapses fired back into action as I compiled my retort.

"I could ask the same about your cheesecake, Sir." I retorted, my voice sounding husky and sultry as it broke slightly.

He smiled slightly as he rose to his full height once more. "I have a friend who bakes the cakes for this place. They always save me a slice. It's a perk of being an almost daily patron." he boldly proclaimed.

"Ah, well my caramel slice was gained through less honest means." I admitted shyly, the smirk returned, playing at the corners of my mouth. Dreamy was relishing the ongoing drama in front of her and she perched on the edge of her seat awaiting my next move.

At this he raised a dark eyebrow and placed a hand on his hip. The paperback slid out from under his arm and slapped the wooden floor with its paper cover. I heard a quiet "damn it" from under his breath. Seizing my moment I quickly bent down and retrieved the fallen book. It's slightly bent cover and dog eared pages felt warm to my touch. I didn't recognise the cover but I knew the book.

"You like fantasy novels?" I queried as I passed the book back to him.

He suddenly paled slightly and tucked the book quickly under his arm. I realised that I had possibly insulted him and moved to correct my mistake.

"I mean he writes novels about other realms doesn't he? I have a friend who has read them all. He told me about all of the worlds and their mystical races. Quite a good escape I've been told."

At this correction the colour returned to his face and his eyes sparkled under the muted lights of the Coffee House.

"You know about Angel Lost?" he asked softly, his voice almost a whisper.

"A little" I shrugged "Only what Scott has told me. I know about the citadel, the Empress and the vampires but not much more than that. He has never gone into story lines in case I read them one day."

"You've never read them then?" His disbelief apparent in both his expression and the tone of his voice.

I bowed my head a little in guilt and shook it slowly dislodging a strand of my hair from its tight bindings. Before I could move to tuck it back in his hand was at my cheek gently tucking the wayward strand of brown hair behind my ear. Dreamy almost squealed like a school girl. Logical looked up, tutted loudly and returned to reading her book.

"You are truly missing out on some extra ordinary story telling." he explained as he quickly collected his plate and cup from his table and to my surprise brought them over to mine.

"May I sit?" he motioned to the chair next to mine. Hastily I lifted my bag from the chair to allow him to sit and to my horror it tipped sideways and spilled most of its contents onto the floor beneath the table.

"Shit!" I muttered under my breath as I quickly dove under the table to retrieve my belongings. As I lifted my head while on all fours I realised he'd dived under the table to help me and was holding my well-thumbed copy of Fifty Shades of Grey on one hand and my note book in the other. I grabbed my pen and purse from the floor and sat back up at the table. Silently but with watchful eyes he passed me the two books and I hurriedly stuffed them back into my bag. I could feel the scarlet in my cheeks as I took a long hard gulp of forgotten tea. Dreamy was holding both hands over her mouth and was a deep shade of fuchsia. I couldn't tell if she was embarrassed or about to die laughing. Logical merely lowered her book to roll her eyes. When I had regained some composure and placed my bag safely on the floor next to my chair I looked back to him. He was smiling at me with an almost knowing look in his eyes. I tilted my head quizzically to the side at his expression.

"Surely you know that everyone on the planet has read this book?" I snapped almost defensively.

"I won't argue that Mr Grey has done wonders for the love lives of many people as well as brightening the days and nights of bored housewives." he quipped almost tongue in cheek.

My mind started to drift slightly to thoughts of that tongue but abruptly I pulled myself together.

"That's a little unfair. It's not just housewives."

We both began to laugh at the ridiculousness of our conversation which had started with one sort of fantasy and lead to another. Mid laugh he interrupted.

"By the way, my name is Carter, Carter Brams."

"Charmed." I said holding out my hand to shake his "I'm Kira Jansent."

I almost jumped at the touch of his hand, it was so warm and firm. His skin was almost searing and yet so soft.

Our conversation over books continued while we both finished our cakes and beverages. We discussed everything from chick-lit to sci-fi, horror and romance. I couldn't remember the last time I'd had such an engaging conversation with a guy over books. The exception to this was Scott, however, playing for the other team rendered him in the neutral and the fact he was my housemate practically made him a eunuch.

Dean came over to our table to collect our dishes and I noticed that all the other tables were empty and only a few staff remained cleaning the floors and tables.

"Sorry to interrupt Kira, Mr Brams, but we are closing up now. Are you both finished?" he stuttered shyly while lifting my used napkin onto his tray.

Carter looked up at Dean and swiftly in one graceful movement ascended to his feet. He paced over to the book case and replaced the paperback and quickly gave the shelf a tidy before answering.

"I guess we are now Dean, if it's closing time."

Dean looked at his feet as he shuffled uncomfortably with the tray.

"By the way" Carter added "Did you offer Sophie a night out for that caramel slice."

My gaze immediately snapped to Carter. I stopped fiddling with the contents of my bag on the table. How did he know about Sophie and the caramel slice? Had he been eavesdropping earlier?

"Yes Sir." Dean muttered quietly his cheeks turning scarlet with embarrassment.

Carter beamed and let out a haughty laugh before taking some pieces of paper from his pocket and placing them on the table.

"You'd better take these then." he offered warmly "She'll be wanting something classy."

I was taken aback at this gesture and slightly confused. My "spider sense" was tingling, how did he know Sophie, know what she liked? Did they date? Was that why Dean was the colour of a scalded cat? Why did it even concern or bother me? A sudden feeling of unease washed over me like I was missing something, something important. I shrugged the feeling aside for now and lifted a note from my purse and gently placed it on Dean's tray.

"That's for my pot of tea and caramel slice, which was heavenly." I smiled reassuringly at him.
"I am in your debt Dean and as a new regular patron I will return this kindness. Oh and the change is a tip."

Watching our exchange Carter was looking quizzically from Dean to myself and back again. Perhaps he was pondering the same questions and his "spider sense" was tingling.
We lifted our belongings and headed to the exit. Dean called after us with a hearty "Good night and thank you."

As we stood outside on the cold street, the wind battering along the road I looked up at Carters face. He was looking down at me with a look of sheer gut twisting torment.
"What's wrong?"
He once again ran his hand along the top of his head pulling gently at his hair and loosening the braid.

"I feel like I should offer dinner or a trip back to my place, but I'm not sure how you would take it." he answered very carefully.

Knowing full well that real life is not a fantasy novel and things never work out like that I smiled shyly and took his hand. Dreamy and Logical began to argue between themselves about which would be better for me and what would be safer. I hushed them and took a deep breath to centre my thoughts again.
"While I appreciate the offer Mr Brams and this afternoon, now evening has been very enlightening with your literary opinions I do have a home to go to. I also make it a personal point not to go home with strange men I meet in coffee houses." I smiled sarcastically and licked my lips waiting for his reply.

"Do you find me strange Ms Jansent?" he quipped back.

I took a few paces backwards into the lane down the side of the coffee house before I answered to give dramatic effect.
"I honestly don't know you well enough after one chance meeting to say if you are or not Mr Brams. Perhaps our paths will cross again?"

He began to follow me down the lane and I started to fear I'd made a bad choice choosing this route back to my car.

Gently he placed his hand on my shoulder and handed me a small card. I almost yelped at his touch. The static in my ears was almost deafening and the heat of his skin could be felt beneath my layers of clothing. The card had his name and mobile number on it.

"If I can't convince you for a drink tonight, perhaps another time?" he smiled softly and with the depth of feeling in his deep brown eyes I melted a little.

"Thank you Mr Brams. I will consider your offer and respond accordingly." I replied cheekily, blushing slightly at my own sarcasm.

"You have 2 days Kira. I'm due to head across the country this weekend for business." he answered in a warning tone. I jumped a little at the new gruffness in his voice. It sent a shiver of both apprehension and excitement through me. No one had ever tried to command me like that in my adult life. I wasn't sure if I felt insulted or stimulated.

I nodded and turned to continue walking down the lane. I noted there were no footfalls echoing my own, although over the howl of the wind it was hard to tell. I briefly turned to see a car pull up outside the coffee house and Carter climbed into the back and it sped off.

That, I thought to myself, was the most unusual coffee pick up I've ever encountered and I've read a lot of weird and wonderful stories in my time! Dreamy was sitting clapping her hands together in excitement while Logical had let her glasses slide down to the tip of her nose and was positively glowering at me. *No. Don't even think about it. This is how all those tragic stories begin. Girl meets guy, guy woos her and takes her away them BLAMO!* Dreamy stuck her tongue out childishly at Logical to make her shut up.

I turned the corner at the bottom of the lane onto the adjacent street and located my car under the bright glare of a street light. I climbed in, turned on the ignition and clipped in my seat belt as the gentle tones of Savage Garden played over the radio. I sang along quietly as I started the drive out of the city centre to home.

Chapter 2

"Oh my God!" squealed Jenny as she danced around the office holding the business card. "Carter Brams, THE Carter Brams and you had coffee with him!"

I nodded removing the card from her waving hand and tucked it back into my pocket.

"I need to take more days off and hang out in coffee shops." she sighed looking wistfully off into the distance and stroking the pot plant on my desk.

"He's the guy my friends have been blogging about online. The one who's hotter than Adonis." I explained, rolling my eyes slightly at the implication of a mythical beauty. I gently moved Gary the pot plant out of her reach and adjusted his pot.

Jenny suddenly snapped me a sharp look while adjusting her glasses on the bridge of her nose. "You don't know who he is do you?"

I shrugged slightly as I opened another window on my computer and began entering the data from the paper copy spreadsheet in front of me.

"Dang it girl. That's what google is for. You went out hunting for some hot guy you thought was imaginary and you didn't google him first?" she practically squawked at me. She was starting to sound a little like Logical who was nodding in agreement with what Jenny was saying.

"I didn't even know he was real, let alone his name until yesterday afternoon!"

"Girl, for someone so bright, you can be thick as a plank sometimes. Running off to find some random guy without doing your research. You could have ended up on crime watch. But joking aside, you honestly have no idea who you've met?"

Dreamy was staring off in her own little world at the memory of tall, dark and handsome.

A silly schoolgirl grin spread across my face as I shook my head at her, infuriating her further. She opened her mouth to give me more of a slagging off when she was cut short by our boss. He'd left his office and was standing in our open plan space.

"Kira, can I see you in my office right now please?"

I got up out of my seat and headed towards him.

"Sure."

I turned back to see Jenny signalling that this conversation wasn't over as she went back to her desk. I was in hot water once I got out of my bosses office for sure.

I sat in front of his heaped desk. Stacks of paper littered with post-it notes were piled almost as high as his head.

They were everywhere, on the desk, on the floor and on the small filing cabinet in the corner of the room. A lonely coat stand stood behind the door, naked except for one small, thin cotton jacket.

Irritated, he began to search through the mounds of deforestation on his desk. He grunted as he trawled through the piles until he pulled out a booklet of stapled pages with highlighted sections.

He stood beside me and thumped the papers down in front of me with such force that he almost toppled the entire load.

"Can you explain this Miss Jansent?" he snorted at me with disgust as he crossed his arms and took a step back from me.

I looked down at the booklet in front of me. They appeared to be a series of emails, but they were from my address and I hadn't sent them.

I nervously picked up the document and began to read through it. Pages and pages of conversation between my email address and some external companies detailing some of our companies plans for expansion and mergers with other departments. I had only been privy to some of this information but news grows legs in open plan offices and everyone knew all the plans via word of mouth.

Logical kicked me hard to snap me back to reality. My boss was accusing me of emailing company secrets.

I turned and looked up at him through my glasses.

"I didn't send these!" I protested, my voice cracking a little as I could feel where this was headed.

His expression softened slightly but the cold steel of his stare remained in place.

"This is your email address Kira" he explained "The time stamps are all from nights where you stayed late to complete tasks so there was no one here to vouch for you."

I nodded solemnly.

"I know it looks bad sir." I started but he raised his hand to signal me to stop.

"It's no longer in my hands." he sighed deeply as he shook his head. "The managers upstairs have decided to fire you and my hands are tied. I can't prove your innocence Kira. The evidence is too damning."

"But my job?" I started to sob slightly.

My boss gently tapped me on the shoulder in a comforting gesture that merely came across as condescending. I inhaled deeply and pushed back the tears as I tried to fathom where this attack could have come from. I had no rivals in my department. I'd happily worked here for several years busting my ass for this company and my department.

"It's out of my hands." explained my boss as he lifted an empty archive box and passed it over to me.

"You should be grateful they aren't suing you for damages for leaking secrets. They've agreed to just let you go. You'll be paid until the end of the month."

"Don't I get to defend myself?" I almost whined.

My boss silently handed me the box and motioned me towards the door.

I rose from my seat and made my way slowly towards the door back out into the open plan part of the office. As I raised my hand to turn the handle my boss began to speak. I stared blankly at the door as I listened, my hand still on the handle.

"And you can't go for unfair dismissal Kira. They will drag you through hell for that. You will end up getting sued."

"Yes Sir." I exhaled as my shoulders slumped forwards, defeated.

As I opened the door I hastily pulled myself together. I

quickly wiped my eyes removing any trace of tears, repositioned my glasses and straightened my posture. I scanned the office as I stood for a moment in my boss' doorway. Who could have done this to me and why? I looked at the faces of these people I'd worked side by side with for years. Did I truly know any of them? That was a truly sobering thought and with that in the back of my mind causing a row between Logical and Dreamy I trudged back to my desk.

Once at my desk, I began cleaning it out. I saw Jenny stand from her desk to come and help me but our boss standing over me watching as I packed was enough to make her retake her seat. I quickly risked pinging her an IM, making out I was closing out of the excel sheet I'd been working on.

I'll explain later, I've been fired. I have to be out of here immediately. Please look after Gary.

Her reply was immediate and thankfully my pc was on silent.

Gary is safe with me. Talk soon.

I was packing my archiving box when I was told I had ten minutes before security would escort me out and I could make any calls I needed to make to get safe passage out of the building. I placed my office crockery and cutlery into the box along with a few personal items and pictures I'd kept on my desk. I lifted the office phone and called Scott, the only person I could think of to help me in my time of great need. Our house phone went to answer machine and his mobile went to a pre-set answer that he was in a meeting. That could mean anything from an actual work meeting to sneaking out early for lunch and donuts from the local indoor market. Dang it, now who was I going to call?

I went into my desk drawer one last time to retrieve my small first aid kit tin which housed all the medications I would ever need, pain killers, anti-histamines the usual. As I stood up to place the tin in my box the business card Carter had given me the night before fell out of my pocket and landed on my desk. Insanity gripped me, I was in a panic. I needed someone to be with me right now before I totally collapsed in on myself and I lifted the phone and dialled the number.

A gruff voice answered sharply "Brams".

"Erm, hi, it's Kira. We met last night at the coffee house. I know this is out of the blue and totally unreasonable but I have no one else to turn to right now and I was wondering..."I started to sob slightly.

He interrupted me before I could finish. His voice was softer and more like the man I had spoken with at length the previous evening.

"Where are you?"

"I'm at work." my voice began to crack as I felt the tears building "The large office on the corner of Moss and Howe."

I managed to get those last words out before the tears filling my eyes started to run down my heated cheeks as I could feel my boss' eyes on my back. I could sense his expression of complete contempt without even having to face him.

My voice came out as a small whispered squeak. "Security are escorting me out in 5 minutes and I need..."

He interrupted me again, with more dominance in his voice.

"I'll be there in two." The phone clicked as he hung up.

Fighting back the now floods of tears I was biting my tongue as I finished packing and tried to regain my professional composure.

What the hell was I doing! Asking a complete stranger to come and pick me up immediately after getting fired. Then again, it was no fault of mine that this was even happening. I felt like I'd just been cast down the rabbit hole and I wasn't sure if wonderland was my destination or hell. I just knew I had to escape and I had to do it with dignity or that was the plan. Dreamy was agreeing with me wholeheartedly, she felt hurt by this whole thing too and knew I needed someone to comfort me right now. Logical would have argued the point with me, but she was too busy hastily trying to figure out who it could have been that sabotaged me. Who else had been in the building those nights and knew I was there? Or who had access to the swipe passes and knew when I'd logged in and out?

As I lifted the box containing the last several years of my career and turned off my computer terminal with my other hand. I started to walk out of the cubicle section of our open plan office when the adjoining office door opened. Out stepped the last person I wanted to see. Maria Miller, head of accounting. She had made my life hell, blaming her mistakes on me and trying to make me look bad any time I picked up on her mistakes before I entered the data into the system for our team to work with. Bitch had a cold streak a mile wide and anyone who didn't pander to her will faced that cold streak. Everyone knew how she got her position and it wasn't for her brains and lack of accounting knowledge but everyone bent to her will because her husband was head of the company. Talk about sucking up to your boss, she did it literally and that's how her affair had landed her a promotion and a new marriage into the deal. I hated her with a passion but as I was now unemployed she was no longer my issue. I could finally take my leave of her. A flash of inspiration blazed across my mind but was quickly quelled. There's no way it could have been Maria that did this to me. She lacked the brains but more importantly she lacked the IT access to find out about the swipe passes. Much as I despised the woman, this hadn't been her doing and part of me hated her even further for that.

"Kira..." she called after me as I decided to dive out the nearest exit that was as far from her as possible. I almost made it until she finished her sentence.

"The IT boys will be sad their little geek girl is leaving. So unfortunate you won't be here for the company night out. I was looking forward to watching your pathetic attempt at being a lady for one night"

I tried to resist it, the burning urge to turn right there and then and gouge her eyes out but her remark had cut deep. I had been secretly worrying about the upcoming company dinner and how I would fare. I'm not the most social of women and am actually quite awkward when it comes to behaving like a lady. I can be polite and flirty when the nerve takes me but I've never described myself as a typical girly girl, or confident.

It was no secret in the office that she hated me with a passion because unlike her I was actually good at my job. What I lacked in personal confidence I made up for in professional confidence, but this display of venom was very unlike her. Mean emails implying I was crap at my job and should stay at home and play video games was her norm, but actually slagging me in public. I must have really done something to get under her skin this time.

I had to think quickly, I was now balancing 3 crisis at once (unemployment, asking a stranger for help and now my public stoning) and it was quickly escalating.

I turned, gripping my archive box like grim death in an attempt not to throw anything in her general direction. My eyes were aflame and I let the venom fill my mouth as I focused all my frustration and anger from months of built up rage erupted out of my mouth.

"This little geek girl might not be very good at playing a lady but at least I can admit to it. Sadly I won't be able to make the dinner, I will miss the snide little snipes I hear in the ladies room about you. But then again, there are only so many times you can hear the story about how your Dyson mouth landed you both a promotion and a husband. Sounds to me like his ex had a lucky escape and now so am I."

I turned sharply on my heels, swiped my pass and pushed the exit door for the last time.

I hurriedly walked through the canteen and to the front desk. Catriona was on reception today. She looked at me with complete shock, her pale blue eyes wide as I tossed my ID badge and pass at her as I ran towards the front door. Tears were now streaming down my face and my mascara was smudged. I must have looked like some sort of nightmarish panda. Catriona stood to yell after me, her face contorted in a look of both compassion and confusion, but I was already half way through the revolving doors.

I was trying to hold on to what little shreds of dignity and restraint I had left when I suddenly realised that I was stuck. I was holding the box sideways and it was jammed in the revolving door. Shit! I pushed the box a little harder being careful not to slip and jam my fingers, the last thing I needed to add to my list was a trip to A & E. It wasn't budging.

Taking what little patience I had left and securing it in my mind for later sanity I gave one more push and the box was free. Unfortunately with the laws of physics a little momentum goes a long way and momentum once freed has a habit of continuing onwards. I flew out of the revolving door and was dragged forward about 5 feet when my heel clipped a paving stone and I pitched forwards, flipped completely and landed beside my box, which unfortunately for me had landed on its side and tipped its contents over the path in front of me.

I bowed my head, finally defeated by shame, anger and frustration I had nowhere else to go but let the sadness wash over me. I was now unemployed, black marked for employment, alone and sitting on the concrete like an ass, crying. I closed my eyes and began to sob uncontrollably.

Within moments I felt a hand on my shoulder and a newly familiar voice in my ear.

"You ok? I got here as fast as I could but there's nothing much you can do about those damn traffic lights"

I opened my eyes and looked directly into those deep pools of caramel and for a moment I forgot everything, I felt reassured somehow. The logical side of me was arguing with the dreamy creative side that this was not sensible but the spike of electricity that I felt run from my shoulder right the way through me argued otherwise. Dreamy stuck her tongue out resiliently whilst screaming "your argument is invalid" and logical me slunk back into her subconscious gloom.

I blinked and he was gone, then he was there in front of me, picking up my belongings and gently placing them back into the now righted box. It only took him moments and he was helping me to my feet. I staggered a little like a new-born calf finding its feet as I realised that in the fall my left heel had snapped.

"Shit!" I wailed "Pardon my language! These were my favourite pair."

Carter motioned to me to wait a moment as he vanished off with my box and reappeared a moment later.

"Well I've checked the car and I definitely don't have a spare pair in there, however, I have made alternative arrangements for you." he smiled a slight chuckle in his voice.

I opened my mouth to speak when he suddenly whisked me off my feet and carried me off down the car park.

"Hey," I squealed "I'm too heavy and this is embarrassing, put me down."

"The lady doth protest too much." he replied and kept walking.

True enough he was carrying me like I weighed nothing, which I was well aware wasn't true.

Luckily the visitor spaces weren't very far from the front door and we quickly arrived at his car. It was a silver Porsche, I wasn't sure on the model as I'd never seen one before. I later discovered, via google, that is was a Panamera. We had plenty of wannabe car guys with their Audi's and BMW's. I'd even seen a Ferrari and a Maserati in the visitor bays before but not many Porsches that weren't Cayenne's.

He flicked the door open for me and gently propped me up on the ground allowing me to straighten out my clothes and get into the car unaided. At least he respected my pride enough for that I thought sadly. I carefully climbed in and let myself sink into the black leather seat. Pleasantly it was heated. Carter climbed in beside me carefully lifting his ponytail (I noted no braid this time) over his shoulder before sitting back to clip in his seatbelt. I fastened mine and our hands almost touched. It felt like a spark arced between us and I jumped in surprise. He raised his eyebrow in query as he turned the key in the ignition and the engine purred to life.

"So, what the hell was all of that?" he asked gently "I won't deny I was eager to see you again after last night at the Coffee House but I wasn't expecting such an eventful meeting."

I looked down into my hands, unable to look him in the eyes and realised that I'd managed to cut my hand. A small sliver of red gleamed in the sunlight streaming through the window.

"Does it hurt?" he said following my gaze and looking at the cut.

I shook my head as the tears began to swell in my eyes again.

Gently he leaned over me and opened the glove box. He pulled out a small travel first aid kit and a cotton handkerchief. Tenderly he cleaned and bandaged my cut and passed me the handkerchief to wipe my eyes and clean my face with my other hand. Once I was patched up and cleaned off I raised my head to look at him. His eyes were wide and he gently licked his bottom lip nervously.

"Better?"

I nodded, unable to speak.

"I'm going to take you to the Coffee House ok? It somehow seems fitting that my sanctuary should now become yours and I know for a fact that Dean is on this afternoons shift. You can ask him how his date with Sophie went last night." he smiled gently and clasped my unwounded hand in his. He was still warm and a sudden rush of blood filled my cheeks. My logical side was back out of her corner again and nagging at me. *This is insane, you chatted to this guy for a few hours yesterday and now you're trusting him to take care of you right now! He could be a psycho, a rapist or worse!* Then Dreamy emerged from her corner arguing that he just patched me up with as much care as a nurse or a parent would have shown a child, I wasn't chloroformed and in the back of the car, nor was he suggesting his place. He was suggesting a safe, mutually public setting we were both familiar with. Once again she triumphed and proudly stuck out her tongue proclaiming *Your argument is invalid*. They both vanished again as Carter spoke again.

"You ok Kira? Is coffee ok? Or tea as I remember you prefer? I would recommend a healthy spoon or two of sugar or honey. Whatever just happened would seem like a shock to most." he gently rubbed my hand as he spoke, his voice was soft and reassuring and his hand stroking mine was sending ripples of warmth through me.

"Sorry." I replied sharply snapping out of my psychosis "Yes, I really do need a cup of tea and I will take your advice on the sugar even though I don't normally have sugar in my tea. Perhaps Dean's love life can help take the edge of today's living nightmare." I looked at the worried expression on his face as he put the car into gear and we moved out of the car park.

I realised he was waiting for an answer to his other previous question.

"I will explain all about it once I've had a mouthful of sugary tea to calm my nerves, although I think perhaps later I might need something stronger." I muttered while I stared out of the window watching the last three years of my life and possibly the rest of my career fade out of sight as we left the building and the industrial estate behind us.

"That can be arranged if you like?" Carter said impassively as he drove on towards the town centre. "I know a man who owes me a favour and we could get a private booth in a quiet bar."

I was taken aback again by this man. I'd meant at home I was going to raid my alcohol stash and drink a little until the ache of losing my job eased a little. I wasn't hinting I wanted to go out for drinks.

Logical side was out of her corner like a flash *that's what you get for calling a complete stranger to collect you. He wants to get you drunk and who knows what else*. Dreamy appeared beside her with a tortured look on her face. *I got nothing* she shrugged.

Shaking my head I turned to look at Carter, his eyes were fixed on the road ahead but he was fully aware I was staring at him with wide eyes.

"I didn't mean..." I started.

"I know you didn't." he interrupted "But it's safer and better company to have one drink in a bar than several at home alone."

I sat back into the warm leather of my seat and watched the world passing swiftly by the window. Carter's body seemed to relax slightly at this. I hadn't noticed until now but he had been tightly gripping the steering wheel and his knuckles were now returning to regular flesh colour instead of the pure white they had been moments earlier. He also slouched back into his seat a little more.

Chapter 3

It seemed like only several minutes had passed when we arrived in the city centre and after a few moments we were parked around a corner behind the Coffee House. I unbuckled my belt and went to step out of the car when I suddenly remembered by broken heel. I looked out the window and Carter was motioning me to a shop right next to the Porsche. It was a small exclusive looking shoe store. I prayed silently under my breath that they had a cheap pair of flats although I suspected this was going to bite my bank balance hard and for the recently unemployed shoes are not a necessity, well not next to food and a roof. I slipped my heels off and set them into the foot well and got out of the car feeling suddenly very awkward about my odd socks choice this morning. I took a few bounds over the pavement and into the store. Carter followed behind me.

The store was small and bespoke. It was lined with wooden shelves that went all the way up to the tall ceiling. Several step ladders of differing lengths were stacked up against the back wall. Every single shelf was stacked with shoe boxes. There must have been hundreds, possibly thousands. Different colours, different labels and letterings adorned each box. I'd never noticed this store before and now I know why. Everything about this store screamed eclectic and expensive! I went to go and look at the shelves to try and find a bargain section when a beautifully manicured and suited woman emerged from the back of the shop and immediately headed straight for Carter.

"How may I help today?" she addressed him politely tossing her perfectly straightened blonde hair over her shoulder.

"My friend Kira here needs a new pair of shoes. We had a horrible mishap with a pair of heels. What do you have in confidence building and pretty?" He looked across at me as if seeking my approval. A playful light glimmered in those deep brown pools as he fiddled slightly with his braid.

My cheeks blushed scarlet as embarrassment overtook me. I should have been angry at him for answering for me and for implying I had no confidence, but he was right on so many levels. My confidence, what little there was, was completely shot and I really didn't want to talk to anyone right now, except perhaps Dean as a distraction. Maybe he'd gleaned more about me than I thought from our coffee conversation about books.

I smiled shyly at the smartly dressed blonde woman and my voice was almost a whisper as I answered "Yes. Size 6."

Carter whispered something into the woman's ear and she disappeared quickly and reappeared with 3 boxes before I had time to resume my search for the possibly non-existent bargain shelf. She motioned to a seat beside Carter in front of the window and placed the 3 boxes down on the beautiful teal carpet. I wiggled my toes slightly as I walked over to the seat, enjoying the feel of the thick warm carpet pile under my odd socks. *It must be a wool carpet* I thought *No way a place like this would have anything less.*

I sat down and Carter knelt beside me eager to see what the boxes contained. I braced myself for what was going to come next.

She took the lid off all 3 boxes, one after another letting me see all 3 pairs before I decided which to try on first.

The first pair were flats, they were a baby pink with dark red roses vined all over. It reminded me a little of the thorn forest from Sleeping Beauty. At the front of both shoes were tiny fabric rosebuds with a small diamante stone in the centre of the bud, at least I was hoping it was diamante!

The second pair were slightly heeled and looked somewhere between and a shoe and ankle boot. They were black suede with a zebra style print along the "collars" of the tops. I noticed the back of each heel had a line of more diamante stones.

The third pair I couldn't actually see right away as the tissue in the box was still covering them. I moved to lift the paper when Carter's hand suddenly thrust forward and he pulled the paper back. Our hands briefly brushed against one another and the spark was there again. Spiking through my body and making the hairs on my neck stand to attention.

"Allow me." he grinned. The expression on his face was so self-assured and confident. How could he read me so well? He knew my style and tastes even though we'd never really touched much on it in conversation.

As he pulled back the paper I gasped. This pair were not lady like and proper, they weren't heels, nor were they flats, well, not in the conventional sense.

"I want to try these on please." I beamed as I lifted the first shoe from the box. I marvelled for a moment at the creation in my hand. The soft fabric of the sneakers brushed my fingertips while my eyes drank in the brilliant colours and forms depicted on the entirety of both shoes. Carefully I undid the laces of one and then the other and softly slipped my feet inside. They felt even better than they looked. I tied the laces and stood up. Carter motioned to a mirror a few paces away from where we were sitting.

"Go take a look." he offered "See what you think."

The sales assistant smiled slyly as I walked over to the mirror. They were so cushioned and soft. They felt almost like house slippers on my feet. A complete comfort after the torture of those heels.

I looked down in the mirror at the sneakers. Small comic book panels greeted me and I could feel myself beaming. I turned back to Carter and the sales assistant who both had the same look of satisfaction on their faces.

"They are perfect." I almost squealed. "I'll take them please."
I was suddenly shot with a sudden fear, I hadn't asked how much they were and I was now painfully aware of how tight money would become without any form of income. I knew these shoes were pretty much one of a kinds. I'd read about them on some websites about how they were limited edition and no two pairs were alike. Every single limited edition pair had completely unique

panels from different comics.

I panicked a little and began to chew on my lower lip. I walked back over to the chair and sat down. Carter walked over to the till with the sales assistant, they were discussing something. I fiddled with the laces for a second trying to hear if he was trying to haggle the price for me. When I looked up the shop assistant was handing him back his card and a receipt. My mouth fell open dumbfounded. I went to say something when he caught my eye and raised his finger to his lips to silence me, a wicked gleam shone in his eyes. I chewed a little harder on my bottom lip. My logical side hadn't retreated into her corner, she was now on full alert with dreamy stood behind her looking quite alarmed.

Carter hugged the sales assistant, much to her surprise, then motioned for me to head back out into the street. I got up, uttering my thanks as I left the store and Carter placed a bag with the shoe box into the back seat of the car next to my box of work belongings.

He offered me his arm after locking the car.

"Shall we? I'm parched. Shoe shopping is more demanding than I remember." he chuckled softly, teasing me.

I blinked disbelievingly at him.

"How much were they? I'll pay you back as soon as I get another job! I can't thank you enough." I stammered as we walked to the Coffee House.

He stopped and turned to me gently taking my other arm.

"Think of it as a thank you."

"A thank you for what?" I asked confused.

"A lovely afternoon yesterday. I really enjoyed our long conversation. I'd had a particularly difficult day. It made me feel better just talking to someone about anything else and it helped me sleep. Something I've been having issues with lately." then he flashed me that killer smile I'd already seen several times today.

I went to argue with him as the afternoon had been as enjoyable for me too, as well as inspiring a less than lady-like dream later on, but he pressed his finger to my lips to silence me and there was that spark again, like a shot of lightning through my veins and I stayed quiet all the way to the Coffee House. Dreamy and Logical vanished into the dark corners of my mind.

As we entered the Coffee House I noticed that there was so much noise in here today. I hadn't noticed but since leaving the office the world had become almost monotone and dull. Single voices and no background noise. Now the sound was full surround. Music played softly in the background on a hidden sound system, a mother with a young baby tried to settle him as he cried loudly on her shoulder. Some school kids were talking incessantly at their table about something related to popular culture or celebrities. An elderly couple stared longingly into each other's eyes as they passed a piece of chocolate cake between each other while their friends sat beside them and chattered nonstop about events in their street. I was suddenly painfully aware of each and every sound in the building. I stopped for a moment and gripped the black book case that had sparked our conversation the previous day. I stood staring at the mish-mash collection of paper backs and hard backs assembled on the shelves as Carter stood behind me and gently held my arm. He whispered softly in me ear, concern spiking his voice.

"You're not going to pass out on me are you?"

I slowly shook my head and as I straightened myself up and turned to face Carter. I saw Dean coming towards us from the serving counter, his badge was straight today and he walked with an air of confidence. His hair was gelled back and looked far more grown up and professional than yesterday. It was like he'd aged several years overnight and matured. He now looked his true age which was actually 21 as I'd learned last night.

"Mr Brams, Kira I have a table for you at the back. Sam called in advance." and he lead us to a quiet table right at the back corner of the coffee house. I hadn't even noticed this back corner yesterday. Once we were seated and Dean had bounded off with our orders I finally spoke again.

"Who is Sam and how could he call in advance?" I quizzed him feeling slightly uncomfortable.

Carter blushed slightly and fiddled with his left cufflink. I was surprised I hadn't even noticed what he was wearing before now. The initial shock from the office must be wearing off as I was now becoming more aware of my surroundings and the people in them.

"I hope you don't mind." he whispered quietly to me, making me lean forward towards him to hear "I had my business associate Sam book us this table for lunch. I left work in rather a hurry to collect you and I had to give a reason for suddenly racing out like that. I said I was meeting a client for lunch and had Sam book us this table."

"Of course!" I gasped, blushing slightly. How could I have been so stupid? Of course if I was at work so was he! I'd never even asked what he did for a living. It was one of the few things we hadn't talked about the day before.

The song on the in-house system changed to one I recognised. The gentle tones of Snow Patrol filled the air and the atmosphere quietened and settled slightly. I relaxed in my chair a little and I wiggled my toes in my new sneakers.

"You like this song?" Carter observed. "Run, isn't it?"

I nodded. This song had many a time settled me when nothing else could, but it had also made me cry. Not today though, it would seem.

Dean returned with our drinks and placed them dutifully on the table then he returned to the counter and picked up another tray and brought us over a plate each containing a large caramel slice. I smiled stupidly at him as the sheer happiness of his kind act stirred my inner happiness. Dreamy nudged logical. *See* she scolded. *Nothing but blue skies so far*.

We ate and drank in relative silence. Once Carter was sure I wasn't going to pass out on him with shock he asked me about the events of the morning that had led to my desperate phone call and even more desperate state on the concrete. I explained about how the day had been no different than any other then I'd been called into a meeting with my boss who confronted me with some emails I'd never seen before leaking business memos and information but were from my email account and date and time stamped on the nights where I'd stayed in the building to do over time. I couldn't explain how I'd been hacked but that must have been it. I'm not that IT savvy but I knew it wasn't my doing. I was privy to a lot of internal goings on within the company but I wouldn't have leaked anything ever, let alone to a business rival I've never even heard of until today.

Carter's brow furrowed as if deep in thought while he listened to my tale of woe. When I finally finished my eyes were red and I could feel the tears forming again.

"And then you found me on the concrete. I had no one else I could think of to contact. Scott wasn't answering my calls and my other friends all work out of the city"

He gently took my hand and stroked his thumb up and down it as he looked into my foggy eyes as I blinked back the tears.

"Sounds like a rough day my dear. Ejected from the kingdom in exile, left to wander the forest barefoot, attacked my heel eating concrete trolls and rescued by a knight on a white steed."

I sniggered slightly. How could I not? Even in all this mess he managed to make me feel at ease and let out my inner geek. I definitely rolled a critical fail on the dice of life at work this morning but maybe I had a saving roll left?

"My life is not a D & D adventure that can be solved by a knight. And I think you'll find your Porsche is silver, not white" I quipped with a smile playing on the corners of my lips. The tears were receding and I wasn't feeling quite as forlorn as I had been.

"I was in no way implying that your life is a game my dear. Simply that now it has become a little more interesting as the path has changed. You've wandered off your predetermined plot and now the world is yours. You're setting the rules now. Where you want to go from here is up to you." The look on his face changed slightly, the smile was gone for a second and a serious tone took his voice as if he was trying to hammer a point home.

Dean came over to check everything was ok with our cakes and drinks. Carter gently gripped his arm and pulled him towards us across the table slightly.

"How were the tickets?" he whispered to Dean loud enough for me to hear. I looked at Dean with complete fascination as his cheeks flared red.

"They were perfect Mr Brams." He then glanced over to me. "Sophie has said you can have a caramel slice any time you are in Kira. She'd been waiting weeks for me to ask her out. Mr Brams 'tickets were the key. Once we were in the club she confessed how she'd wanted to go out with me since I started working here, but she was too shy."

Carter nudged Dean with his elbow. "I bet she was anything but shy last night?"

Dean flushed a deeper shade of scarlet.

"How vulgar!" I blurted out suddenly. I didn't even realise I was thinking the words until they came out. "Debasing a lovely girl like that. She's a person with feelings, not a conquest."

My cheeks flushed red with momentary anger.

Carter and Dean both paled suddenly as they looked at me across the table.

"We were only playing!" Carter started defensively.

"I really do have feelings for her Kira. It's not like that." Dean finished.

I felt the anger recede and I was now flushed crimson with embarrassment.

"I'm sorry. I don't know where that came from. I didn't mean to accuse you both of being womanisers." I whispered shamefully. "It's not been a very good day for me!"

Dean and Carter both smiled at each other and then at me.

"Sometimes it's easy to forget that women don't always take things men say the way we meant them." Carter started again.

"I'd stop while you're ahead Mr Brams." interrupted Dean as he left the table. He looked back over his shoulder as he headed towards the counter. "Thanks again though, both of you."

"Seems we're match makers now." joked Carter as he downed the last of his coffee.

I fiddled with the last drops of tea in my cup as I forced down the last bite of caramel slice.

Logical and Dreamy were standing arm in arm looking accusingly. "*We?*" they both chorused inside my head.

Chapter 4

Carter and I sat for a while longer furthering our conversation from the previous night and expanding a little into our interests and likes until his phone rang in his coat pocket. Excusing himself for a moment he got up and left the table to continue his conversation. I suddenly got an icy chill, what if it was his boss? What if he was getting in trouble because of me? I spent the next several minutes in a mild panic until he retook his seat in front of me. He took one look at the expression on my face and his brow furrowed and his eyes darkened.

"What's wrong?"

"Was that your work?" I asked timidly.

He nodded, still regarding me with a furrowed brow and a concerned expression.

"I haven't gotten you in trouble have I?" my voice was almost a cracked whisper.

Immediately his face lightened and he began to laugh.

"No, I'm most certainly not in trouble. Sam was just wondering if I was done for the day or not. I'm off the clock now so we're ok to chat for a while longer. If you like?"

Relief flooded me. Losing my own job for a crappy reason was bad enough, but I couldn't cost someone else their job. Especially when they'd rode their mighty steed to save me and put shoes on my feet, which reminded me of an unresolved matter.

"I really like my shoes" I began to broach the subject "How much am I owe you?"

Carter shook his head. "A gift, I insist. They were worth it to see you finally smile after your event filled morning" The tone of his voice told me he wasn't going to accept no for an answer.

My phone suddenly chirped in my bag, alerting me to a text message. I lifted it from my bag and unlocked the screen. I had 2 texts. One from Jenny and one from Scott. I decided to read the one from Jenny first as I was still mad with Scott.

Carter left the table under the premise of fetching us refills to fuel our conversation with a promise of further caramel slices to follow. I saw him at the counter having a conversation with Dean and a pretty strawberry blonde girl who emerged from the kitchen. That must be Sophie I thought as I glanced back down at my phone. She was hugging onto Dean's arm too tightly to have been anyone else.

Jenny: **What the hell has happened? Where are you? What was that with Mrs Miller? The office is like a church this afternoon, no one is talking at all and everyone is avoiding eye contact! I saw Marc from IT at lunch. He's was sad to hear you were going and to ask if he could keep your fantasy American football team for the office sweepstakes? Whatever that means! Jen.xx**

I quickly typed as brief a response as I could about it being a misunderstanding I had to leave and that the bitch had just pissed me off too much lately. Marc was welcome to my team as long as he stuck to the season plan I had discussed with him one lunch time when we were blowing off steam after a stressful morning. I explained I'd meet her to further explain at some point.

Carter was walking back to the table with our tray when my phone chirped in my hand.

Jenny: **Did you google Carter Brams yet? You should really do more research coffee girl!**

Quickly I tucked my phone back into my bag and smiled nervously as he sat back down and offered me a fresh pot of tea and another caramel slice.

"Who was that?" he asked casually as he took a bite of his cake. Crumbs cascaded down his shirt front and he tried not to draw attention to himself as he dusted them off as best he could while holding his coffee cup in the other hand.

"I had a text from Jenny at work and one from Scott." I replied very matter of fact.

He raised an eyebrow whilst he quickly cleared his mouth to speak.

"What did Scott have to say for himself?" He asked in a slightly irritated tone.

I suddenly realised I hadn't read his message yet.

"I...erm...don't know. I didn't read his yet."

Carter motioned to me to read his message.

"Better see if it's a good excuse or not." he almost growled.

I lifted my phone from my bag once again and unlocked the screen. I opened the message from Scott.

Scott: **Hi, sorry I missed your call. I was out at a business breakfast with a potential new employer. Does your call have anything to do with your late night at the coffee house last night?**

I quickly sent a response suggesting that we talk and that I'd lost my job, hence calling this morning. I was ok and would speak to him soon as I was currently out with a friend calming down. I got a brief "ok" back as a reply.

Carter was looking expectantly at me when I put my phone back down.

I shrugged as I replaced my phone in my bag.
"He had no idea why I'd called. I said I'll catch up with him when he's free. He's currently trying to get a new job. He was out at a business meeting/breakfast."

"I'm actually quite glad he wasn't in when you called him earlier." offered Carter honestly as he took a large mouthful of coffee. "I wasn't sure I would get the chance to see you again after your exit last night."

I tiled my head at this statement. I didn't think I'd been that cool with my response the night before. "Really?" Taking another mouthful of coffee he simply nodded. There was a bare honesty in his eyes that suggested he was sensitive about this for some reason.

I couldn't get my head around this. My tall, dark knight was actually bothered by the fact that I might not call him up for another coffee date! He was everything a woman could want, he was tall, had eyes you could melt into, he was a very articulate speaker with a broad range of interests, from what I had gathered so far and he was kind. On the opposing side you had me. I was short, over weight and while I wasn't the elephant man, I wasn't exactly what you'd call hot either. Oh, then there was the matter of my low confidence and self-esteem killing sarcasm!

Dreamy and Logical both looked at me and shook their heads. I knew I was a little prettier than I gave myself credit for, but I'd never admit and they knew that too.

"It really bothered you that much that I might not call you for another coffee date?"

He nodded solemnly and finished the last bite of his slice with the last gulp of his coffee.
I took his lead and launched into my caramel slice, revelling in the soft texture of the caramel and the sugary gravel of the base. I sipped at my tea as I chewed, melting the caramel further. If I closed my eyes right now I could imagine I was anywhere as the sugar kicked up my happiness a notch. I was so distracted by the sugar rush that I didn't notice Dean taking the empties from the table and Carter whispering something in his ear. I was taken back to earth by a jolt from my hand as Carter gently stroked it. What was it? I'd never felt this electricity with anyone before. Dreamy was looking at me with a "go on" expression while Logical was scowling with her "don't you dare" expression. I dismissed them both with a toss of my head. I shook loose a brown strand of fringe that drifted down over my left eye. I blew gently to move it over a little.

Carter watched in complete curiosity as I began to feverishly blow at this strand of hair to convince it to lay anywhere but directly over my eye. After a few attempts I was feeling light headed and gave up. Instead I pulled out my hair tie and let my shoulder length hair fall free a moment before I gathered it all up again. I pulled it back and was about to put the hair tie back in when Carter stopped me.

"Wait a second Kira." he pleaded "Could you leave it down a while longer?"

I wasn't sure what exactly I was meant to make of that request from a guy who had butt length hair to die for. I merely nodded and left the hair tie around my wrist. Gently I teased my hair out with my fingers until it sat nicely on my shoulders and regained some shape.

"Wow your eyes are a really brilliant shade of blue. I didn't notice that with the lighting in here last night." Logical dug Dreamy in the ribs with her elbow in an "I told you so" gesture.
"Err...thanks. That was a little bit random wasn't it?" I stated, trying to lighten the tone. I was suddenly feeling a little claustrophobic. Coffee fine, the shoes were a bit too much but now we were going a completely different direction and I wasn't sure I was ready to fall down another rabbit hole today.

Carter withdrew across the table and slouched a little in his seat.

"Sorry, that was a little forward wasn't it. From now on I'll behave. I hope my reputation preceding me isn't going to ruin this."

Now I was confused, his reputation preceding him! What the heck did that mean?

Suddenly all I could hear was Jenny's voice in my head. "Did you google him?" What did I not know about this man? Surely our legal system wasn't the kind that would let him wander about free if he was some kind of sicko! I took a deep breath and calmed myself. I was letting logical take control a little too much. She saw the worst in everything and was mainly the reason I hadn't been able to maintain a stable relationship since my teens. I decided to ignore the slight tingling of my "spider sense" and see where this path was going.

I shrugged and playfully stuck the tip of my tongue out at him. He seemed startled at first then smiled and shifted a little in his chair.

"I have no idea what you're talking about, but as long as your intentions are honourable dear knight, I accept the compliment. My eyes are a nice shade of blue." in all honesty my eyes were one of my only features I truly liked.

Suddenly his eyes flashed like fire and he leaned right over the table until his nose was inches from mine. He whispered in an almost rasping hiss.

"And what if I said the next time you stick out your tongue at me I'm going to bite it. Then I'm going to suck it until you beg me to stop"

I was in shock at his boldness and a little unsure of what my reaction should be. I looked to Dreamy and Logical for back up but both of them stood there in my psyche totally dumbfounded, their jaws on the floor. I should have been offended or at least slightly disgusted but to my own surprise I was actually quite flustered and hot. A knot formed in my stomach that tugged at my groin and then my mind went blank and my body took over. An unseen force moved me forward towards Carter and my lips met with his. I closed my eyes and an explosion went on around me. All my senses were on fire and to my pleasant surprise he kissed me back. His lips were soft and warm and the slight stubble on his top lip grazed me gently as he kissed me more deeply. I parted my lips slightly and invited his warm, probing tongue. As soon as our tongues touched the spark was there again. Jolting everything in my body, tingling its way through all of my senses. As quickly as the moment had taken me it ended. I gently pulled back and opened my eyes. Carter's pools of chocolate brown were barely visible as his pupils were so dilated and his lips were still slightly parted as he looked at me in complete amazement.

He opened his mouth to speak and I lifted my finger to my lips to stop him. He watched in fascination as I moved chairs so that I was now sitting next to him rather than opposite.

I put my arm around his neck and kissed him gently once again on the lips.

"I have no idea where this rabbit hole leads" I whispered shyly "But it's sure as hell got to be better than the world I came from"

Carter's expression brightened further as he pulled me into a tight embrace.

"Kira, you have no idea!"

We stayed in the coffee house like that for a while longer before my stomach started to complain. I hadn't really eaten today and my sugary snacking had only filled the gap for a short while and stoked the furnace in my belly.

Carter must have heard the monstrous growling as well as he gently let me go before asking if I would like to have dinner with him. I nodded and returned to the other side of the table to grab my bag. Dean came over again and asked if we were done with our table. Carter spoke to him while I pulled my coat on and grabbed my purse to pay. Carter immediately shot me a black look and I put my purse back into my bag. He was going to be stubborn about this whole employed vs unemployed thing. Chivalry is not something a woman finds often, so for now I decided to let it slide. I could make it up to him later either with cash or with help with something. You never know when a favour will come in handy.

As we left the coffee house behind us her lights slowly went out one by one until she was a dark shape behind us. I quickly rang Scott as we walked along the main street looking for somewhere to eat. Carter stared off into the distance as if trying not to listen to my call. He had a strange expression on his face as we walked slowly.

The phone picked up on about the 8th ring.

"Yeah" said Scott's deep voice, he sounded sleepy.

"Long day?" I asked, only half caring.

"You know how it goes hun. What can I do for you?" he chatted back. I could hear a TV in the background and knew he would only be paying me half attention.

"Can you please check on Malakai? His timed bowl should have fed him, but just double check ok. I'm going out for dinner with a friend."

At the sound of this Carters eyes darted to me and a sly smile played on his lips as he wrapped his arm around my hips and tugged me closer to his side. This action made me giggle slightly at the childishness and possessiveness of his action. My knight wanted to make sure I knew I had his attention.

Scott sounded puzzled. "Who you with?" he asked.

Before I could reply Carter lifted the mobile from my hand.

"Hello. I'm Kira's new friend. I'm taking her to dinner as she's had a lousy day. Could you please go and check on the cat for her?"

I heard Scott stammering on the other end of the phone and then agreeing.

"Good evening Scott." Carter ended the call and gently handed me back the phone.

I looked at him quizzically for a moment and returned my mobile to my bag. He smiled back at me, his eyes full of happiness and he took my hand letting me walk again at my own pace beside him.

"What was that for?" I asked "And how did you know Malakai was a cat?"

"Ahhh my dear, for someone who reads so many novels you haven't picked up the skill of observation very well. Your coat has some small puncture marks on the sleeve and there are a few strands of fur on the fabric cuffs. Cat hair is hell to get out once it's embedded."

"Could have been a dog." I quipped trying to throw his staggering confidence off.

"You don't strike me as a dog person." he smiled.

I wasn't sure what to make of that until I heard the jokes
Dreamy and Logical were having.
Less bitch and more pussy!

"Anyway," he interrupted my thoughts as a stupid grin
had grown across my face "I wanted to reassure Scott you
weren't hanging out with an undesirable."

"How can I know that for sure?" I teased a sly smile
playing on the corners of my mouth now the stupid grin
had dissolved.

Suddenly we stopped walking and Carter ducked me
quickly into the alley between two businesses. He pinned
me to the wall with his hip and took both my wrists in one
hand above my head before I could blink. His eyes were
dark and shone with a strange light in the alley.

He bent his lips towards my ear and whispered in a low
feral growl.

"You can't know for sure."

He took a moment to almost glare at me before taking me
into the most passionate embrace I've ever been held in.
My heart was beating so loudly it was like a deafening
ocean roar in my ears. My skin flushed and I could feel
myself glowing scarlet.

There was almost an urgency in the way he kissed me. His
hand held me fast against the wall, both hands bound
above my head. He moved his hip slightly and pinned me
with his left knee between my legs. I was startled at first
then as I softened into the kiss a deep tugging sensation
radiated from my groin. I don't think I'd ever been this

turned on and never by someone had I known so little about.

His tongue was like fire in my mouth as it darted, searching for mine. As our tongues met and began to dance, the same familiar strike of lightening took me. The energy pulsed between us like invisible electricity. I groaned softly as his free hand gripped my waist and pulled me towards him until I was almost straddling his left thigh. He gently let go of my hands which immediately worked their way into the length of jet black hair. I tugged his braid free and gently tugged his hair trying to claim him. Softly he moved and ground against me as he kissed me more deeply. My eyes had remained closed the whole time, bright lights and sparks flashed before me. I was losing myself completely in his embrace, surrendering myself to these feelings that had long laid dormant in me when suddenly a cough from the other end of the alley interrupted the moment, shattering it and causing us to suddenly separate.

A couple were walking past and had stopped to enjoy the show for a moment but had let us know they were there. As they realised they had our full attention they scuttled off. I heard the woman muttering to her beau as they vanished out of sight.

"Wasn't that...." her voice tailed off into the distance.

Carter was tying his hair back into a loose ponytail when I turned back to him.

He looked down at me shyly as he tucked my hair back behind my ears and straightened my jacket.

"I must apologise." he whispered softly. "I don't normally take such forward steps with ladies I have just met."

All I could do was nod slightly, the breath slowly coming back to me, as we entered back onto the street in search of food.

After a several moments of walking in silence we stopped outside of a quiet looking little Italian restaurant. Carter moved to enter the building but I tugged him back for a moment.

I looked up at him shyly from under my eyelashes before admitting shyly "I enjoyed it."

He offered the crook of his elbow towards me which I gladly took and we stepped inside just as the first drops of rain dotted the pavement outside.

Carter led us to a table towards the back of the restaurant. We were greeted by a short happy Italian man who introduced himself to me as Ignatius. Carter felt the need to inform me that Iggy and himself had known each other for years and kept an eye on each other's businesses, especially in the current economic climate. The smiled knowingly at each other as Iggy told us the evening's specials. I opted for the seafood ravioli while Carter went for the house special. He ordered a bottle of house white while we waited. Iggy bounded off into the kitchen to personally deliver our requests.

I sipped slowly at the cool bubbles in my glass. They fizzed gently on my tongue and the temperature of the wine sent a shudder through me.

Carter moved his hand to my shoulder.

"Are you cold?" he asked sympathetically.

I shook my head and lifted my glass.

"Cheers."

"And what are we celebrating?" he laughed gently.

"To the kiss in the alley and wherever it leads." I smiled.

Carter clinked his glass to mine and gently gripped my empty hand on the table.

His eyes glittered with promise in the half light of the restaurant.

"I should like very much to find out where this path leads."

We continued on with our evening together laughing and conversing over wine and good food with Iggy checking in on us to ensure everything was to the expected standard. We finished off with chocolate dessert and coffee.

As we left, Iggy bid us good evening and gave Carter a knowing pat on the back as we sauntered off along the damp street. The rain had stopped half way through dinner and now the stars twinkled silently in the chilled evening air. We stood briefly on the overpass bridge and watched other couples and singles milling around the walkways between bars, restaurants and clubs as the city seemed to almost throb to its own beat as life went on.

We stood hand in hand watching and listening, absorbing as much of the evening ambiance as possible as well as drinking in each other's company. I hadn't dated anyone in a while and I hadn't been looking for anyone but somehow this evening felt right. I could hear Logical kicking and screaming that it was illogical and potentially fatal to just take off with someone in this fashion and I could hear the subtle reassurances from Dreamy to follow my heart and do what felt right. How different they both were, the two sides to my personality. I wondered sometimes if they would ever agree on anything.

As I snapped back to reality I was painfully aware of Carter staring at me. His lips were parted slightly and he slowly licked his upper lip with the tip of his tongue. It was oddly erotic. He was looking at me like a dying man in the desert who'd seen his first drink of water in days.

"What next?" I smiled, breaking the awkward silence and whatever thoughts were crossing his mind.

That dark glimmer was there in his eyes again as he whispered softly to me.

"Where would you like to go next?" he said in a hushed husky voice as he offered me his hand. A silver and ruby ring glinted on his middle finger. I hadn't noticed that before. It was masculine but with an almost feminine beauty with the delicate filigree work on the shoulders.

At his words heat rose in me. Logical was screaming at me to call it a night and go home, feed the cat and deal with these newly awakened feelings with my vibrating friend under the pillow. Dreamy was urging me on the side of caution but to pursue this as far as I dared.

I took Carters hand and swallowed a little harder than usual. I felt like an insecure child venturing into the playground for the first time.

"Wherever you take me." I whispered.

A short walk and we were standing outside a large glass and steel building. It looked like it was possibly an office building or something of that ilk. Carter urged us forward to the large revolving doors. I hesitated remembering my earlier bad experience with the last revolving door I had met. Carter gently placed his hands on my shoulders and pressed up behind me. He urged me gently forward and we walked as one through the automatically turning door. Once inside he nodded to the night guard before leading us to a small lift door to one side of the massive reception area. He took a key card from his pocket and swiped it over the security panel beside the lift door. He quickly punched some numbers into the keypad and the lift door opened.

"Err." I stuttered "Do you need to work late?"

Carter burst out in laughter as he turned to me tugging me into the lift.

"No Mon Chéri." He said tenderly, stroking my cheek with the back of his hand. "I need to collect something from home."

Instantly I blushed. No one had called me anything like that before. I knew it was French but I wasn't certain what it meant. *Wait, did he say his home? He's taking me home!* Suddenly I felt a sliver of panic creeping in. This suddenly felt too fast, too sudden. I'd only met him in the Coffee House yesterday and with all the events of today I was suddenly weary. Logical goaded me from the back of my mind about how bad an idea this was and I was sure to end up on the front page of the papers in the morning in a body bag. Dreamy had fallen silent as if she too wasn't sure I had chosen correctly.

The lift doors opened onto a small dark corridor and I had no further choices. This was it, no turning back now. We left the lift, its metal doors closing soundlessly behind us and paced silently and quickly to the front door of Carters home. He fished a key out of his pocket and after soundlessly unlocking the large dark wood door he threw it open to reveal the lavish expanse of his home.

Chapter 5

After blinking blindly for a moment at the light I stood breathless at the view. The apartment was a massive open plan expanse. It was modern and mostly monochromatic. The far side of the room was made almost entirely of large windows giving a panoramic view of the city. It looked beautiful from here at night. The lights at the harbour twinkled like stars. I knew they were the deck lights of several cargo vessels docked for the night but they still stirred my imagination. Stories began to build in my mind about voyages and adventures they had seen and where their next journey would take them.

As I looked around the room I saw a small kitchen and breakfast bar to my left and a huge black curved couch with cuddle chair in the centre perfectly positioned to take advantage of the views through the windows. To the far right the room seemed to almost stop dead, there was a solid wall of white with two doors. I was guessing one was a bathroom and the other was his bedroom. The hair at the back of my neck tingled with the thought. I slowly spun around taking in the entire room. There were a few works of art on the wall and some small framed photographs. I wanted to investigate further but I didn't want to appear a rude houseguest. Carter had left my side and gone over to the breakfast bar where he was sifting through a pile of papers, looking for something. He must have sensed my eyes on him as he looked over his shoulder and smiled.

"Have a look around if you like. I'll only be a few moments"

I took his permission as a cue and began a more thorough inspection of the place. The floor beneath me looked like black marble. It seemed to have sparkling specks that caught the dimmed spot lights that Carter had turned on, they twinkled periodically at me as I walked across them.

I went to the wall with the framed photographs, curious to learn more about the fascinating man who had treated me so kindly today. I noticed a spiral staircase tucked into the wall before the kitchen area, it seemed to lead up to a mezzanine floor from what I could see. I focused back on the pictures in the heavy looking wooden frames.

The people in the photographs appeared to be of family, or were they friends? They looked too similar in age to be family members surely? There was Carter, another man who looked to be his younger doppelganger only in blonde and a woman who only looked to be in her late 50's. Was she an aunt? All 3 of them were smiling in what looked to be a forest at dusk, the last beams of sun caught beautifully between the background of woodland. I stood transfixed, they all had the same eyes. Soulful and deep with a hint of hidden pain. I recognised that look immediately. My mother had died when I was young and I remember growing up, that glint at the back of my father's eyes. The hint of a long buried pain that sometimes clawed at the surface tormenting him. I resemble her in so many ways it must have been torture for him as I was maturing into a young woman.

"They are my family." Carter whispered in my ear.

I almost jumped out of my skin, I hadn't heard him cross the room or even noticed his movement from the corner of my eye. The wine at dinner must have been more potent than I'd thought, I normally never get caught out this way.

I turned to face him and nodded. Gently he placed his arm around my shoulders as he continued to explain the photographs. The feeling of his against me soothed my slightly jangled nerves.

"My mother Isobella and my brother Caleb. That was taken while we were on holiday in the Black Forest." he explained as if reading my curious thoughts.

"Did your father have dark hair?" I blurted out before I could think.

The glint of hidden pain appeared in his eyes and he nodded once.

"He died when I was young. My mother never spoke much of him when we were growing up. She figured it less painful." he said with definite sadness in his voice as he turned away from the picture and headed towards the couch.

"Would you like to join me in taking a moment to enjoy the view?" he said, watching me as he took his place on one end of the couch.

It looked so warm and comfortable. I'd first thought it was a leather couch judging on the rest of the modern style of the apartment but closer up and in better light I realised it was actually some type of fabric, a type of microfiber maybe? I took a seat next to him and followed his lead in staring out into the night beyond the large windows. The city was still buzzing with life outside. I knew, from experience of this city, the wind was whispering down alleys and through the trees. People were chattering happily whilst wandering from pubs, bars and restaurants to night clubs or making their way home. Seagulls were calling their brood home down by the harbour as the soft sound of waves lapping the hulls of boats blurred into the background. The heartbeat of the city pulsed beyond the glass but all I could hear was the rushing of blood in my ears as I turned to look at Carter. He had taken his hair down and it spilled freely across his shoulders. He was staring straight out towards the horizon, the lights from the harbour reflecting in his dark eyes. He seemed deep in thought and I turned silently to look once again at the view.

Logical and Dreamy were both stunned as they watched the events unfolding.

Several silent moments pass as we both sat staring out at the nightscape beyond the glass. Carter was lost in his own thoughts. His brow creased slightly as if he was trying to decide on something. I started to feel a little uneasy and shifted in my seat. What was he thinking about?

He turned to face me once more. His deep eyes filled with a look of yearning.

"Do you dance?" he finally asked in a hushed voice.

I sat mute, blinking at him like I've just been asked a complicated maths problem.

"S..Sorry?" I finally manage to stammer.

He quickly stood and offered me his hand.

"Do you dance Kira?"

I nodded shyly as I took his hand and he pulled me to a stand.

He looked relieved.

"Good, then we should go dancing." he stated very matter of fact "I know the perfect place."

We were moving again, leaving his apartment. Logical was breathing a deep sigh of relief, if I hadn't known better I'd have sworn she'd been holding her breath. Dreamy on the other hand was sullen and quiet in silent disappointment.

We departed the building out into the rain. The cold drops of water on my skin seemed to awaken me from the trance I had fallen into on Carters couch. The stagnant feeling in my head was clearing and I was alert and awake once more. We walked swiftly along the streets, passing other couples giggling and holding hands in the darkness. We darted between the awnings of buildings and granite doorways to stay as dry as we could. Like two animals in a concrete forest we frolicked and played between the structures to stay dry and reach our destination. We stopped under a bank's awning while waiting for the crossing to turn green, once it had we both darted across the road like school children, giggling and hollering as we went. I got a stitch and had to stop in a shop doorway. Carter was instantly at my side.

"You ok?" he gently bent over me. I held my knees waiting for the pain to pass. I nodded and tried to hand signal "stitch" and failed miserably.

"Oh, that sounds bad." he chortled at me. "Your lungs just did what to your liver?"

"Don't make me laugh." I scolded as my breath returned "My stitch is starting to fade."

"Oh, that's what that meant?" he teased as he mimicked the hand gestures I'd just tried to do.

After a few moment my breathing had returned to normal and we continued our path towards our promised dance.

We headed down a large alleyway with a dead end. The dead end was a large grey granite building comprising of a pool hall and a night club. The pool hall was in darkness already but the bright lights illuminating the club's signage and the pulsing beat spilling out into the night told me that it was just getting started for the evening. I turned and looked at Carter as we headed towards the queue.

"Night creatures? What kind of club is this? I've never heard of it before."

"Mon Chéri, it's as old as the hills and twice as cultured as any club in this city. Follow me."

He tugged me out of the line and straight up to the front door. A large bouncer looked down at me. He must have been about 6' 8" easily with a long well established beard and long hair which was tied in a number of small braids at the front. He looked almost like a Viking. I then noticed the tattoo showing just under the low neckline of his netted style top, it was a torc. Dreamy was paying attention and whispered nonsense to me, *perhaps he IS a Viking!* Logical abruptly slapped her and told her to pay attention and stay alert.

Carter nodded politely to a smaller bouncer to the left of us who I'd completely failed to notice. He was barely taller than me, smelled of damp and had slicked back hair which I suspected was to hide the start of a male pattern baldness bird's nest at the back of his head. Carter then turned his attention to the tall Viking I was currently transfixed on. He opened his arms and gave the man an overfriendly hug. To my surprise the man's expression softened and he returned Carter's hug.

"Evening Carter. Fine night for it." he smiled. "Who is your charming guest this evening? I will get her added to the list."

Carter smiled and nodded.

"Thank you Griff. Her name is Kira Jansent. She is to be added to tonight's VIP's."
The bouncer scribbled my name onto a clipboard they held at the front door and we were immediately let inside. Confused I followed Carter inside the club, feeling the thrum of baselines pulse in my chest as soon as we crossed the threshold. I instantly recognised the Foo Fighters track and softly tapped by hand on my thigh.

I looked about for the cloakroom to unburden myself of my coat but Carters tight grip pulled me off towards the dance floor. We walked around the edge of the wooden dance floor and headed towards the bar. I was just starting to think that a drink was in order with how surreal things seemed to have gotten in the past hour but instead of going to the bar we ducked inside a small mirrored door next to the bar.

The room was pitch black and again I was startled by the light when Carter turned it on. It was a dim bulb but as soon as I turned around I could see why. I could see through the wall next to me. I could almost touch the dancers on the other side if I reached out my hand. I could still feel the baseline of the music pulling at me through the floor but the room itself was almost sound proof. I looked back towards Carter and he was sitting behind a small desk sorting through some papers. I wondered if this had something to do with the paperwork he'd been looking for at his apartment. He glanced up and caught me staring. He patted the empty patch at the front of the desk.

"Sit?" he asked softly "I just have a small matter to deal with and then we can dance. I did promise you a dance and I'm a man of my word."

I coyly padded over to the desk and perched on the front of it, my legs dangled off the edge and swung slightly. I was aware of Carters eyes on me from behind but I was caught up once again in watching the dancers through the one way glass. I was suddenly feeling pleased that my workwear choice for today had been smart but casual. The song changed and so too did the dancers. The new baseline was heavier, louder and more aggressive. Metal, I was guessing. Dancers were replaced by moshers who bobbed their heads up and down and crashed into each other and spun off in different directions. One such mosher took a tumble and slammed into the wall right in front of me. I squeaked and jumped back on the desk almost knocking Carter's paperwork over. Swiftly he caught the paperwork and almost in the same instance he managed to grab me around the waist and stop me from hurtling backwards off the desk. I quickly righted myself and shuffled forwards off the desk. I turned to apologise to Carter but he was smiling at me.

"I think that's possibly enough paperwork for one night." he sighed gently. He produced a brush from the filing cabinet next to him and quickly brushed through his long dark tresses and retied his pony tail this time a little higher on his head.

"Before we go out and dance." Carter asked "I need to know. Do you have any idea of who I am?"

Confused I nodded slightly. "Carter Brams." I stated very matter of fact.

A bemused look came over his face as he cupped his chin with his thumb and forefinger.

"And?" he prompted. His tone was serious and a slight growl.

I fiddled with my fingers while I tried to think of an answer.

"You work here?" I offered sheepishly.

Carter erupted in laughter as he approached me from behind the desk. He gently cupped my cheek and softly kissed my lips. His eyes were full of longing and what looked like a glimmer of hope shone in their dark depths.

He gently nuzzled into my neck as he muttered "You honestly don't know do you?"

I pulled back from his embrace and studied his face for a moment. Logical and dreamy were both at a loss and slightly concerned, as was I.

"I don't know what you mean." I whispered feeling the crimson begin to flush my embarrassed cheeks.

He took a deep breath before continuing. His arms were now around my waist and his face was inches from mine.

"In the coffee house, why were you there? Truthfully." he asked softly.

I lowered my eyes and looked at my feet while I answered him. I felt so foolish that I couldn't face him.
"Some of my friends online who live in the city had been talking about you. About the Adonis that graced this little coffee place. I had a day off work and being the sceptic I am, I decided to see you for myself. That's why I was there. I'd been there for hours waiting to catch a glimpse of you so I could confirm or deny their rumours."

I raised my eyes to his once again and there was a smile to greet me. Gently and more slowly and purposefully this time Carter kissed me. This time there was a slow urgency to his kiss, I let the sparks of electricity wash over me as I fell into his kiss. A slow burn began in my belly that slowly spread throughout me. Igniting every nerve ending and setting me on edge. When we surfaced for air I looked at him quizzically. "What was that for?"

"Kira, I am Carter Brams, of Brams-Grace Incorporated. I own this club, the building I live in and have shares in several companies' right across this city and beyond. I'm no millionaire but I am fairly wealthy by modern standards and I had to be sure on why you were waiting for me."

For a moment I can't move and then suddenly panic grips my chest like a startled rabbit. I dart for the far side of the desk to put a physical barrier between us. My head is still full of static, my concentration is shot.

"You what?" I gasp completely horrified.

He moved to the front of the desk and fanned his hands out in front of him as he leaned towards me. My heart was hammering in my chest.

"You honestly had no idea did you?"

Suddenly I hear Jenny's voice in my head along with Logical and Dreamy *"You really should google him."* She knew who he was, why didn't she tell me, warn me! I'd made such a fool out of myself.

"I am so sorry." I apologise fiddling with my fingers once again. I look down at the desk. A submissive gesture by any standard but also to prevent him seeing the full scarlet hue that has bloomed right across my face and is snaking its way down my neck.

He is confused I can hear it in his voice as he speaks again. "Mon Chéri, Why would you be sorry? It is I who owe you an apology."

"Me?" I look up. My eyes were watering, I was so embarrassed I could have cried.

"I have many people hunting me for many reasons Kira. I wasn't sure if you were a reporter looking for a scoop or after something else. I am so relieved you are just a curious innocent."

Curious Innocent, Dreamy and Logical snort together. They felt insulted but oddly I didn't.

Carter approached me around the desk. I didn't run this time. My heart rate was steadying as panic gave way to embarrassment and acceptance.

He gently touched my shoulder. I turned to him and he kissed me again.

I narrowed my eyes and furrowed my brow.

"Why are you still kissing me? I just made an absolute ass of myself."

"I can always stop if you'd prefer." he shrugged.

He laughed as the shocked expression crosses my face.

"Permission to speak freely now that I know you're not trying to get a front page exclusive or something."

"Of course." I nodded.

Carter sits on his office chair and soundlessly pulls me onto his lap before I can resist or protest. Despite the short length of time I've known him there is an odd familiarity about being with him. It's almost like I've been here before. It felt strangely right and the familiar crackle of electricity between our touch made it feel even more right.

Gently he stroked my hair away from my eyes and tucked it behind my ear.

"I have been pursued, hunted if you will, for so long, by many women who only aim to get something from me. An exclusive, money, power, you name it, I've had to fend them all off. But I've always had a feeling deep down that no matter how pretty their lie, that's all it was, a lie. Then I met you in the Coffee House. You were honest and pure.

You asked nothing of me except knowledge. You sat with me, spoke with me, bonded with me. I can't explain it, there's this sort of spark between us. It's familiar and comfortable and it doesn't make me feel like I'm pushing too fast."

My mouth fell open at his words and Dreamy and Logical both fell silent.

Carter gently pushed my mouth closed with his finger as he finished talking and looked at me for confirmation of all he'd just said.

I slowly shook my head trying to think a little clearer. Carter frowned a little fearing my answer was no.

"I can't explain it. It's like a novel. This familiarity between us. You coming to my rescue, the fear I feel over the strength of emotion I'm feeling right now. I hardly know you and yet it's like you've always been a part of my life. I feel the spark too but I can't explain it. It scared me Carter. Things like this don't happen in real life. I'm worried you'll think I'm some woolly headed girl with wild ideas of romance. We met, we've discussed books and you've come to my rescue after a terrible work related incident." Carter raised his finger to my lips before I could go any further. He raised an eyebrow while a smile played at the corner of his lips.

"A terrible work related incident?" he said slowly with a quizzical tone "That's what we're calling this event?"

I nodded, steadfast in my decision in what to refer to this awful unemployment mess as.

"I'd more call it some spiteful bugger trying to screw you over and get you out of a job you were overly capable of doing." he sneered. A dark shadow fell across his face as he lowered his head and spoke. "Mon Chéri, I could investigate this further for you if you like. Unfair dismissal. I have lawyers."

I smiled and laid my head against his chest. He radiated warmth even through his clothes.

"No, its ok." I cooed gently "I'll figure it out. Play detective and get my revenge."

I felt a laugh rising in his chest, a deep rumble that suddenly burst forth from his lips.

"Like Batman." he chortled.

I sat up and looked intentionally offended.

"Yes, like Batman, what of it?"

He shrugged and gently lifted me from his lap as he stood.

"Well then, before you become a vigilante and ask for my help to fund your tech habit we should have that dance, before you need a secret identity."

He walked towards the door and reached for my hand. He turned out the light and carefully led us back out into the noisy night club. The music had softened again, a light rock tune I didn't recognise was playing and most of the dancers were now off to the sides of the dancefloor enjoying their drinks and each other's company. Carter left my side for a moment but I didn't notice until he returned with two drinks in his hands. They were small shot glasses filled with blue liquid. I recognised it from the colour and sticky sweet smell immediately.

"Sourz?"

He nodded and Logical and Dreamy began to argue over how he would have known that, did he have stalker tendencies? I'd never been to this club before so it's not like it was a regular order for me. Right on cue, like he was reading my mind he answered my thoughts.

"You like blue drinks." he stated "It's listed on your Facebook profile, along with the music you like, some of the books and movies you like and," he blushed slightly "your cat Malakai."

I felt myself glowing red slightly and I downed my shot to try and avoid dealing with how stupid I'd looked. It's the age of social media and he could have found that info from almost any social media site I was part of. Most information I keep private but things like drinks and books, what's so personal about that?

Carter tossed back his shot and sat our glasses on a small table a few steps away in front of the one way glass wall. He turned to me and reached for my hand again.

"Dance?"

As I took his hand the first few notes of Learn to Fly by the Foo Fighters came over the speakers. As we joined the dance floor so did many other couples, all slow dancing to the gentle melody and soothing beat. The evening was wearing on and the day was coming to a close. I relaxed completely into Carter's shoulder as he softly held me round the waist, swaying in time with the music and almost performing a slight waltz, as much as is possible with a beat that isn't 3/3. The song played out and the moment ended. It was getting late and I was starting to feel exhaustion catch up with me after today's events. Carter must have felt me starting to fade on him as he suggested we get a glass of ice water and then organise me some transport home.

After my ice water I felt slightly more awake, but the ache deep within my muscles told me that I really did need to get home to my bed. My battery operated friend would have to stay hidden tonight, I was too exhausted to think of anything except sleep, despite the several occasions this evening the electrical jolts through my body had gone straight to my groin.

Lack of familiarity I heard Dreamy sigh as she snuggled up in a corner with Logical.

I dismissed her comment entirely as I realised that Carter was on his phone to someone. Seeing me watching, he ended the call and took my hand. There was that zap of lightening again and the warmth of his skin. I was now a little more awake and the ache in my body changed slightly, yearning for something other than sleep.

"I've called for a car to take you home Mon Chéri, the light in your eyes is fading and I'm pretty sure today's events are starting to take their toll." He explained as he gently held me close and kissed the top of my head.

Wearily I walked towards the front door as the DJ announced the last song and last orders at the bar. Carter kept in step with me and held my shoulder to help keep me upright. We reached the pavement and the two bouncers were still standing obediently at the door like suited and booted guard dogs. Both nodded to us as we passed and smiled. Carter walked me down the street towards the crossing where we stopped just shy of a taxi rank. I was surprised when a moment later his Porsche appeared being driven by an older gentleman of broad build and silver hair. I looked at Carter with surprise as he opened the rear door and let me in, then shuffled into the back seat beside me.

"It wouldn't be very gentlemanly of me not to see you home would it?" he stated.

I nodded as I put on my seat belt and then rolled my eyes at him as a thought dawned on me.

"I've seen yours now you want to see mine." I said teasingly.

A shocked expression flashed across Carters face as he clipped his seat belt into place which was then replaced by a wicked grin.

"Well, if you're offering Miss Jansent, who am I to refuse?"

He motioned to the gentleman behind the wheel and we moved off from the kerb.

"How does he know where we're going?" I whispered trying not to seem rude.

Carter laughed and explained that the man driving was Sam, more than a work associate than I had previously been lead to believe. Sam was actually a chauffeur, body guard, gopher and close friend to Carter. His wing man so to speak.

I bid Sam good evening as I lay my head back on the seat and recited my address off without even thinking about it. Logical kicked me in the head. *Our address, you're openly telling him where we live!* she bellowed. I dismissed her with a quick wipe of my hand across my brow.

We drove out of the city limits and the sparkle of lights fell behind us as we headed out into the country and towards home. Scott was waiting for me at the front door when we pulled up outside the house. Carter gingerly helped me out of the car, I truly was exhausted now and was seriously starting to flag. Scott met us at the bottom of the front steps. There was a brief and mutually brisk introduction from both sides and then Carter kissed my cheek gently as he said good evening and paced back to the car. He waited for Scott to help me inside and start closing the door before he climbed into the passenger seat of the Porsche and it sped off back into the black countryside, back towards the bright lights of the city centre.

Scott was full of questions as he led me upstairs to my room. I answered as many as I coherently could as I quickly slid out of my clothes and into my cosy fleece pyjamas. Seemingly confident I had been in no real danger and demanding we have breakfast tomorrow at a pancake place that had just opened on Belmont Street in the city, his treat, he left me to tuck myself into bed. Malakai pushed the door open as he softly padded into the room and jumped up onto the foot of the bed. Happy to sleep now his mistress was home. The light from the open door made a line across the duvet and it was the last thing I saw before falling asleep. Totally exhausted with the day's events, I felt my body fall into the black.

Chapter 6

Carter's hands are firm but soft on my skin. Gently he cups my cheek as he kisses me. He is carefully lying on top of me, his hair cascading down over his shoulders like a curtain sheltering us from the world outside. The soft light of evening shines through the window and gently colours the room in soft glowing whites and ambers. Carter's black cotton shirt is crumpled in a heap next to my head, I can smell him on it. His scent is everywhere right now, powerful and intoxicating. My skin pulses with the electricity that is always there, like static holding us together.

Carter lowers himself slowly until his chest is gently brushing my torso, his chest hair gently tickling from my stomach right up to my bra. I stare up at him, his eyes are black, his pupils completely dilated. His stare is intensely matching mine, my breathing is rushed. I can hear my heart beating in my ears. The rest of the world has melted away beyond the curtain of black surrounding me. Suddenly Carter rises to his knees, my body yearns for the weight that's just been lifted from it. His long black hair is flicked back over his broad shoulders and my eyes trace a line from the stubble on his chin, down his neck and across his torso down to the buckle of his belt. With one hand and very little effort he unhitches the buckle and the top button on his faded blue jeans. The top of his happy trail is showing and my blood begins to burn in my veins.

I close my eyes as the thrumming of blood in my ears becomes over powering. Carter begins to plant butterfly kisses gently from my belly-bar upwards. My back arches, pushing me towards him. His lips are hot and his kisses sear my skin but in all the right ways. I keep my eyes closed and my arms still as he traces a roadmap of kisses across my body. I can feel the length of his hair trailing gently up the side of my body as he continues kissing. He pauses for a moment at the border of my skin and the fabric of my bra, then continues kissing up across my collar bone and my neck. He nips playfully at my neck and ends finally at my lips. His kiss lingers there for a moment and is then gone.

I open my eyes to stare up into those dark pools again but they are gone. He is gone and I am lying alone in my bed. My tabby cat Malakai looked up briefly from the bottom of the bed as I tugged my duvet tighter around myself. It was just a dream. Luckily Dreamy and Logical are both still sleeping soundly or I'd be getting ridiculed by now. What is that man doing to me? I rolled over and flicked the duvet for a quick blast of cool air. My skin was damp and overly warm. I tossed and turned a little to settle myself back into sleep. As I drifted off, I thought it didn't really matter, it's not like I had a job to get up for anymore. Then I contemplated Carter's offer to look into the real reason behind my sudden unemployment. The thought was still lingering as my eyes closed and I entered another dream.

It is evening and the stars are all out, twinkling like diamonds in the black sky. I am standing on a bridge with

Carter. We are looking down into the rushing river below us. As I stare down into the burbling and crashing water flowing quickly under the bridge I fail to notice Carter climb up on the stone balustrade on the bridge until he is almost in front of me. Silently he holds out his hand reaching for mine. His eyes are pleading with me to trust him. Slowly I hesitantly hold my hand out and feel the sudden warmth of his fingers as they wrap around my hand and wrist, pulling me up onto the balustrade. We gingerly turn and face the river. There is a cool breeze blowing past us. It smells sweet and fresh. I turn and look at Carter. His eyes are dark pools reflecting the heat I feel inside. He is smiling at me as he suddenly steps off the bridge. My fingers intertwined with his I'm pulled off the bridge with him. For a second I am scared but then a feeling of calm washes over me, I glance down to see the water rushing up towards me. There is no river below us now, there is a train track and what's worse is there is a train hurtling towards us. The cooling breeze is now a hot wind, scorching my skin and all I can smell is burning flesh. I look for Carter but he is gone. I brace myself for the oncoming train and then I fall, absorbed by the tracks which have turned to liquid. The river? No, this liquid is sticky and it's dragging me down. I look at my hands as I flail to keep my head above the surface, they are red, blood red. I'm drowning in a river of blood and Carter is nowhere to be seen. I feel myself going under, the metallic taste of blood fills my mouth and nose as I try to break the surface. By the time I am going under for the third time I'm exhausted, there is no fight left in me. I close my eyes and hold my breath as I let myself slip away.

I woke with a gasp into my pitch black room. I was struggling to breathe so I sat up on the edge of my bed, legs hanging limply above the floor. Malakai had vanished from the end of the bed, no doubt disturbed by my dream thrashing. I tried to gather my scattered thoughts as fragments of the nightmare slowly faded from my mind's eye. I was soaked with sweat, my hair was sticking to my face and neck. As my eyes slowly focused and my breathing calmed I heard Malakai meowing from the bathroom. Curiosity got the better of me, he doesn't usually meow at Scott in the middle of the night. I padded slowly down the polished bare floor boards of the landing towards the bathroom. The meowing got louder as I approached and I heard a loud growl and hiss. Fearing Malakai may be hurt I dashed into the bathroom. Malakai was in the sink staring defiantly at the bathroom window. For a second I was in complete confusion and then a movement caught my eye. There was a shape at the window, beyond the frosted glass. I screamed and fell back against the bathroom wall, landing in the towel basket as I did. I was frozen for a second, my mouth stuck in a perfect "O" as a blood curdling scream continued to flow from me. Logical and Dreamy were immediately awake and looked at the shape that was dashing away from the frame of the window. Suddenly Scott's hand was on my shoulder and I struck out at him. Expertly he deflected my flying fist and caught me in his arms.

"What the hell?" he yelled, still half asleep.

I was still staring at the frosted glass window and all I could do was point and utter "there was a man." I shook uncontrollably as I tried to regain control of my limbs and voice.

Like a shot Scott was up and ran down the stairs in his boxers.

"Stay there and don't move." he bellowed as he vanished out of the front door to confront whoever or whatever had been at the window.

Malakai had now jumped down from his defensive position in the sink and was curled on my lap purring reassuringly. I listened intently for Scott to re-enter the house. The shock was beginning to set in as I sat shivering in the towel basket, which I realised was incredibly uncomfortable. After what seemed like eternity Scott came back to the bathroom. He instantly hugged me tightly and stroked the matted hair from my face. I felt the tears begin at that moment. Hot, burning and stinging in my eyes. They ran like small rivers down my cheeks, uncontrollable and free. The niggling memory of my nightmare was still with me and it was beginning to feel like too much.

Scott gathered me up out of the basket and helped me back into my room. Malakai dutifully followed and pounced up onto the bed as Scott tucked the duvet back around me. He said something about treating shock and vanished out of my room. I must have dozed off for a few moments as he returned, wrapped in his robe, with a warm cup of tea with far too much sugar.

"I need to make a call." he said with a far too serious expression on his face. Scott had always been the happy go lucky, fun loving one out of the pair of us, but right in that moment his sombre expression shocked and upset me further.

He only went out onto the landing. I could hear him pacing the floor as he talked hurriedly in hushed tones. As he ended the call he re-entered the room, his expression slightly less concerned. I was downing the last of my too sweet tea. I placed the empty mug on my bedside table.

Scott perched on the end of the bed next to Malakai who groaned slightly at his presence.

"We're gonna have to skip breakfast and have brunch instead." he informed me. "The police are on their way to have a look around the property and see if there are any signs left by anyone. We will have to go and give statements tomorrow about what we saw or heard. I'll stay up and help them when they get here. You try and go back to sleep for a while if you can. I'll sleep in here once they have gone if you like? I can crash on the floor and use the camping mat. It'll be like old times."

I nodded mutely. I was now feeling totally drained and now the adrenaline had worn off I just wanted to sleep. Scott kissed my head and then turned out the light and let me settle down to sleep again. Malakai padded up the bed and snuggled up in front of my chest as I lay on my side. I gently put one arm around him and pulled him closer drawing comfort from the soft rumble of his purr. I once again drifted into the black.

When I next woke my room was filled with bright sunshine and Scott was asleep on the floor next to my bed. He was lying on his back with his right arm over his eyes fending off the sun in his sleep. He was half covered by a pale blue sleeping bag but I could see he'd slept in his boxers and an old gym t-shirt. If not for his preference to men I could have found him attractive. In all honestly when we'd met at University, we had dated and I had always found him attractive, there just wasn't any spark between us. Permanently friend zoned by each other.

I carefully stepped out of bed and gingerly tiptoed off to the bathroom. After checking the window thoroughly before entering the room I rush to get washed and sorted before heading back to my room. I'm just drying my hands as I hear my alarm going off on my mobile. Damn it, I thought I'd turned that off yesterday. I rush back to my room to find Scott sat on my bed with my phone. He smiled at me as I entered the room.

"Sleep any better?" he asks as I climb back into bed next to him and snuggle up to him from under the covers.

"A little." I confessed.

"What the hell was that last night?" he asked, honestly at a loss to explain any of it.

"I'd had a nightmare and when I woke Mali was growling and meowing from the bathroom. When I got there, there was a shape at the window. It moved when I came in to see what was wrong with Mali and then when I realised there was someone or something there I screamed and fell backwards into the basket where you found me. What did the police say?"

He shrugged and sagged his shoulders.

"They said there were marks in the mud on the grass like someone had run across it, but the print was so pulled with slipping in the mud that they couldn't identify anything from it and other than a small tuft of fabric on the window ledge that's all they have."

"Fabric, foot print" I squeaked, "It was a person, not an owl or something?"

I had honestly hoped it had been my sleep addled brain exaggerating things in my mind's eye and it had possibly just been a big owl perched on the windowsill. The thought that there was someone at my bathroom windowsill, upstairs no less, terrified me!

"Seems we had a peeping Tom." said Scott very matter of fact. "Sad really, the dumb son of a bitch wouldn't have seen anything through frosted glass in the dark!"

His tone became more teasing and he fired off another couple of sarcastic remarks aimed at our peeping Tom. I start to feel a little more at ease as Scott left the room to go and get showered and dressed. My phone bleeped in my hand and I reached down to silence the snoozed alarm and realised it was a text message from Carter. My heart skipped a little with both excitement and slight panic as the shadow of last night's nightmare was still in the back of my mind. I opened the text message.

Morning Sunshine. I hope you slept well after yesterday's events. You looked exhausted. I hope you can join me for coffee the day after tomorrow. Unfortunately I have meetings all day today. Dean was asking for you this morning when Sam was picking up my morning coffee. He'd love to see you too. Let me know. C

I smiled down at my phone as I started to type my response. I could hear Scott's singing blaring from the shower and giggled a little to myself. I typed with one hand as I walked around my room collecting items of clothing in preparation for my own shower.

Morning C, my sleep wasn't as good as I'd hoped. I will explain all about it over coffee as you've suggested. I hope your meetings aren't too boring. I will text you again later on to see ☺ K.

I set my phone down on my bedside table as I went into my drawers to collect some underwear when my phone almost immediately alerted me to a new message. I ignored it for a moment while I selected some comfortable yet sexy underwear. Anything to make me feel better and take me away from the memory of last night. I wasn't sure how long the waking nightmare feeling was going to last but it hadn't faded much since I'd woken up. Shimmying into my underwear and fiddling with the catch for my bra I looked down at the phone to see who had texted me. I nearly jumped out of my skin as a new message came in and the phone flashed to life in light and sound in front of my nose.

Laughing at my own stupidity I picked up the phone and unlocked the screen. One from Carter and one from Jenny.

Hiya Kira, How are things going? Seen Mr Brams again since you left the office? By the way, WTF? Want me to do some digging for you? When are you free for a catch up coffee/tea? Jen xx

I quickly type a response about being free for tea anytime she is, let's face it, I'm not exactly fighting off job offers yet. Logical gave me a frown, *you can't be chased until they know you're out there!*

I await your next text Miss Jansent. I must confess these meetings would be a tad more interesting with you under my desk! C

I smirk to myself as Logical gasps disapprovingly. Dreamy is reflecting my saucy smirk. What an indecent proposal, am I really that kind of girl? Knowing his playful yet kinky thoughts I decide to respond the only way I can think of for now.

Yes Sir. That would be agreeable. K

Feeling I've accomplished the basics for flirty texting for the day I throw on my torn jeans and a black vest top. I'd just pulled on my, still new, comfy trainers and walked out of the room when I almost bumped right into Scott on the landing. He was soaking wet, his ginger locks flopped over his face, dripping onto the dark blue carpet that matched his eyes. A large bath towel was loosely wrapped around his waist concealing his secret weapon. Many a friend at university had remarked on Scott's "gift" but it was like damp gunpowder to me. I knew what side he batted for so having a larger than average appendage did nothing for me. Logical reminded me I'd always thought of Scott more as a brother I'd never had. So many late nights in his halls watching late night wrestling and discussing the evenings failed conquests while spooning in his bed. Not once had I thought about testing the waters to see if I could "convert" him. I was happy with the status quo and so was he.

"You all ready to go?" he asked as he scooped his dripping ginger tendrils back over the top of his head.

I nodded as I fiddled with my MP3 player in my pocket. Music always calms me down no matter what has happened. Had I been forced to get the bus home after my disastrous final morning at work then my MP3 player would have been my best friend but I had needed human companionship right at that particular moment. It was like Carter had been meant to fill that role. I'm a firm believer of everything happening for a reason. I still hadn't figured out the universes plan for last night's scare yet though.

I hopped down the stairs with Malakai at my heels as Scott called down the stairs after me that he'd be ready in

15 minutes. I automatically added on an extra 15 minutes as Scott always took double his estimation for any given time for anything. I bounced into the kitchen with the tones of System of a Down ringing in my ears as I grabbed a cat pouch from the cupboard under the sink and crouched down to feed Malakai. I ruffled the top of his head as he bent down to eat from his bowl which proudly proclaimed him as the "Boss". He purred gratefully as he crouched to eat and tucked his tail underneath himself. He closed his eyes while he ate as if savouring every mouthful. I gently bent down to him so I didn't startle him as he ate. I softly ruffled the fur on the top of his head as he ate. He emitted a loud smacking rumbling sound as he tried to purr as he chewed. I stood up and flicked the kettle on as I passed it on my way to the bin. The lid swung closed after I deposited the foil pouch. I looked back over at the vibrating form that was still wolfing down chunks of meat in gravy. I was so grateful for Malakai. He'd seen me through some difficult times and felt like my own personally furry grounding force.

The kettle boiled beside the sink, steaming up the kitchen window slightly. I watched the birds on the tree outside the kitchen window as I automatically dropped a tea bag into my awaiting cup on the work top. A mother sparrow was teaching her youngsters, still balls of fluff, how to fly. Several times she dived from the tree branch and returned before the first youngster was brave enough to follow her lead. By the time the kettle clicked off the steam was already starting to clear and the sparrow family were all but gone. That was when I noticed the broken branch. A shiver ran through me. Was that how the shape had reached the bathroom window? Perhaps the branch had already been broken and I'd just never noticed it. I shook off the nagging doubt in my mind as I brewed my cup of tea. I deposited the tea bag on the side of the sink and left the view of the tree to grab the milk from the fridge. Settling at the small kitchen table I sipped gingerly at my hot tea while I watched Malakai finishing the last of his breakfast. My stomach growled in response but Scott's promise of breakfast in the city meant I'd have to wait, at least a little longer, for food.

By the time I'd finished my tea and placed the cup in the sink Scott was standing at the bottom of the stairs fiddling with the laces on his trainers as he held the car keys in his mouth. He looked up as I stepped out of the kitchen.

He straightened and removed the key fob from his teeth.

"Ready to go?" he asked quizzically

"As I'll ever be." I responded, my voice full of doubt.

"I know you don't want to do this..." he began

"I know." I interrupted him "This isn't the same as what happened at university. We have a peeping Tom. That's all. I was just startled, but we need to go and make a statement. I know the drill."

He nodded sympathetically as he held out his arm and I hugged into his side. His arm wrapped over my shoulders and gave me some comfort. Despite knowing Scott for years and thinking of him as family I couldn't help but notice that I'd felt safer in Carter's arms. Logical chastised me from her corner and Dreamy gave me a mental hug to prepare me for giving a statement to the police. An eerie memory surfaced in the darkness at the back of my mind.

It had been a late night for all of us. After we'd left the club we had all returned to our separate university halls. Most of the girls I shared with were still out. Now it was coming up for half term everyone was winding down and enjoying themselves a little more than was probably advisable. I reached the safety door into the building and smiled to myself as I could hear Scott's baritone voice around the corner still belting out a Foo Fighters song we'd all taken great delight in moshing to only an hour or so earlier. I opened the door and wandered slightly tipsy into the dark front hallway of the building. I heard the safety door slam shut behind me as I climbed the stairs to the third floor to my flat. The security lighting flickered on beside me at each floors landing as I kept walking to my flat. My feet were now starting to hurt even though I only had a pair of old scuffed trainers on. I was far luckier than our friend Pam who had been wearing heels. She'd ended up being carried home by one of our other friends Martin as her feet were so painful she couldn't get rounds from the bar anymore. That was our cue to walk home. Still my feet were swollen from a night of dancing and traipsing from pub to pub all night. I was looking forward to getting into my cosy PJ's and giving my feet a quick soak in essential oil before bedding down for the night. As I passed the second floor landing I checked my watch. It was approaching 2am. I'd never been so glad my Chemistry classes had been moved so I had nothing to worry about today.

I finally reached the door to my flat and turned the key in the lock. The internal safety light flickered on as I closed the front door behind me and opened the internal door. I sluggishly paced the hall past the living area and towards my room. My door was wide open, which was odd. I was sure I'd locked it when I'd gone out. I sauntered in and turned my back on the room as I flicked the light switch on and tossed my keys onto my desk beside the door. Sleepily I shrugged out of my coat and hung it on the hook on the door. As the faux leather tugged on the peg my CD player sprang to life behind me with Ava Adore by the Smashing pumpkins. Before I could turn around there was a large hand across my mouth and my legs gave out from under me as I was dragged backwards to the bed. Terrified I kicked as hard as I could but it was for nothing. The hand still clamped over my mouth I was tossed onto the bed face down and still unable to see my attacker. I couldn't see him but I could smell him as he bound my hands behind me with what sounded and felt like thick tape. I recognised the smell of cigarettes and recognised the brand. Only one person I knew smoked them. I could also smell alcohol, strongly, like he'd bathed in it.

The hand over my mouth was quickly replaced with a thick band of tape and I was flipped over onto my back. I blinked a little as my eyes readjusted to the light. Big Davey, as everyone called him, perched on the end of my single bed like a looming ogre. His eyes were slightly bloodshot and his face was contorted in a look of hatred and disgust. He looked like he'd been crying.

"You!" he began, his voice low and angry. "You told me she'd not reject me. You said she'd see the good in me. You lied!"

He lunged at me and struck me across the face, hard. I shook my head as my eyes rolled a little from the force of the hit. He wasn't pulling his blows. He was furious and I couldn't figure out what I'd done. I continued to stare at him with confusion and fear.

"Don't look at me like that." he continued. "I asked her out, told her I was a different man from the reputation she knew. Do you know what she did?"

He was keeping his voice low In case anyone else was in the flat but his anger was increasing and he was seething with venom. The spittle was collecting in the corners of his mouth as he spouted his venom. As he spoke he kept leaning closer to me, the smell of alcohol and cigarette smoke was becoming nauseating but there was nothing I could do. His thigh had my ankles pinned and was making it increasingly painful to lay in this position.

I shook my head, wide eyes in fear of his response.

He struck me across the face again, turning my head towards the wall before he answered. I could feel the blood surging to my cheek. The blood was singing in my ears as my pulse raced.

"She laughed in my face. She fucking laughed and rejected me. She didn't hear me out like you said she would and she had me fucking thrown out of the club for following her." he growled.

The scenario he was describing was now starting to spark a memory. A few weeks ago after a few pints and several games of pool at a local pool hall Davey and I had gotten talking. He was in some of my classes but I'd never really spoken to him much before. He was known as the local "Lord" to many of the students. Connected and able to get anything a student could desire for the right price. Drink, drugs and other items flowed through him and into the halls. He had people under him to collect payment and extract payment when it wasn't forthcoming. He was a junior gang lord in the making but that night at the pool hall he'd approached me as a sympathetic ear. Damn my caring nature. If I hadn't listened and actually given a shit then I wouldn't be here. Dreamy was mentally rubbing my shoulders and Logical was sadly giving me that "I told you so" look with remorse.

I could feel the tears starting to well up in my eyes as I remembered our conversation. The pool hall had been closing so he walked me back to my flat as we'd continued to talk about this girl he was crushing on badly but was beyond his reach. I'd advised him to show her he wasn't a force to be feared, more that he could be her protector and that she'd never want for anything. Turn his reputation on a positive spin to give him a chance to win her heart. I never knew anything about her only that her name was Rose and she was training to be a physiotherapist. We'd arrived at my flat and he was almost in tears. I'd taken pity on him and invited him in for a coffee to finish our conversation. We'd talked until about 3am when he'd left to return to his own flat before classes. That had been a few weeks ago and I hadn't even seen Davey in class. There was a rumour going around that he'd been arrested on suspicion of something. I never did find out what, but it turned out that he'd gone home to deal with a family matter.

My lip was bleeding underneath the tape. I could taste it in my mouth and feel it pooling between my lips. Salty and metallic. Slowly I turned my head back from the wall to look at him, fully expecting another blow. He shifted on the bed freeing my ankles. Quickly I pulled my legs up underneath me and lay in a tight ball on top of my pillows, watching him as he stared at his hands. I wriggled my wrists slightly behind my back testing for any weakness in the bindings but the tape was holding tight, even if I could get off the bed I had no way of getting out of the room before he would be upon me.

"You said she'd listen!" his voice cracked as another emotion crept into play. "You said she'd give me a chance. But you lied. She was just like the others and so are you."

He raised his fist and brought it crashing down towards me. I instinctively closed my eyes and braced for the impact. I heard the shattering of wood beside my face and opened my eyes. The tears were flowing freely now. I was terrified and I could no longer hide it from him. His fist had broken through the headboard of the bed inches from my face.

"You are going to pay for the humiliation you caused me." he spat in my face. His pupils were dilated and he couldn't focus properly. There was a concoction in his blood more potent than alcohol and nicotine and the ball in my stomach knotted tighter. I said a silent prayer in my head, this was not a situation I had ever wanted to find myself in and I had no idea what I should do.

He grabbed my ankles from under me and yanked me off the bed. My hands behind me caused my back to arch in a painful position and my head struck the ground as he threw me on the floor. With no care for my discomfort he fumbled with the fasteners on my jeans and ripped them off, throwing them onto the desk behind him. They clattered noisily as they knocked my high school award off of the desk. It smashed on impact with the floor and more tears fell from my eyes. It was like the smashed pieces on the floor were a prediction for what was about to happen to me. Whatever he had planned it was going to damage me in ways I couldn't imagine and I knew I was powerless to do anything about it. I looked up at him as he crouched over me. My eyes pleading with him to let me go. I began to mumble beneath the tape making sounds like a tortured puppy in the hope something in him would realise that this wouldn't solve anything. He struck me in the face again, this time with his full fist and my left eye filled with static momentarily. I blinked and shook my head but the pain in my eye wouldn't subside and I kept it closed. I watched as he stood full height and turned off the light behind him before crouching over me once again. He leaned in to whisper in my ear as his hands tugged at my t-shirt. With my good eye I could almost see his outline in the dim light filtering through my thin curtains.

"I'm going to make sure you never forget wronging me. I'm going to make sure you look like my favourite steak when I'm finished."

Suddenly out of nowhere he punched me right in the stomach and I could taste vomit in my mouth. I tried to scream out but despite the blood and vomit the tape was holding firm. Another punch struck me in the dark, this time in the side. I twisted in the dark trying to lessen the pain that was now spreading across my torso. His large hands were suddenly clambering at my bra yanking it down exposing my breasts. I turned my head away so my good eye could no longer see him as he drunkenly fondled them. The nausea rose again and I fought to keep it down. I was tortured with blows and caresses. I wasn't sure which made me want to vomit more. I lay there on the floor of my room, bound, gagged and unable to move, being punished for something I hadn't done.

After what felt like hours I was contorted on the floor, everywhere hurt and everywhere felt violated. His filthy hands had been everywhere and I started to wish I could vomit as there was a chance I might choke and end this. I opened my good eye to find him above me, watching me. I pleaded with my expression, begging him to stop. This just angered him further.

"Frigid bitch. You think you're better than me! I'm going to make you pay!"

He brought his fist down one more time and this time there was no static, there was only black.

When I finally woke over 24 hours later I was in a hospital bed and then had to relive the ordeal over when the police arrived to question me. Once discharged I moved into Scott's flat and finished out my year doing coursework online and safe in the knowledge that Davey wouldn't be doing that to anyone ever again. It emerged that Scott had taken my mobile home with him and as soon as he'd realised he'd come to return it. Unable to get an answer at the flat he'd bumped into one of my flat mates who'd explained about the "surprise" my friend had planned for me so she'd let him into the flat to wait for me. She'd had no idea of who he was or what he could possibly be planning but Scott knew immediately that no good could come of the situation so as a precaution he'd called the warden of the halls to let him in. That was how they came to find me black and blue and bleeding on the floor semi naked and Big Davey standing over me, jeans at his ankles.

I shuddered as the memory began to fade back into the black space at the back of my mind. The feeling of nausea wasn't fading as quickly and I gagged a little at the memory of that night and I leaned away from Scott holding my mouth. I suddenly felt dizzy as the thought that memory had brought back coupled with the shape at the bathroom window last night tightened the ball in my stomach. Scott caught me as I fell to my knees.

"Honey, you ok?" he instinctively held my hair back as I retched again.

Tears formed in my eyes and began to spill as I looked up at Scott.

"We don't have to do this today sweetheart. If it's bringing back too much."

Defiantly I shook my head and used his knee to push myself to my feet.

I took several deep breaths in through my nose and out through my mouth and the knot lessened a little. I grabbed my bag from the shelf by the door and walked out to the car.

"I can do this." I called to Scott as I went.

I reached the car and heard the doors click open as Scott fiddled with the front door lock.

I sank into the passenger seat and let the soothing smell of sandalwood wash over me as I tried to gather my scattered thoughts as Scott climbed into the driver's seat. The ignition turned over and the reassuring sound of the engine purred as the Golf rolled away from the house. I watched Malakai's face vanish from the living room window as we pulled away and headed into the city.

Scott put on some random music CD that a friend had made for him. It was his favourite made up of bands I'd never really heard of. My favourite on this CD was a band called Be Like Pablo. The music was gentle and ballad like.

It reminded me a little of Idlewild with North East accents. We listened until we reached the outskirts of the city and then turned the volume down as we approached the police station.

I kept the music from the CD in my head as I gave my statement. I played sections of it over and over to help me keep the darkness at bay. It wasn't as bad as I'd thought but I'd unwittingly released a demon in my mind that I'd kept caged for a long time and now the monster was there, always in the corner, waiting.

Scott was sitting out in the hallway when I left the interview room. He tilted his head at me as I walked over to him.

"I'm ok." I reassured him as I grabbed his hand. "It wasn't as bad as the last time"

I could feel the tears sparkling in the corner of my eyes when a voice calling my name suddenly snapped me back to reality.

"Kira Jansent?" asked the officer as he came towards us. He must have been a detective or something as he was in a suit not a uniform.

I nodded slowly, unsure of what he was going to ask.

"Could I have a word for a moment please? Nothing to worry about. Just a formality."

I gently stroked Scott's hand before following the detective into a nearby room.

"Please take a seat. This will only take a moment and is off the record." he reassured me as he perched on the edge of the desk against the wall.

"I'd prefer to stand if that's ok." I rebelled.

"It has come to our attention that you have recently been in the company of a Carter Brams, is this correct?" he asked, very matter of fact.

"I don't see what that has to...."

"Mr Brams has had a few high profile girl friends over the past several years. All of whom have ended up missing, never to be seen again, or dead just shortly after finishing with him."

His voice was serious and his eyes were locked onto mine with all seriousness as he continued. I swallowed hard as a lump formed in my throat.

"I know you've had a scare with a trespasser last night. This is just some friendly advice. Too many young girls in this town make the wrong choices and I have to write up the reports. Please don't become another one."

He opened the door and motioned for me to leave. Gingerly I walked past him. As I did he whispered in my ear and made me shiver.

"Just some friendly advice from an old man."

I didn't look back. I walked past Scott holding out my hand and as he took it I wrenched him out of his seat and kept walking. I didn't stop moving until we got back to the car.

Scott went to ask me about what had just transpired with the detective but I silenced him with a single look.

"Please just drive." I said flatly

"Pancakes?" He offered as he started up the Golf.

I shook my head a little too fast to try and calm myself.

"No, just home please! You can always make pancakes." my voice cracked as I felt the monster in the shadows moving.

"Too much for one day?"

"Yeah, you could say that." I laughed nervously. "Too many demons awoken for me today."

I could feel Scott's eyes dart to me every now and again as we drove home. I knew he was dying to ask me what had happened at the police station but I couldn't even try to answer that. I was still trying to filter it all myself. Tonight maybe my best friend would be Google. Perhaps Jenny's advice hadn't been so farfetched after all.

Once we'd arrived home Scott made his wonderful breakfast pancakes with bacon and we sat down to eat. As with everything in our lives breakfast needed a soundtrack. Scott plugged his phone into the docking station on the speaker on the kitchen windowsill. As the speaker sparked to life the familiar tones of "Waiting for superman" by Daughtry brought a smile to my lips. Scott and I had spent many a night in listening to songs like these. Songs that told a story and pulled at our heartstrings, but also songs that were great for karaoke in the living room.

Scott began to sing as he put the dirty dishes into the sink to soak as we ate. As he sang he began to dance a little and wiggle his ass as he moved gracefully about the kitchen until he finally sat beside me to stuff a pancake in his mouth.

"These are pretty good." he mumbled through his mouth of pancake.

I smiled and playfully swiped at him. Finally the dark cloud from last night and this morning was starting to lift and my thoughts turned to more enjoyable things.

"I think there's a classic Kevin Smith marathon on that movie channel this afternoon." I managed in between mouthfuls of pancake and bacon. "Would you like to play with me?"

Scott pretended to be offended and muttered something about the forwardness of today's girls as he stuffed the remaining pancakes into his mouth. It never ceased to amaze me the sheer volume of food Scott could pack away in that mouth of his. It never showed on him either. I was quite jealous of his athletic build at times.

After he'd swallowed his last mouthful he turned thoughtfully to me and waving his fork about thoughtfully he considered my offer of a drinking game.

"I'll fetch the mixers and you can be Dante." he chirped excitedly as he left the table.

He laughed at my playful groan as he left the room. He always thought he'd win these games, but he never did and never would. I'd been watching these movies almost religiously since university and there was no way, no matter how drunk I was I would fluff my lines. I got up from the table and deposited my plate into the sink. I tried not to look at the broken branch on the tree and headed into the living room. Malakai followed at my heel like an ever watchful shadow.

Scott and I drank the afternoon away taking shots and quoting our favourite lines from the Kevin Smith movies they'd included in their marathon. I knew they'd missed out a couple but I didn't want to give Scott "the rant" again so I let it slide.

As the closing credits of Clerks 2 ran I felt my eyes becoming heavy and the last thing I saw was Scott smiling and placing the throw over me as a comfortable blackness washed over me and everything was suddenly warm and dark.

Chapter 7

I awoke to the sound of Scott's voice as he recited lines in the kitchen. I could smell bacon. My eyes fluttered open and a ray of bright sunlight streamed in through the window and past the sofa. Malakai lay purring on his back, all four paws in the air as he rejoiced in the warmth on his tummy.

I moved to sit up and my head started to throb. This was my punishment for over sleeping.

Scott bounced through from the kitchen, a large cup of tea and a biscuit in his hands. He placed them down on the coffee table as he watched Malakai rolling about on the floor to regain the sun his shadow was blocking.

"He looks better than you today." he mocked playfully as he headed back towards the kitchen.

"Oh," he called over his shoulder "You left your phone in the hallway. It's been going demented for over an hour now. I left you to sleep because frankly you could do with it. I hope I've not cost you a job, but health comes first."

I sipped at my tea as my mind came back to the waking world. Who would be texting me this early? I looked at the clock on the wall. It wasn't early at all. It was nearly lunchtime and I remembered my meeting with Carter had yet to be finalised due to me falling asleep! I quickly grabbed my phone and gulped down the last of my tea. Malakai positioned himself on the back of the couch knowing the sun would move to warm him again soon.

I unlocked my phone and opened the messages. One was from Jenny wanting to arrange our catch up. The other three messages were from Carter and there was a missed call from a few minutes before I woke up. I was about to formulate a reply and make my excuses for not messaging back when my phone lit up with an incoming call. I jumped at the sudden sound coming from my phone and answered. It was Carter.

"Afternoon Mon Cheri. How are you today? I hope I didn't wake you. I only just realised that you may be asleep." He sounded concerned.

"Afternoon handsome." I yawned "sorry, excuse me. I have just woken up. Scott let me sleep on the sofa as I dozed off yesterday and I didn't sleep well the night before."

"You're certainly having an eventful week. Are you still up for coffee? Can we move it to this afternoon?"

"Definitely." I chirped a little too excitedly "I won't be ready for a bit though. I really need to go and grab a shower. Dean would throw me out right now. I've smelled nicer litter trays!"

On cue Malakai yawned and let out a defensive meow. I could hear Carters deep laugh resonating on the other end of the phone as he held it away from his mouth. I gave Malakai a reassuring pet as he repositioned himself on the back of the couch.

"That's actually kind of fortunate as I won't be able to meet you for a little while either. I've had a slight emergency that needed tended to and I'm going to be tied up until about 3pm. However I am assured that Dean is on the later shift today and both he and Sophie will keep a table for us around 3:30, if that's ok?"

"Yes that's perfect." I nodded like an idiot as logical reminded me I was on the phone and not Skype, he couldn't see me.

"Do you have any dinner plans? I happen to know a very exclusive place that is serving a very special menu tonight?" he asked, his voice deep and seductive.

"Hmmm, that sounds intriguing." I said in a contemplative tone.

"Would you like Sam to pick you up about 3pm?" he asked, ignoring my attempt at a tease.

"Yeah, that'd be fine." I replied a little deflated that he didn't play along with my tease.

"Good girl." he replied "I expect no argument about dinner. Wear something smart but casual, heels are optional."

He was now taunting me. I bristled a little at the insinuation that I couldn't handle a pair of heels, despite the awful show he had previously seen. Logical reminded me I'd always looked like a new born calf in anything taller than a few inches and I conceded defeat.

"No arguments here Sir." I hissed down the phone only to be greeted with more laughter.

"Right, you shall be collected at 3pm and I'll meet you at the Coffee House. Until then."

"Bye for now." I replied shyly, feeling like I'd just been reprimanded by a teacher.

I placed the phone down on the coffee table and ate the biscuit Scott had left and decided to dig out my tablet for a little Google snooping. The nagging warning from the Detective had resurfaced in my mind along with Jenny's advice about Googling strange men before meeting them. In my heart I honestly felt no fear about Carter or that he was hiding anything from me, much as logical chastised me for it.

I fired up my tablet from its slumber and Googled Carter Brams. Most of the results were to be expected a few interviews from business magazines and the likes. There were a few gossip pages remarking on the eligible bachelor and his infrequent and short lived love affairs. I scrolled down one page's list of past girlfriends and decided to google a few of them further. I was a little shocked to discover that indeed a couple of them had gone missing but on further exploration of their online pages discovered they were notorious gold diggers and known for causing trouble and wrote them off as a bit of a non-event. People who made mistakes went missing all the time, it was a fact of life. If you wanted to be lost after a massive mistake then you could hide, from friends, family and the media. I found one listed ex had died but on further inspection of that case, through the wonders of online information, she had died sadly from diabetic coma. There were no records on the other ex's and I decided to stop digging. Logical had to admit that this seemed to all be above board and more like conspiracy theory from an over protective old man. I packed up my tablet and put it into my messenger bag in the front hall. I ran upstairs to grab a shower and chose something to wear for coffee and then dinner. I chose a smart but casual skirt and blouse combo. The skirt was a dark olive green and was knee length. The blouse was white but not see through, which was a relief as my only good bra was black lace with pink padding above the underwire. I chose a skimpy pair of black lace shorts that near enough matched. My mother had always taught me to wear clean and matching underwear in case I was ever taken away in an ambulance and needed undressed. I had to laugh at the whole scenario as it played out in my head. How likely was it that paramedics would care what my underwear looked like? If they had undressed me it would be to save my life, not be impressed that my underwear matched!

I was still laughing at the thought as I went into the shower. I wasn't in for too long before Scott came up asking what my plans were. I explained from the other side of the bathroom door I would be out for dinner and would be back later on at night. There was a long pause before Scott next spoke.

"Mmmmmhmmmm." he replied.

"What is that meant to mean Scott Fitzgerald? I can feel you judging me from the other side of this door!"

"I'm not judging you darlin'." he squeaked defensively. Scott's voice always shot up an octave when he felt he was being blamed for something. "I've just not seen you this into anyone since, well, forever. It's nice to see you finally have that sparkle back in your eye again."

His words hit a soft spot full of the memories of my friends after my attack. It took several weeks for most of them to feel comfortable talking to me and until the bruises had mostly healed. We all went out to Slain's Castle for dinner and drinks one evening before the end of Easter term. Everyone I was friends with in Aberdeen from both high school in my home town and University were there. We were a party of about 10 and took up the largest table Slain's could put together. There were meals, drinks and madness as we reminisced about the past and looked to the future. We didn't talk about what had happened to me, only focused on the positive and the fond memories we shared. Looking around the table I was overwhelmed by the friendship I felt. Old friends and new altogether and getting along so well and all in support of me. We ended the night with a few Karaoke songs in the Triple Kirks before heading back to a well-deserved sleep in the halls. It was that night that Scott had remarked on the spark being reignited in my eyes which had seemed like stone since the night my life turned upside down.

"It's nice to have my spark back again." I smiled from behind the bathroom door. I finished rinsing the conditioner out of my hair and set about shaving. No sense in wearing nice underwear if I looked like a fur ball. Logical scoffed at my vanity and Dreamy looked off into the distance as if she were seeing into the future.

Once I was dry and presentable again I set about straightening my hair. I had just finished when my phone bleeped with a message. I grabbed it off the bed and eagerly unlocked it, hoping it was Carter.

The message was from an unknown number but contained no attachments so I opened it, fairly sure it wasn't spam. It simply read: **You will know me again.**

I shrugged. It must have been a wrong number. I did occasionally get random texts meant for a lady named Persephone and judging by the previous texts meant for her, this was very probably one for her as well. I deleted it without giving it a second thought and put on some light make up before going downstairs and assembling my bag. I had asked Scott to print me off some CV's which I intended to post through some office doors between coffee and dinner. Multi-tasking while in the city was a good plan, even if it cramped Carter's style a little.

By the time 3pm rolled around I had sealed the last of my envelopes complete with C.V's and covering letters along with a few essentials for a night out. I grabbed my phone from the hall table where it had been charging and pulled on my kitten heels and went into the living room to check for Sam.

As I looked out if the window I saw the familiar shape of the Porsche as it rolled to a stop outside the house.

"That's my ride." I called through to Scott. He was still busy slaving away in the kitchen with his newest pulled pork recipe. He came through and gave me a tight hug and a kiss on the forehead before stroking my cheek with his oven glove and dusting off his apron.

"Are you my mother now?" I joked "Stop looking at me like that."

He tilted his head to one side thoughtfully before sighing. "My wee Kira's all grown up."

I playfully punched him in the arm before I walked towards the door.

"Just remember to use protection!" he called far too loudly as I opened the front door.

Sam was standing there waiting for me and I blushed scarlet as I shot Scott a very angry look as I walked down the steps and into the waiting car.

Sam was his familiarly quiet self as we drove into the city. I sat in the back seat of the car, playing with the keyrings on my messenger bag. A small silver pair of handcuffs with a grey ribbon hung from the d ring on the side of the bag. I stroked the grey ribbon and giggled to myself. What would Ana do with my situation?

I contemplated all of the books I'd read, the ones with damsels in distress being rescued by knights in shining armour and the strong female leads who try as they might found themselves falling for a strong and determined man and enjoying a little power play in the process. Which one was I? I was definitely stronger for all my life events but I was still broken, damaged goods in a way. Was I something to be fixed?

All too soon we were in the city. We passed several small stores on the way to the Coffee House. I caught the shop sign of one which was a pet store. It was having a sale on cat scratching posts. I would have to remember that one. Malakai was taking liberties with the back of the couch and could use a distraction before we needed to repair it or replace it altogether. I quickly typed a small memo on my phone to remind me later. I seemed to be needing more and more memos to remind me of things when my thoughts were on Carter. He had a habit of making all other thoughts melt away into the ether.

Sam pulled up in the small side street behind the Coffee House and let me out of the car. He walked me to the corner and silently bowed allowing me to enter the Coffee House alone. We had made good time and it wasn't yet 3:30. I walked up to the counter only to see Carter waving me to our usual table at the back. I nodded to Dean as he appeared behind the counter then smartly and seductively I paced over to Carter in my kitten heels. He looked impressed as I took my seat opposite him. I nodded knowingly at him.

"I believe I owe you a double for that performance Miss Jansent. That was a lovely catwalk in those kitten heels."

I turned and waved 2 fingers over at Dean, luckily he knew exactly what I meant with my motion and started brewing two drinks. I turned back to Carter to find him watching me with a huge grin on his face.

"What?" I snapped playfully.

"The difference in you today is almost astounding." he remarked watching me place my bag under the table and remove my coat. I hung it gently on the back of my chair, painfully aware of his eyes tracing every move I made.

I turned back to stare straight into those brown pools and for a moment I lost my train of thought.

"What do you mean? How am I different?" a small alarm sounded at the back of my brain. Could he tell I was putting up a front? I was still reeling from the events the previous night and day.

"You seem more confident and like the events of the other day are like water off a ducks back. But I can't help but feel you are only putting a face on it. Tears don't seem far away."

How could he see right through me like this? I checked my body language and nothing I could see betrayed my true feelings. I shot him a questioning stare but before I could get my answer Dean arrived with our drinks.

"Your usual coffee Mr Brams and your tea Kira." he beamed as he placed the cups down.

"Sophie will be right over with the cake." he chirped before I could open my mouth to ask.

Carter returned his smile and took hold of my hands across the small table.

"What's troubling you Kira. You can't hide it from me." he said in a stern tone that almost startled me.

"I'll be fine. I just need to put a front on it for a little while. Work and everything is just getting to me today. Honestly I'm just having a bad head day. I'll be fine."

He almost sneered at my response as he took a sip from his coffee cup.

I'd never seen this side to him before. He seemed ruffled and slightly on edge like he could read me like an open book and was angered by my protective lies.

"I know you're not being honest with me Kira." he muttered from the lip of his cup.
"I don't appreciate that. I thought we were building something between us and this endangers that."

His tone was a warning and his words came as a low growl from deep in his throat.

I sat totally bewildered for a moment as I stared across the table at Carter. His warm brown eyes seemed suddenly sharp and cold. His shoulders were raised slightly. His fingertips were whitened where they gripped the sides of the coffee cup. He was angry with me for not trusting him with the truth but I hardly knew him. I had never trusted anyone with my secrets, except Scott. Could I entrust my burden with him? Could he ever look at me the same way when he knew how much I was truly broken? I'd already put so much trust into this sexy but virtual stranger.

Our staring contest was momentarily broken when Sophie arrived at the table with our two pastries. They looked and smelled delicious. My mouth began to water as I smelled the freshly baked treat. Carter's expression too lightened as he inhaled the spiced aroma of our food.

Dreamy was tugging at the back of my mind, reminding me of the spark and the emotion I felt around Carter. That hadn't happened before and I was starting to feel that it may not happen again. Logical wasn't even arguing with her. After the events so far this week I was emotionally exhausted carrying this all on my own and the warning from the Detective no matter how false was still wearing on me. Perhaps I did just need to stop trying to protect my heart. I would never know how deep the waters ran with Carter unless I took the plunge. The fact he seemed angry and hurt at my lie made me feel guilty and like I owed him a bigger piece of myself. My only worry was where the tide was going to take me once I dived in.

We sat in silence for a long while as we ate the pasties and sipped at our drinks. Carter's eyes never left me. His gaze was piercing and intimidating. It was like he was trying to burn the truth from me with his eyes. Yet at the same time there was still a flicker of inviting warmth in them. Like a shelter from the storm I was battling inside.

Finally Carter broke the silence once we had both finished eating.

"I'm sorry Kira."

I was surprised to find myself responding to him while having not formulated a response in my head first.

"No. I'm sorry." I paused a second then the rest just came pouring out of me.

"I was lying. I'm not ok but I'm trying to deal with it on my own. I'm not used to sharing my burdens with anyone, especially well to do nightclub owners who pick me up in coffee houses and treat me to Michelin star dinning on a whim."

As soon as I said it I realised how harsh it sounded. Carter recoiled slightly in his seat, worrying his napkin between his fingers a second before responding. He took my hands again across the table.

"It can't be helped. It's not often I meet genuine people. Especially pretty ones who have an open soul and a pure heart. I see something in you Kira. Something I've not seen in a woman for a very long time. I'd forgotten I'd even missed it until that first night where you made me laugh. You had no idea who I was and yet you stayed in my company all evening and it was me you called for help at your most vulnerable. That means a lot to me. You can't begin to understand."

His eyes were warm dark pools once again. Enticing me in with promises of safety and security. He never let go of my hands as he spoke. His thumbs softly massaged the delicate skin between my thumb and forefinger. His skin was searing mine in all the right ways. The buzz of electricity flowed through both of us. I shuffled slightly in my seat as my skin began to feel hyper sensitive and the look in his eyes was igniting my veins. Butterflies fluttered up in my stomach, stirring a heat that sank and settled between my legs. Logical was nowhere to be seen and Dreamy was perched on the edge of her seat, her eyes like saucers at the scene revealing itself before her.

At exactly the same moment Carter and I stood and leaned forwards over the table and met, lips first. A jolt ran through me and I closed my eyes as I melted into his kiss. His skin burned like an aching desire on mine. His soft lips opened as his probing tongue softly searched for mine. As they met, they entwined and drew our kiss in deeper. I remembered our kiss before in the alley way. This was slower and more purposeful but it still had the same burning passion and desire. I felt Carter's hand gently stroking my arm and I opened my eyes. Slowly and purposefully he backed away a little watching for my response. My eyes darted from side to side looking for any reason that Carter would have broken off our kiss. I could see Sophie and Dean stood arm in arm at the counter looking wistfully at us as an elderly gentleman stood at the counter muttering something about the poor service he'd been receiving.

I retook my seat as Carter pulled his wallet from his pocket and headed off towards Dean. I watched him go, wondering what the hell I was doing. I felt suddenly lost. Did he want me or not? Could I share my truth with him? Would he recoil from a creature he thought of as an angel but was actually a hideous beast, broken and torn in more ways than he could imagine? I glanced out the window at the bustling street outside to try and gather my thoughts. There was a large guy leaning on the window lighting a cigarette. As he took his long first drag he stared right into the coffee house and right at me. A shiver ran through me. I felt like someone had just severed my spine with ice. I was instantly cold and paralysed. My eyes were wide and my expression frozen with complete terror. Something burned as it snaked its way down my back. The figure at the window was Big Davey.

Carter gently touched my shoulder and I jerked in fear, swiping at him with my right hand. He dodged back and grabbed me by the wrist pulling me into his chest and softly stroking my hair. As my head cleared and I was suddenly able to move, I inhaled deeply and realised I'd been holding my breath. I looked up at Carter who stared down at me with a worried expression on his face. I turned my head back towards the window and the figure was gone. There wasn't even a mark on the window where he had been leaning. Was the recent stress of events starting to manifest as hallucinations? I suddenly felt incredibly foolish and I struggled from Carter's grip. I bent and grabbed my bag from underneath the table. As I straightened Carter was still regarding me with the same worried expression. I tucked a stray strand of hair behind my ear as I bit my lip and looked him deep in the eye.

"Ok, I know I was a little angry that you lied but I don't think I deserved that did I?" he quipped.

I smiled, feeling like a complete idiot then thought of something witty to say.

"You just made me so "palm twitchingly mad"." I giggled, starting to feel the fear melting and giving way to the warm thrum of energy between us.

He raised an eyebrow at me as he lifted his hands behind his head freeing the braid he'd had tied and letting his hair flow in waves from his shoulders. My breath caught at the sight. I'd always been a sucker for guys with long hair but Carter's long, dark waves were the dream of any woman. Perfectly conditioned and the way it fell from his shoulders just pronounced his firm frame even more. I felt myself biting my lip again. Gently he raised a finger and popped my lip back from behind my teeth. He then restrained his flowing mane in a looser pony tail.

""Palm twitchingly mad" huh?" he teased.

I fully stuck my tongue out at him childishly as I tried to rein in my thoughts. Carter's eyes narrowed for a moment as he focused on my tongue bar.

"How long have you had that tongue piercing?" he asked.

"About three years now. I did it for a dare."

He shook his head and smiled as he reached out his hand for mine.

I took his hand and felt the safety of the static buzzing between us. My shoulders slumped slightly as I let the last of the tension flow out. I took in a deep breath and slowly exhaled all the negativity from my body.

"Where are we headed?" I asked as we made our way to the door.

"I thought you might like some dinner before we head out this evening. There's a theme night at the club tonight and Dean and Sophie have been invited as my VIPs. There's space for your friend Scott too if you'd like to invite him along."

There was a slight edge to his voice as he mentioned Scott. I got the feeling it'd take him a while to fully forgive Scott for not answering my call that morning, but on the plus side, all of this happening between Carter and I was because of his absence.

I nodded and quickly grabbed my mobile from my bag. I sent him a brief text asking if he'd like to go clubbing tonight and possibly invite a friend to tag along. I wasn't sure these days if Scott was actually seeing anyone or just "sampling the local cuisine" as he put it. He could be such a slut.

A smile played on the corner of my lips as I replaced the mobile in my bag and I braced myself inside as we exited the coffee house. The image of Big Davey hadn't left my mind, but there was no way it could have been him. He was still locked up wasn't he?

Chapter 8

The fresh cold wind bit into the skin of my face as we exited the coffee house. It refreshed me and chilled me to the core at the same time. You have to love Scottish weather. I shivered and pulled my coat tighter around me. Carter must have seen me as the next thing I knew his arm was around my shoulders pulling me into his side. Even through clothing the heat he exuded was warming my side.

The wind buffeted both as us as we began to walk down Union Street. Carter's pony tail was wildly whipping around and just narrowly missed my face on a couple of occasions. I giggled slightly as I batted it away with the back of my hand. I felt like a cat with a piece of string.

Carter tucked the unruly length inside his collar as we headed on towards the traffic lights. We looked just like any other couple out walking on Union Street. Carter did tower over me slightly but no one took any note of who he was, despite being the most eligible bachelor in Aberdeen. As we crossed the bridge over the railway I resisted my usual urge to look down. The disturbing images from my nightmare the other night still felt raw in the back of my mind. We kept walking a little longer and turned down Market Street. As we passed the indoor market the sweet smell of freshly made donuts and pastries filled the air. I stood for a moment and took in the sweet scent. It stirred memories long dormant in the back of my mind from my younger years when my dad would take me with him for work and we would get a donut at lunch time. Those days were long gone but the donuts remained. Even at night when the market was closed the smell still lingered in the air, much to the annoyance of the sports pub across the road.

It was now becoming evening and the bustle of the city was becoming more apparent as people left their offices and the streets became busier. Market Street was becoming grid-locked as per the norm for this time of day. We weaved in and out of people never breaking contact. We kept walking until we were right in the middle of the office blocks by the harbour and not far from a shopping centre.

"Where are we headed?" I ask as we slip in between two large office buildings.

"Dinner, but with a twist." Carter answered with a sly smile played on the corner of his lips.

As we emerged from between the buildings I recognised the large building we are now in front of. Carter's home is the penthouse on the top floor.

"Your place?" I almost squeaked. A shot of adrenaline fired through me, vanquishing the chill I'd felt since we left the café. I was suddenly nervous.

He nodded and tugged at my arm, drawing me towards the building. It was bigger than I remembered it and it was more stunning in the light. There are some beautiful architectural features on the building including some stunning gargoyles above the massive doorway but I was quickly ushered into the building and away from the piercing gaze of the stone creatures. As we entered the front foyer a rush of people in suits and smart skirts bustled out into the cold wind and darkening skies.

We paced over to the lift and Carter swiped his card. The ride up was somewhat silent and slightly awkward. I could feel Carters eyes on me as I stared down at my feet. I gently clicked my kitten heels together 3 times as a low rumble bubbled up from Carters throat. He laughed softly.

"There's no place like home." he mused as the lift stopped at the top floor and the doors opened up on the corridor to the penthouse.

It had been dark previously but today it was bathed in soft artificial light. There was bold red and cream striped wallpaper with a strong fleur de les emblem repeated within the pattern. A deep blood red carpet ran the length of the corridor. I could feel my heels sinking slightly into it as we walked. As with everything about Carter it felt expensive. I tried not to drag my heels in the carpet for fear I'd pull the pile.

Carter unlocked the door and we slipped inside. The view from inside his home was just as breath taking as I'd remembered it. The living area with its wide panoramic windows looked out on the darkening harbour. Carter vanished from my side and headed towards the kitchen area. I found myself drawn to the view and I paced over to the massive panes of glass. Gently I laid my forehead against the glass and I looked down at the street below. The street was far busier now. People frantically rushing around. Some were leaving work, catching buses and heading for parked cars. Others were meeting friends and partners and heading for dinner. I saw a few families heading towards the shopping centre round the corner. The food court there had a good variety of eateries and at this time of day would be totally packed and I could imagine the queue for the cinema extending out of the cinema and past a few restaurants. As if prompted by my thought my stomach let out a large growl. Embarrassed I looked around for Carter, I could see his back just beyond the edge of the living area. He had taken off his jacket, his loose pony tail was wild down the back of his shirt, dark as tar, messy and as sexy as any rock star I'd ever seen. Now it wasn't only my stomach that was hungry. As he moved about behind the kitchen counter, my eyes drank in every inch of him. His shoulders were taut beneath the thin fabric of his shirt. I could see the definition of the muscles in his forearm as he lifted a bottle of wine and two glasses from a shelf beyond my line of sight. As he turned his eyes locked with mine. Those deep liquid chocolate pools sent fire through my blood. I could feel the searing heat of his touch through his stare. Embarrassed at my unashamed staring I turned away from him towards the window. He left the kitchen and joined me at the window. I noticed he was barefoot but still dressed in his suit trousers and shirt. He extended a glass towards me.

"Dinner should be ready in five minutes. I thought you'd like a glass of wine."

"Are we eating in?" I asked shyly as I took the glass from him.

Slowly the white wine half-filled my cup before he answered.

"I thought it'd be a little more romantic to be alone." he smiled.

I took a fairly big swig from my glass as this revelation was reviewed by Logical and Dreamy.

Instead of the usual bickering and disapproving looks they both remained silent and happily my spider sense wasn't tingling so I decided just to relax and see where the evening took us.

After a little more wine there was a knock at the door. I took a seat at the kitchen counter as Carter answered the door. In walked Ignatius with a hostess trolley followed by a young waitress also pushing a trolley.

"Dinner is served Carter, Ms Jansent." he called cheerfully as he entered.

Carter helped Ignatius and the waitress to unload the two trolleys. Decanting food into various bowls and plates and then storing them either in the fridge or onto a small heated plate on the work top. Once all the dishes had been removed from the trolleys Ignatius and his assistant bid us good evening and Carter saw them both out. Ignatius whispered something to Carter about not forgetting about the dessert as he closed the door behind them.

"Dinner is ready if you would like to accompany me to the Dining room?" Carter asked as he extended the crook of his arm for me to take.

I stood and placed my arm in his.

"I didn't realise you had a Dining room."

He flashed me a devilish smile as he led me up a small flight of stairs by the front door.

"I'm full of surprises Kira. Tonight you will discover quite a few."

As we got to the top of the stairs I realised it was a mezzanine floor. A large, ornate wooden dining table adorned with candle sticks and silverware awaited us. The first course was already laid out expertly for us to start. Carter pulled out my seat as I looked around me. There was another stair case that led to another floor from this one. I was guessing that was where the bedroom was. A flush graced me cheeks as Carter took his seat opposite me. He raised his glass towards me.

"Here is to an insightful evening."

"Cheers."

As we ate we spoke more about hobbies and interests. Mainly about books and the unrealistic portrayals of both men and women in popular fiction. We discussed movies and music over the main course and over dessert we discussed the theme for tonight's club evening.

"Seriously. You're running a masquerade evening at the club?" I almost spat out my mascarpone ice cream.

Carter nodded. A wicked smile across his face as he took another mouthful of tiramisu. As he swallowed he answered me fully.

"We sold tickets for this about a month ago. You'd be amazed how fast we sold out. Not one booth is free this evening and the VIP lounge is full too."

I tiled my head slightly as I wondered how we were all going to fit in if all tickets were sold. As if reading my mind Carter answered my silent thought.

"As the owner I always keep a handful of tickets and my own private booth for friends to come along and join in the fun. Dean and Sophie booked their tickets weeks ago."

A thought suddenly struck me and I opened my mouth to speak just as my phone began to ring downstairs in my bag. I excused myself from the table and darted back down the stairs to answer it.

Scott's picture smiled at me as I lifted the phone from the front pocket of my bag.

"Hey stranger. You coming tonight?" I chirped.

"I'd love to Hun, but erm, something has come up!" Scott squirmed on the other end of the line. I could hear breathing behind him.

"Does it have a hard cock right now and it's beside you?" I snapped, a little hurt that Scott would ditch me for a random so soon after the bathroom incident.

"Ouch. That was sharp, put those claws away Missy. I'll owe you one ok? This evening's entertainment is too good to miss." Scott retorted trying to sound hurt as the heavy breathing vanished and was replaced by an audible sucking sound.

"Yes, you damn well do owe me Scott." I almost shouted at him "Go enjoy your hoover. You're missing a good night out in town and my boyfriend. I hope it's worth it."

I clicked the call end button just as a confused stammer escaped Scott's lips. Boyfriend, did I really just describe Carter as that? Logical peaked her eyebrow. That wasn't a term I'd used in quite a while. Dreamy clapped her hands together excitedly. I took the phone back up to the table with me, but tucked it under my napkin to be polite and polished off the last of my ice cream.

"Where were we?" I asked Carter as I placed the last spoonful of ice cream in my mouth.

"You were just about to ask me about the dress code for this evening when Scott rang you. How is he?"

I swallowed the cold lump in my throat and sat aghast.

"I have excellent hearing Ms Jansent. Good thing too in the nightclub business. You never know what you might hear that becomes useful or that helps save other patrons."

I closed my mouth and consciously swallowed.

"As for dress code. I took the liberty if that's ok?" He stood from his end of the table and extended his hand towards me as he pulled out my chair. I took his hand and the familiar jolt of electricity flowed between us. The searing heat of his skin on mine set my mind aflame and adrenaline immediately sped through me.

He took me up to the next floor. It was more like a long corridor with three doors coming off it. A large sky light lit up the corridor. We passed the first door and the second and stopped at the third. Carter asked that I close my eyes, a request I quickly acquiesced to. He threw open the door and gently pushed me forwards.

"Ok, Open them." he commanded softly.

I opened my eyes and sharply took in a breath at the sight before me. This was Carter's bedroom. It was as large as I'd imagined. The tones were all dark. Crimsons and deep purples on the wall. The centre piece of the whole room was the massive wooden four poster which was draped with white satin, in stark contrast to the rest of the room. At a guess it was a queen size as it was bigger than any bed I'd ever seen. A matching dark wooden wardrobe dominated the furthest corner of the room. A door stood slightly ajar showing a hint of a tiled floor. It must have an en suite I thought silently to myself. My eyes were immediately drawn back to the bed as Carter perched on the edge of it. A tingle shot through my entire body. I wasn't sure if it was apprehension or fear but I shivered slightly.

Carter raised his hand and pointed over to the large wardrobe in the corner.

"Go and look on the inside of the door. I wasn't sure what sort of mood you'd be in for this evening so I took the liberty of making sure you had a choice."

I took my cue and walked over to the wardrobe, stealing a quick look out of the window while I pulled open the heavy door. It was getting dark now. The street lights were beginning to illuminate the streets below.

I looked on the door and three dress bags hung there. Slowly I opened all three individually and was taken aback at the beauty of each dress contained inside. They were three different lengths and styles but the colours remained the same, silver and black. I opted for the mid length dress which had a sort of informal and modern style. I lifted it from the door and walked back over to Carter who sat beaming on the bed.

"Do you want to try it on?" he asked, pointing me to the door of the en suite.

Without a second telling I vanished into the adjoining room and tried on the dress. I excitedly bounced back through to Carters room like a small child on Christmas morning. He padded over to me and zipped the dress at the back then took a step back towards the bed to admire how I looked. The dress fitted like a glove.

"How did you know my size?" I asked a little sheepishly. I was more than aware I wasn't a size 10.

"Sophie advised me. I hope you don't mind. I knew you wouldn't have time to get anything in time for tonight." he apologised

I dropped the dress on the edge of the bed and threw my arms around his neck pushing us both backwards onto the bed. Gently he rolled me over until he was on top of me, bracing himself on his arms above me.

"That was one hell of a thank you." he gasped slightly.

I blushed beneath him, slightly embarrassed by my overzealous thankyou that had sent us both flying backwards onto the bed.

He stared at me a moment in silence before speaking again.

"You are very beautiful Kira." he said softly as he leaned down to kiss me.

As our lips met I felt my skin begin to melt once again. My heart began to pound in my chest and the buzz of electricity through my veins began to pulse with a force I'd never felt. Carter gently stroked my cheek as our kiss deepened. I felt the warmth and strength of his tongue as it gently danced in time with mine. Searching and probing ever deeper. I felt his fingers tangle further into my hair as I gripped tighter onto his forearms. The world felt like it was tumbling away from me and the room was spinning. I closed my eyes for a moment and wild colours dashed about me. I'd never had this feeling before. I'd felt lust before but this was different. This wasn't lust, it was a form of longing. Each touch, each burst of electricity between us, it was a connection that I craved, needed. It was enflaming but it was also healing. The troubles of the week were finally starting to sink into obscurity and all I could feel were Carter's arms around me, his fingers wound in my hair and his firm body against mine. We broke our kiss momentarily for air. I opened my eyes and realised we'd tipped and were now lying side by side on the bed. Carter lay unmoving, almost inhuman, his eyes burning with desire. He was lying with his arms beside him but my skin still burned with his touch, a delightful scorch that left my body yearning for more.

"I want this Kira." he whispered to me. I never even saw his lips move.

I opened my mouth to speak but quickly he silenced me with a single chaste kiss.

"You have to understand that I'm not really one for relationships. I have quite a secluded life with a few exceptions. It's been a while since I've let anyone in close. We've not known each other long but I honestly feel like I can trust you. Like we're almost kindred spirits." he had propped himself up on one elbow and his eyes burned with such honesty and emotion I couldn't help but feel the tears pooling at the corners of my eyes. Softly and without a word he wiped the tears from my eyes before they could fall.

"Men like you only exist in books." I sobbed softly. "There are no real men who care so deeply about damsels they've just met over coffee and then saved, heelless from the savage work machine"

"We do exist." he smiled reassuringly "We are an ancient breed and not exactly like the billionaires in your novels. But we are real."

He traced his fingers down the length of my thigh and toyed with the hem of the dress where it spilled off my skin. Instinctively I traced the line of his shirt buttons and effortlessly undid the top two buttons.

"Are you sure you want to do this? Want all of me?" Carter asked. He sounded slightly breathless. His hand was now gripping the edge of the dress and lifting it slightly allowing him access to more of my skin. As his fingers pressed softly into the flesh on my thigh my heart rate shot through the roof. Every beat pulsed more adrenaline and energy through me. I looked deep into those dark pools, sensing every bit of longing and desire reflected in my own eyes. Swallowing hard, I nodded.

"I think I wanted you the first night we met in the coffee house." I admitted shyly.

"I'm still worried if I share all of myself with you that you're going to run screaming." he confessed.

"No, I'm a big girl Carter. I want you. All of you. I'm just amazed you want me."

"Why wouldn't I?"

"I'm not exactly a catch am I? I'm a plus sized geek."

"I don't go in for pigeon holes Kira. It's a beauty inside that I find captivating."

I could feel my cheeks flush a shade of crimson.

Carter sat up and carefully began to remove his shirt. I watched in complete fascination as he performed a perfect strip tease for me. His well sculpted muscles causing him slight issue in discarding his shirt as effortlessly as a stripper would. Slowly and purposefully he began to remove the suit trousers. His eyes never left mine and with complete skill he slid both layers of material from his body in one slow fluid movement. I gasped a little as, now freed from its cloth prison, his erection stood proud and free. It bobbed slightly as the thick veins throbbed in sync with the pulsing of fire on my skin.

Still never taking his dark, chocolate eyes from mine he climbed back onto the bed and lifted his hands behind his head. A second later his hair cascaded free from the pony tail that had held it. The long dark tendrils of hair slid silently over his shoulders and down his back. As he stalked across the bed like a big cat I could see that his hair reached down as far as the firm curves of his buttocks.

I was staggered by just how inhumanly beautiful he looked now. His dark eyes framed by this perfect mane of dark locks. His voice was almost a purr as he motioned for me to sit up.

"You've got me now Kira. The man and the monster. Be careful of the choices you make." he warned.

A slight chill ran through me as the Detective's voice sounded in my head for a second. Logical had headphones in and was reading a magazine, Dreamy was watching in complete awe, her tongue lolling out of her mouth like an over affectionate puppy.

Carter's hands gently curved around me to the zipper at my shoulder blades. His mouth hovered inches from my bare shoulder. His hot breath teased my senses in ways I couldn't describe. I closed my eyes to the sensation of his arms around me gently sliding the zipper down my back, allowing the straps to fall completely from my shoulders and letting the front fall forwards exposing my breasts.

As he continued to peel the dress down to my waist he started to plant butterfly kisses across my shoulder, down across my right breast. Gently he raked his teeth across the now very hard point that had formed. A small moan escaped me as his teeth vanished and further kisses ran down my torso to my waist. My skin burned with a delightful torture that I was starting to relish. I was on the border of pleasure and unbearable teasing. I didn't have to think twice and impulsively wriggled free of the fabric around me. Gently I let it roll down my leg to my knees then I gently tugged it off completely and let it pool on the floor beside the bed. Carter then continued his kiss trail south once I sat back onto the bed. His kisses scorching my skin and quickening my pulse as they went. He bypassed the centre of my heat as he softly kissed and caressed his way down my thigh, round the back of my knee right down to my ankle and then worked his way back up the other leg in the same pattern.
I was now writhing on the sheets. My hands bunched in the fabric and I was biting my lip to avoid making a sound. His hair tickled as it fell like a veil between us. As I lay

back on the bed I realised this whole scenario was starting to feel like my dream. My heart began to quicken as the sound of my pulse surged through my ears. I could feel the heat rising in my cheeks as his kisses triggered every sensual point they touched. Logical and Dreamy were a million miles from my thoughts as a new creature emerged. Caged and frustrated it was pounding inside my chest to be free. It wanted to do all the things that I was trying to rein in within my imagination. Sparking all the emotions I was trying to suppress, they bubbled to the surface and burned with the heat of his kisses.

I felt Carter's fingers catch on the edge of my underwear, a small, lacy black thong that I'd decided to wear went perfectly with the matching bra that I had been wearing when I'd left my house earlier. One swift tug in Carter's experienced grip and it was rolled to my ankle and after an expert flick on my part it landed beside the dress on the floor. Now completely naked and at his mercy I was starting to feel a little nervous. I only had a moment to feel a spike of fear as I suddenly felt Carters mouth brush against my sex. His hair was splayed across my thighs and from my point of view, as I chanced a quick glance, looked like tendrils of pure darkness were radiating out from between my legs. I closed my eyes and threw my head back as I felt his warm tongue flicking across the top of my clit. His fingers were suddenly inside of me and I couldn't stifle the sounds any longer. Unwillingly I let out a pleasurable moan as his fingers probed deeper and he gently sucked my clit into his mouth. The flames within me grew higher and my skin felt like a blissful inferno.

I'd read many novels and seen many movies and nothing described the feeling I was having right now. My skin burned and tingled at the same time. My whole body felt like an electrical pulse ran straight through it, concentrating on the single point that Carter was currently expertly caressing with his tongue. His fingers worked a little faster and I could feel an orgasm already starting to build. I could hear animalistic growls and sighs echoing in my ears as my breathing became more erratic and I realised the sounds were coming from me.

Carter released his hold on me for a moment and drew himself level with me on his side. I opened my eyes and I could see my own eyes reflected in his dark pools. I could see the need and desire and the sparkle of a promise of things yet to come.

A sudden boldness gripped me and I shot Carter a sly smile as I whispered to him in a feral growl.

"My turn!"
I slid down the bed until I was between his legs. I saw him tuck his hair behind his head as he lay on his back, his eyes burning into me with wonder and a hint of fear.

I licked my lips as I gently took his head into my mouth. My tongue softly flicked and rolled around, my tongue piercing having its desired effect. He bucked slightly in my grip so I knew I was hitting the right chord. I took more of his length into my mouth and ran my tongue up and down the length of his shaft. I felt flutters of delight as he writhed and bucked in my grasp as I started to pump my hands up and down rhythmically in time with my tongue flicking more firmly now across the tip of his head. It wasn't too long before I was starting to hear appreciative growls as Carter's hands found the top of my head and guided me to what he wanted me to do. Carefully he pushed me deeper onto his cock, my tongue gently swirled from side to side accommodating the rest of his length into my throat until I was almost at my breaking point. Once I had him down to the root I closed my throat on him, making him call out in surprised shock. I backed off again slightly for a moment before deep throating him entirely again. Carter's hands were now no longer on my head but were balled in the cotton of the sheet on either side of him as I hollowed my cheeks and began to suck on him. All the while I maintained the rhythmical motion with my hands. I could taste the saltiness of him in my mouth and it just heightened the desire within me. Dreamy was positively in her element, screaming at me to claim him as mine and slapping Logical across the ass.

I drew him out of my mouth and softly nuzzled his head with my lips and continued to lick him gently. I was about to engulf him again when I felt his hand on my shoulder to stop. I sat up and looked quizzically at him. He merely motioned for me to come towards him.

As I crawled back up the bed as seductively as I could he raised both hands and placed them on my shoulders as I was directly above his now very engorged erection. Without another signal he bucked his hips up to meet me and pushed me down with his shoulders. I was so slick with desire that he slid into me and his searing warmth filled me as I let out a roar of pleasure. We started off slowly and gently but as he began to buck faster beneath me we picked up pace. Slow and gentle gave way to urgent and rough. I could feel my stamina starting to falter as my legs started to cramp up. I was loving everything but the cramp was starting to affect my performance. Suddenly Carter sat up and flipped me over onto all fours beside him.

"Let's try this way." he growled in my ear as he positioned himself behind me. I tried to look back over my shoulder but I could only see Carter's torso behind me. Suddenly there was a loud crack and a jolt of electricity buzzed pleasantly through me. It took a moment for the sting of Carter's slap to register on my right buttock. Another crack and this time it was my left cheek that sang out in pain. Then he was inside of me again. The heat of his cock felt like my insides were melting. I could feel his hands on the rise of my hips to steady himself as he slammed into me over and over. The depth and the force of his thrusts were both maddening and amazing. As he continued to pick up his pace I could feel him rubbing inside me, reaching places that no battery operated friends had ever reached. I could feel the pressure building within me and I started to claw at the pillows as the feeling began to build like a wave I was longing to wash over me.

The motion suddenly stopped and the wave began to subside. I raised myself onto my knees and turned around straight into Carter's kiss. I could taste the slight metallic tang on his tongue which I recognised as myself and I was sure he could taste the salt of his loins on my tongue. As he held me and deepened the kiss he pulled me onto his lap. He sat cross legged on the bed and dragged his nails lightly down my back as I mounted him once more. I gasped into his mouth as he filled me completely and we began to move again. As the kiss faded and we sat face to face, the gentle rocking of our hips was the only movement, I could feel my wave building again. He was rooted in me and gently occasionally bucked a little to push himself further in. I purred low and deep in my throat as he kept hitting my sweet spot. My fingernails bit into the flesh of his shoulders as I could feel the wave reaching its apex before it came crashing around me. Carter's hands were in the small of my back and as I tightened around him as the wave began to surround and engulf me completely his nails bit into the soft skin. I cried out and rested my head against his shoulder as the last of the wave left me drenched and exhausted. I heard Carter find his release and then I felt a sharp sting in my shoulder. A fire I'd never felt before ran through me charging my entire body and making all my senses razor sharp. It was the fine line between pleasure and pain. The sharp sting radiated out from my shoulder and caused my breasts to tingle, my blood to surge and my groin to go into overdrive. Out of nowhere another wave came crashing down on me and I was engulfed once again as every nerve ending in my entire being fired off. Colours exploded around me as I tried to buck against Carter but I was held fast. I could feel his mouth on my shoulder, his tongue gently lapping at the source of the initial sting. The feeling was intense and like nothing I'd ever experienced before. I felt Carter's grip on me loosen and I leaned back a little. In the dim light of the rising evening I could see crimson droplets on Carter's lips. Gingerly I raised my hand to my shoulder and touched the spot that had brought me both pleasure and pain. When I looked at my fingers there were smears of blood.

"Did you just bite me and draw blood?" I squeaked in a voice that surprised myself.

Licking his lips to remove the last of the blood Carter's smile faded and he nodded solemnly before replying.

"There's something I really need to explain about my earlier statement about the man and the monster".

Chapter 9

I sat staring at Carter in the half light of the evening unable to move. His revelation had shocked me slightly but it hadn't had the effect on me he thought it had. I didn't want to run screaming from the room and I wasn't afraid despite the lecture I was currently getting in my head from Logical. I was the opposite of afraid, I was filled with curiosity and fascination. This man who had found himself in my life, my knight in shining car who treated me so kindly had just shared an earth shattering secret with me and expected me to run.

"Ok." I said as I stood up out of bed "I just need to go freshen up first and I'll be right back."

I bounced up from the bed and sauntered slowly into the adjoining bathroom. It was a lovely surprise when I padded into the tiled room only to find my feet warmed instead of chilled by the tiles. Of course he'd have underfloor heating in the bathroom!

  As I freshened up a series of thoughts began to string together in my head, it all made sense. The wealth amassed over time through investments, the secrecy, the good looks, the strength and the sparkle in his eyes. I'd read plenty of romances but I'd never contemplated a supernatural being coming into play in my boring life! The

beast he'd spoken about was just an extension of himself, a facet of who he was as a whole, not a definition.
I finished up in the sink and headed back into the bedroom.

Carter was perched on the edge of the bed now with his suit trousers back on. He had tied his dark expanse of hair back into a pony tail much to my disappointment. He watched me re-enter the room with an expression of fear and apprehension on his face.

"Aww." I pouted "You tied it up again." I motioned to his pony tail. His face remaining expressionless he simply nodded.

"Could we put it in a braid at least?" I asked very matter of fact pointing to a brush resting on the bedside table.

A curious yet cautious smile crossed his face as he reached for the brush and passed it over to me. I knelt behind him on the bed and freed the pony tail once more then set about brushing and separating ready for braiding.

"What are you doing?" Carter asked in complete amazement.

"Braiding these fine locks of yours Mr Brams. It suits you more than a plain ponytail as there is nothing plain about you."

I could hear the smile in his voice as he spoke again, this time any trace of uncertainty was fading.

"I bit you and you aren't running?"

"Should I? I'm pretty sure if women took off every time a partner tried something different we'd all be spinsters or at least prudes." I giggled.

I finished the braid and bound it with a hair tie at the bottom. Even braided his hair went a fair length down his back and from brushing it, it was in far better condition than mine. As I let the braid fall against his back he turned to face me. Those dark pools had a tinge of sadness to them now.

He took my hands in his as he continued to look into my eyes.

"I wasn't joking about the monster as well as the man" he stated very seriously, his eyes gauging me for an answer.

I couldn't control my impulse to laugh and a small giggle escaped me. A smile played on Carters lips as he drew closer until we were nose to nose. My skin prickled with the static between us and I could feel the waves of heat rolling off of him. My muscles all tensed slightly and butterflies fluttered in my stomach.

"Are you laughing at me Ms Jansent?" There was a low growl in his voice as he spoke. It struck a chord with my core and I could feel myself flush all over.

"And if I am?" I challenged.

Without warning he pounced on me, pinning me onto the bed. His mouth covered mine and I playfully tried to resist but it was futile. I was hopelessly intoxicated with Carter. As I gave in to his kiss I kept my eyes open, staring intently into those deep pools. My tongue gingerly seeking out his fangs and delighting in the slight prick of them. I found it strange I hadn't noticed them before now. I'd seen Carter smile after all.

Carter raised himself up onto his arms over me and looked down at me, his head tilted to one side questioningly.

"Are we going to talk about this or merely pretend it didn't happen?" he asked, that tone of uncertainty reappearing in his voice.

I lay there a moment contemplating the "ignorance is bliss" theory before answering.

"You're a vampire. What is there to discuss?"

Carter backed immediately off of the bed. All colour had drained from his face and he stood stalk still regarding me with a sense of horror frozen across his face. I perched on my elbows and watched as he lifted my dress and underwear from the floor before placing them next to me on the bed.

"You're still here?" he queried, watching me with an expression of terror that caused a knot in my stomach.

"There's a lot you don't know about me Carter. I don't scare easily and trust me, there are far more frightening things in this city than vampires."

Complete surprise shone in his eyes along with a sense of relief. His shoulders sagged slightly and he took a deep breath.

"Yes." he almost belly laughed "There are werewolves too!"

I sat bolt upright on the bed.

"Wait, what?" It was now my turn to look horrified.

Carter was now almost rolling with laughter as he perched once again on the side of the bed.

"Seriously Kira! You can accept that I'm a vampire but you have trouble accepting werewolves?"

I shrugged my shoulders. I didn't make any sense that I could be so relaxed with one concept but not the other.

Carter continued to talk to me as we dressed for our night out. Going to the club now seemed so surreal considering the revelation that had just unfolded. I pulled on my underwear and slipped the satin dress back on over my hips and Carter zipped me up. He then set about dressing himself in a stunning dark grey suit with silver pin stripes. A lavish black silk tie adorned with tiny silver stars completed the look. He continued on with his story the entire time we dressed. His family were very old and had settled here from Europe around the time there was a mass exodus of vampires from the continent due to some ancient pursuers. Hunters on our island were more interested in Witches and Celts to be preoccupied with fantasies of vampires and werewolves invading the shores and so the Brams legacy had begun. I listened with complete fascination as Carter tied my hair up for me while I applied some make up. There were indeed more vampires in the city and werewolves too along with a whole plethora of other supernatural entities. Hidden away in folklore they were secretive and with good reason. I came to understand that there was a war being conducted under our very noses and there were more endangered species on this planet than I had ever imagined.

"So you know other vampires?" I queried.

Carter simply nodded as I replaced all my make-up back into my tiny bag. I was still unsure how it ended up in Carter's bedroom but I had bigger things to comprehend right now.

"And werewolves?"

Carter sighed a little as he helped me choose a coat from the wardrobe to match my dress and then held open a drawer at the bottom of the wardrobe with a small selection of clutch purses and bags that would also match my ensemble. As I gazed into the drawer he continued to inform me.

"My cousin is married to a werewolf actually. He is my eyes and ears in the Highlands and she has managed to land herself as pack alpha. Uncommon for a female but she handles it well. They've had some unrest lately so I've not heard much from them."

I selected a small silver shoulder bag, I always found clutch purses a bit of a liability when out and about, especially now! I closed the drawer and turned to face Carter. He was now fully dressed in a dark suit, a silver tie around his neck and silver cufflinks on his sleeves. He looked stunning and for a moment our conversation completely vanished from my mind. I leaned up to kiss him and he greeted me with a chaste kiss on the lips.

"Don't want to smudge your lipstick." he smiled. "Not yet anyway!"

I flushed a little and grinned like a Cheshire cat.

"I was brought up to know a gentleman should only ruin a girl's lipstick, not her mascara."

"I'll take that as a sign you've no intention of running away in abject terror then?" Carter teased as we walked back down to the living area. The city was under darkness now and a glow with a million lights. I looked out of the windows at the amazing panoramic view of the harbour. Fishing boats were docked and their massive flood lights added to the amazing ambiance of the harbour at night. Twinkling lights contrasting with the overpowering black of the water. I could imagine the sound of the water lapping at the quayside and the occasional calls of the gulls as they retired for the evening.

Carters hand was suddenly on my shoulder and I flinched a little at his touch.

"Are you ok?" he asked, gingerly stroking the spot where my revelation had begun.

"Yes." I stammered "You just startled me. My thoughts were somewhere else."

He had a pained expression on his face again.

"In a world less complicated?" he sighed as he took my hand and led me towards the door.

I stopped him and wrapped my arms tight around his firm torso.

"No." I spoke into his chest "I was just thinking about the beauty of nature and how I now have even more to marvel at."

He tenderly caressed my hair as he held me tightly.

"We can stay up all night talking and I'll answer any questions that you have. But for now, let's just go out and have fun. This evening is meant to be about mystery and enjoyment."

I leaned back to look up into his eyes. I smiled reassuringly as I spoke.

"And there will be a million questions I promise you. Before we head out though, I just need to know."

Carter cut me off before I could finish.

"Sam is the only one who knows. Dean and Sophie are completely unaware of anything. I'd appreciate your silence on that part." His brow was creased a little as the seriousness of his tone chilled me a little.

"Want me to sign any silencing paperwork Mr rich pants?" I teased.

The seriousness faded from his face, replaced with a raised eyebrow, a wolfish grin and a swift slap across my buttocks.

"No paperwork required Ms Jansent. Just know that my punishments are swift and timely should you get out of hand."

I giggled as I danced out of the way, dodging his arms as he tried to capture me in his embrace again.

"You're going to have your hands full now Mr Brams. I'm quite good at playing the obstinate wench."

Carters smile shone as he reached out his hand for mine.

"Come on or we're going to be late."

When we arrived at the club we were fast tracked to the door and I once again met that striking Viking bouncer, Griff, who had been on the last time I was here. Tonight he looked even more impressive as his broad form was bound in an expensive looking suit in a charcoal grey with pin stripes. He was wearing a masquerade mask that covered one half of his face. It was quite ornate looking and fascinated me. I couldn't see an elastic strap holding it on and as I looked closer I realised that the mask had an eyebrow piercing just like he did. Then it dawned on me, the eyebrow piercing was his and it was holding the half mask in place.

"Impressive." I remarked as we passed him and headed into the club.

He shot me a sly smile and fired a return remark as we headed out of view.

"Not so bad yourself Ms Jansent."

I could have been wrong but I could have sworn he winked at me from behind the mask.

Carter effortlessly twisted his hand behind his back and playfully flicked the bouncer the bird.

I could hear his deep laugh as we arrived at the cloak room.

The familiar feeling of a deep base beat rumbled up through the floor and up into my chest. I let the beat settle within me as Carter checked our coats in. Before we entered the main room Carter produced two ornate and matching masks. One was shaped like a wolf and one was shaped like a cat. Both were adorned with lace and shimmering sequins to highlight brow lines and muzzles.

Carter carefully lowered my mask over my face and tied the satin ribbons at the back before he repeated the process with his own. I motioned for him to turn around as my voice couldn't compete with the volume of the music. I untangled his braid from the satin ribbon and let it fall heavily against his back, confirming what I'd done. We then linked arms and entered the main room.

The club looked so different tonight it was almost unrecognisable. A large disco ball hung from the ceiling and was lit up with hues of purple and pink. The booths were all draped in laces of black, silver, grey and white. Everyone was wearing smart yet casual attire and everyone was adorned with a masquerade mask. There were several large silver helium balloon clusters located about the room and many of the tables had suggestive centrepieces, silver hand cuffs, rope, locks and keys, hearts and more masks. There were a few of the waitresses serving tables in full leather outfits while some were dressed more conservatively. Everything was above board and nothing was on show, but a lot of things were suggested and that was Carter's way around the theme. It all depended on your imagination and interpretation.

We walked through the crowd over to Carter's private booth which was above the masses on a slightly higher platform. It was level with the DJ's booth directly opposite across the room. Our table was adorned with the same suggestive items as the other booths. Absentmindedly I picked up the silver handcuffs in one hand and the length of silver rope with the other. The weight of the handcuffs made me do a double take. I stared down at the cuffs in my hand. They were real! Carter moved to stand in front of me. A devilish smile playing on his lips.

"So you can't escape later." he said, his face completely serious as the grin spread and I could see the glint of his teeth. A shiver ran through me as the thought of the pleasure and pain that his bite had brought me earlier, or should that be his dark kiss? Either way, my train was derailed as two familiar voices shrilled above the deafening baseline. Dean and Sophie had arrived. Carter greeted them both warmly whilst removing the cuffs from my hand and tucking them into the back pocket of his suit trousers.

"I'm so glad you could both make it." Carter said shaking Dean's hand.

Not even trying to talk I embraced Sophie in a hug and after the initial shock she reciprocated with a smile. Carter and Dean vanished for a moment and reappeared with a bottle, some glasses and a waitress. The waitress carried a tray with snacks on it and placed it down on the table. She said something about being our waitress for the evening and took her leave to attend to her other tables.

Carter poured us all a drink and as I sipped the cool white wine from my glass I watched with interest as the throng danced below us. There was something magical about seeing everyone in such formal looking attire all adorned with elaborate masks and feathers moving in time with the music. It was almost like a step back in time. Ball-gowns and short dresses alike bobbed and swayed to the music. Rhinestones glittered and everyone seemed to sparkle in the reflections of the disco ball. As one song seamlessly blended into another Sophie let out a high pitched squeal that made us all recoil in pain. Even over the loud music her pitch was still audible. She grabbed Dean's hand and dragged him unwillingly towards the dance floor while screaming something about this being the first dance at her wedding. The look of terror that flashed over the poor boy's face only served to make me laugh uncontrollably. I carefully pulled off my mask and laid it down on the table in front of me. Carter immediately turned to look at me as soon as I began to laugh. He leant closer to my ear.

"That is a truly wonderful sound you know." he whispered sweetly to me.

I smiled and whispered back to him.

"I know a sound that I can make that is more wonderful."

I cheekily raised an eyebrow as I took another mouthful of cool, bubbly refreshment. Carter shot me an evil grin that was full of promises for later. The black and silver patterning on his mask only served to accentuate the shape of his eyes as they smouldered sensually behind it.

A waiter in black and silver uniform approached Carter. I noticed how his whole body language changed as the man neared us. Carter shoulders squared and he straightened. He gripped his braid and tightened the end of it before casting it over his shoulder and fiddling with his lapels. Carter the employer was in full operation now. The waiter whispered something in his ear and he immediately bristled. The waiter left and Carter softened slightly as he turned his attention back to me.

"I'll be back shortly." he apologised "I've got to tend to something for a moment. I'll bring you back a surprise. Feel free to stay in the booth or dance with the others. It's a private booth so no one else will be up here except us tonight."

As he walked down the steps I watched him go. Marvelling at just how dignified and managerial he looked while still maintaining that air of sexuality that rolled off him in waves. Those friends on their blogs hadn't over exaggerated him at all. Even the masters would have been in awe of him as a subject to paint or sculpt. Even Logical was agreeing with me tonight as her and Dreamy also appreciated watching his firm frame wandering out of view.

I looked over the railing of the booth down to the dance floor below and tried to locate Sophie and Dean. I easily spotted Sophie with the large feather on her head. Her arms were flailing about above her head as she danced to the beat of the baseline and didn't care who saw her dance. Her eyes were closed and a complete look of euphoria shone in her smile. Dean on the other hand had a strange awkward smile on his face. He was enjoying the glow of her happiness but all the time was keeping a watchful eye on everyone else around her. As if he read my thoughts he moved closer to her and linked his arms around her dainty waist. Her arms fell around his shoulders as she plunged him into a deep kiss. I felt the blush rise in my cheeks and turned my head from them so I couldn't be accused of watching. Carter was still out of sight and I hoped that he wouldn't be too long. I was starting to feel a little vulnerable up here by myself in the fortress of solitude. The next song began to play and after a moment when Dean and Sophie hadn't returned to the crow's nest, as I'd now dubbed the booth, I looked back over the railing to see where they were. They were further across the dance floor now and almost indistinguishable from the mass of swirling skirts and masked suits on the floor. I only managed to spot them due to Sophie's tendency to raise her arms above her head like a ballet dancer and due to the large solitary black feather that adorned her mask. Logical has shaken off her sex shock from earlier and was now starting to ring the alarm bell in the back of my mind. Carter posed no danger to me but the image I'd seen outside the coffee house had seriously knocked the ground from under me and I was still on edge. It might not have been Big Davey that I saw but I wasn't too keen on taking the off chance that I should bump into him to find out and alone in the crow's nest during a busy night with everyone in masquerade masks just seemed like asking for trouble. I was suddenly struck with a brilliant idea. I could try and seek out Carter, if I was unable to find him, I could always find my friendly Viking by the door to help me out. I was fairly certain that magical walkie-talkie on his hip would be the answer to all of my problems. Logical couldn't fault my idea. I had safety points I could reach in event of an emergency that I was praying wouldn't happen. As I replaced my mask and counted silently backwards from ten I walked towards the steps and regained my composure. As I slipped past the thick red rope at the top of the crow's nest I silently took a deep breath before starting my decent towards the dance floor. As I started to cross the floor between songs luckily people moved aside to let me past. That was until the next song came on. I recognised it immediately and literally froze. The familiar riffs that announced the arrival of "I want you bad" by the Offspring pulsed through me and I scampered across the floor like a startled deer as a mosh pit began to form behind me. It was a surreal site watching a group of people in almost fancy dress begin to head-bang and flail about in time to the beat. It almost looked undignified in their attire. I smiled slightly as I continued my exodus of the floor when I ran right into the back of Dean. Sophie spotted me immediately and, before I could apologise to the startled form in front of me, had dragged me back into the centre of the floor, just out of reach of the mosh pit. The mosh pit was now in full flow and men in suits were now being flung back and forth in the throng of head-bangers. Sophie raised her arms and swung her hips in a hypnotic motion rather like a belly dancer. Dean was now right behind me and simply watching as his love was radiating sensuality as she mouthed the lyrics to him behind my shoulder. I clasped my hands behind my back and gently swayed from side to side in time with the music and bounced a little as the chorus played once again, all the time looking for Carter around the edge of the dance floor. My eyes quickly scanned past all the swaying and dancing bodies until I locked eyes with someone familiar. Unfortunately for me it wasn't Carter, even more unfortunately for me, it was Maria Miller. Her hair was loose and wild, totally unlike her stuck up secretary look from the office. She was wearing a tight black dress and heels that should be illegal. I had to admit she looked stunning, she had the figure and the angelic face that was perfect for being spotted in a nightclub where as I was kind of the opposite. I tried hard not to let my confidence issues cloud my brain as I continued looking for Carter. Maybe if I looked away she'd walk away and find her next Mr Moneybags as I doubted this was the sort of club her husband would frequent. I turned my back to her and faced Dean and Sophie who were so involved in their slow dancing together that they didn't even notice when I pushed past them to escape back to the crow's nest. Suddenly painfully aware of my awkwardness I tried to walk with a slight wiggle as I quickly paced across the dance floor, suddenly desperate for my sanctuary. I could look for Carter from its safe vantage point. I didn't want my evening ruined by that woman's aura.

I reached the bottom step and nodded to the bouncer who was guarding the red rope to ensure our perch wasn't disturbed. I took the first step when I felt a small hand on my shoulder, then I heard the voice.

"What the hell are you doing here?" Maria squawked over the sound of the music. Her face was contorted into an expression of sheer disgust. Her mask was perched atop her head like a crown of self-importance. I could see a couple of the other woman from her office floor standing a few feet behind her chattering between themselves and unsubtly pointing in my direction.

Be calm, Logical soothed gently, *you are better than this. Let it go. She can't hurt you anymore. Take the next step, climb to the crow's nest and look for Carter. You don't need to answer her. You owe her nothing.*

Logical's voice of reason subdued the swirling storm that had started to brew in my stomach the moment I'd spotted Maria. I lifted my foot onto the next step, keeping my back to her as if I hadn't noticed her.

In a flash I was on my ass on the bottom step with the bouncer moving to pick me up. It took me a second to realise that Maria had pulled on my shoulder to turn me to face her and I'd lost my footing on the step. She loomed over me, in my crumpled heap, before the bouncer could offer his hand.

"I said, what the hell are you doing here Jansent? This club is reserved for the elite and the sophisticated. A night as special as tonight doesn't need to be tainted with geeky little bitches like you. Go foul up someone else's club. I believe the old fisherman's pub down the harbour is doing karaoke night. I'm sure you could make some new friends down there, possibly even pick up a new job. They'd love a bit of you!"

She snorted to herself as she laughed at her own taunt. The bouncer politely moved Maria out of the way as he helped me to my feet. I dusted myself down and thanked him and winked as I noticed he had his hand over the call button on his walkie-talkie. It wouldn't matter if I made a retort or not. In a few minutes I'd be safe.

The DJ put on a new song, one with a very primal and stirring beat and that was when Dreamy woke up. My mouth moved without my permission and I began to spit fire. I was suddenly in the back seat with Logical. She shrugged at me as we watched the fireworks display Dreamy was putting on.

"Firstly, I think you'll find that this club isn't owned by you. Secondly I think you'll find that this club allows anyone in who respects the rules and follows the dress code. I happen to be a VIP tonight and I am enjoying the evening with my new friends, a term you and your little coven of sycophant's should probably look up. Isn't your husband here with you this evening? After all the cock sucking and ass licking you did to snare him you could at least have taken him out for a bit while you bleed his bank account dry."

Maria stood for a moment completely dumbstruck, an expression I felt she should wear more often as it looked more natural on her. She opened her mouth to speak, but Dreamy wasn't finished yet. I looked blankly at Logical. Again she shrugged her shoulders and mouthed *Didn't know she had it in her!*

"Oh no, you're not interrupting me. You did plenty of that in meetings when I worked in the office. Let me get this straight for you. I am not and never will be your bitch. I will expose your petty little secrets that you thought you'd hidden so well. The thing about treating everyone like crap is you never expect that shit to hit the fan and come back on you. Payback is a bitch and you are about to learn that I am not some mousey little geek girl you can fuck with."

Dreamy had seen Carter's approach and had nodded slightly to him to draw his attention to the situation in front of us. As he approached he stepped soundlessly past Maria and high fived the bouncer before standing next to me and wrapping his arm around my waist and kissing me passionately on the lips, which was slightly awkward due to the masks. The world vanished for a moment as everything slipped into blinding light where all I could feel was Carter's searing warmth on my skin and the raising heat within me as the electrical crackle of static filled my ears.

As I snapped back to reality with the heat of the kiss slowly fading Dreamy had given me back control and I now felt completely energized by Carter's presence as he wove his fingers between mine to let me know he was backing me up.

Maria was stood with her mouth open looking completely aghast as Carter gently kissed and nipped at the junction between my neck and shoulder. I could feel the heat flowing off of me in waves and my confidence had just been given a billion kilowatt power boost.

"Carter." I said absently reaching for his cheek. He lowered himself towards my hand and released a low growl which startled Maria and set a fire burning between my belly and my nethers.

"This is Maria" I continued showing no chinks in my new armour. "Maria, this is…."

"Carter Brams" she blurted out, interrupting my sentence.

"My boyfriend." I growled feeling a fierce sense of possessiveness spike through me. Carter remained close by my side, his hand still entwined with mine.

She stood like a small child who had just had her balloon popped. Her confidence drained from her face and her posture slumped. Her cackling horde were now silent and stood in complete confusion as I turned on my heels to face Carter, grabbed him by the lapels, tossed our masks down and pulled him into the most passionate public face sucking session I'd ever been proud enough to own.

As I broke the kiss which left us both panting for breath I didn't even stop to look at Maria. I tugged commandingly on Carter's hand pulling him up the stairs towards the crow's nest. Carter however fired the parting shot.

Bowing his head slightly towards them as he retrieved the masks he started the climb and left them with a glowing smile and a single word.

"Ladies."

Then we were gone, ascended to the crow's nest, our sanctuary away from this scene and more importantly away from Maria and her cronies.

As we returned to the table I was shocked to find Sophie and Dean sitting at the table with fresh glasses of champagne raised towards us. They put their glasses down and began to applaud.

"We saw it all from up here." Sophie confessed. "That was amazing."

"Yeah," agreed Dean enthusiastically "You really showed that posh cow who was top bitch."

Sophie instantly looked offended and elbowed Dean sharply in the ribs causing him to wince and yelp in pain. I giggled slightly and smiled up at Carter who was focused only on me. His grip tightened on my hand a little and his other arm wound round my waist as if claiming me as only his.

"I'm not offended Sophie, its ok. It was fun being a bitch." I explained while making sure Dean was ok with a head tilt towards him. His instant thumbs up told me he was ok and the wicked smile playing on the corners of his lips told me he liked the physical contact from Sophie.

We all sat back down at the small glass table and lifted our glasses to make a toast.

"To bitches." beamed Dean shooting a cheeky grin to Sophie who merely grunted her disapproval before breaking into laughter.

"To knowing what we want in life and how to get it." proposed Carter shooting me a knowing smile.

"Cheers." we all yelled over the music pounding below us and gently clinked glasses.

We sat like that for a while just enjoying each other's company and sipping on the slowly warming champagne. Dean sat with his arm around Sophie's shoulders whispering in her ear and making her flush red occasionally. Watching them made me smile. It felt nice to be in the company of people who just wanted to be together. No hassle, no agenda just friendship and a love of a good evening out.

Dean and Sophie got up to go back to the dance floor as another couples song began to play. The evening was starting to wind down and my confidence power boost was starting to lag out. I raised my hand to cover my mouth as I yawned and caught a glimpse of my watch as I did. It was nearing midnight and I was suddenly overwhelmed by how tired I suddenly felt. Carter caught me yawning.

"Are you ok?" he asked tenderly as he pulled me closer to him.

I nodded sleepily.

"Just starting to get a little tired." I admitted.

"Do you want me to take you home?"

"I'd rather go home with you." I cheekily whispered as I snuggled into his shoulder.

"That could easily be arranged." Carter seductively whispered into my ear as the reality of what I'd just said struck me like lightning.

"Oh shit, did I say that out loud?" I gasped with horror as I sat bolt upright.

Carter erupted into laughter. The sound of his deep growl softened the edge on the shock of what I'd said. I looked into his eyes. Those deep inviting pools of molten chocolate that seemed to call only to me. The usual sparkle of light was there, luring me in, telling me that the water was fine and I could dive right in. I could lose myself in his eyes. There was a depth to them that I didn't understand when we'd first met, but now made perfect sense.

"You didn't say anything I didn't already know Mon Chéri." he smiled.

"If you want to stay over I have made the necessary arrangements."

I moved towards my bag but Carter took my hand and stopped me from reaching my phone.

"Scott already made other plans for tonight and won't be home for you. Don't worry about him missing you." he stated simply, a wicked grin forming on his lips.

"Are you kidnapping me now Mr Brams?" I teased swatting his hand away as I delved into my bag for my phone. As I looked at it there was indeed a message from Scott confirming his evening's entertainment would indeed keep him occupied all night. He'd also left a small apology for not being able to feed Malakai in the morning should I decide to be a "dirty stop out".

"Did you check my phone?" I asked Carter nervously.

"No Mon Chéri. I don't have stalker tendencies despite my creed's reputation. I called Scott earlier after I'd dealt with my "situation" earlier. I have to admit I did copy the number down from your phone. Scouts honour though, I did nothing else" he admitted, still smiling.

"Scouts honour?"

"You think the scouts would ban vampires?" he whispered in a totally flat tone, a smile shining in his eyes. "Who do you think helped everyone with their tracking badge?"

I erupted into a fit of the giggles, unable to be angry for the slightly stalker like number grabbing. Logical was lecturing me on the signs of danger and how I was ignoring them. Dreamy then pointed out that my date was a vampire and she went instantly mute.

"Ok Mr Brams. I shall give you the benefit of the doubt as I know a scout would never lie or be anything except helpful and kind. Lead on."

We stood and linked arms. Silently Carter led me from the crow's nest and down towards the dance floor. We waved farewell to Dean and Sophie who were slow dancing at the edge of the floor. Carter made a phone hand gesture to Dean and he nodded his comprehension as Sophie laid her head softly on Dean's shoulder.

As we passed the doorway we nodded goodnight to our Viking friend on the door who bid us good evening.

We walked slowly round the corner from the club to where Sam was waiting with the car. Carter opened the door to let me in before climbing in himself. We slumped together in the centre of the back seat as Sam started the car. As we were about to pull away there was a knock at the window beside Carter. Letting out a slight growl of frustration he moved towards the window and peered through the blacked out glass to see who sought his attention. With one glance he threw open the door with a more audible growl of disapproval and slammed the door behind him before I had a chance to see who was there. I heard another door open and realised that Sam had turned off the car and joined his employer outside the car. I sat still in the back seat, unmoving, listening intently as a dark feeling coiled its way around my stomach, causing it to turn slightly. The feeling was cold and dark and was making me feel nauseous. I could now hear raised voices outside the car and I inched slightly to take a glance out of the window. I could see a man in a suit, still wearing his masquerade mask, gesticulating wildly towards Carter and yelling incoherently. A woman was by his side but I couldn't make her out as she was shadowed by this angry man by her side.

Sam was obviously trying to mediate and keep the situation calm as he stood in between both Carter and the angry man. I couldn't make out much of anything from inside the car. The glass must have also been soundproofed. I could make a distinction between voices but that was about it.

The uneasy feeling in my belly was now becoming unbearable. I began to rock from side to side slightly to try and encourage the feeling to ease off. Logical and Dreamy were both alerted and watching the unfolding events with keen interest. Who was he talking to and about what at this time of night? My pain was now making me grumpy and reminding me further of how exhausting the day's events had been.

I was so wrapped up in what was going on inside the car that I didn't realise my phone had received a message. It bleeped loudly once again to alert me to another incoming message. I almost jumped out of my seat as it lit up my bag and vibrated hard against my leg.

I pulled the annoying device angrily from my small bag and unlocked the screen as I silently cursed it for interrupting my spying on the outside situation.

It's almost show time. I felt like my blood instantly froze.

I quickly returned my attention back to the window. Carter was stood with both hands balled into fists at his sides. He hadn't sent the text. The knot tightened in my stomach and the cold feeling deepened causing me to feel slightly numb. I'd forgotten about the random text from the other day. I'd written it off as a wrong number or some random trying to scare people but now I was starting to feel like these texts weren't from some random person and were aimed at me. Carter and Sam continued to try and calm the situation outside the car. Carter was now inching his way backwards towards the door and Sam was now at Carters side. I was still feeling uneasy but the tense feeling was starting to ebb as I realised they were coming back to the car again. My phone once again lit up the dark interior of the car and I shrieked as it bleeped in my hands. I looked down at the screen and felt like I was going to throw up.

I've missed you Kira. Your boyfriend can't protect you.

I felt the blood rush to my head. My hands felt numb but my head felt very light almost dizzy. I was aware of my breath coming in short sharp bursts. I wasn't hyperventilating but I wasn't far from it. Panic seized my mind as I manically scrambled to the other side of the car and began frantically looking out of the window. Where was he? I could see drunk couple and friends leaving the club now and starting to fill the localised streets hunting for taxi's and buses to make their ways home. He had to be nearby somewhere, watching to know that I had a boyfriend. I knew it made no sense but there was only one person who could be texting me like this. Big Davey Grigor. The thought of his name made me shudder and brought me to the brink of tears.

It made no sense, he was in prison, wasn't he? My mind started to conjure up a million and one scenarios where he had gotten out of prison and hunted me down. I was after all the reason he had been locked away in the first place. Whatever the reason was, he was out now and he did indeed seem to be hunting me to settle the score.

I almost screamed as Carter climbed into the back. Immediately he picked up on the fear coursing through my veins. Another perk of being a vampire I guess, the ability to sense others emotions. Carter laid his arm gently across my shoulders and I meekly snuggled into his side and began to sob. He said nothing but gently with his other arm reached behind his head and untied his hair. It cascaded down and formed a barrier around me, shielding me from anyone looking into the car. I doubted very much anyone could see through the blackened glass but it was reassuring none the less. I rested myself completely into Carters side as Sam once again started the car and this time we moved forward away from the lights of the city centre.

Once I had managed to control my almost endless sobbing I unshrouded myself from Carters hair. He sat back against the seat watching the street lights passing as we drove along the dark streets. I looked up at him and he turned instinctively towards me, his deep brown pools full of concern but still he said nothing to me. His free hand slid across his lap and gently stroked away the few stray tears from my cheek.

"Where are we going?" I finally managed to say through my broken voice.

"To my country home." he stated flatly "The city is not safe for either of us tonight and I'd rather you weren't home alone this evening."

I remembered the earlier conversation about Scott not being home tonight. A sudden flash of panic shot through me. I opened my mouth to speak but carter silenced me with a finger to my lips.

"Malakai is waiting for you at my place. He is currently in his own basket in the utility room as its warm and gives him enough room to wander but not to be scared. Sam moved him across earlier when I found out about Scott."

I could feel tears in my eyes again but this time they weren't through fear.

"You've moved my cat in!" I squeaked.

Carter raised a quizzical eyebrow and pondered this thought for a moment before tipping his head back and roaring with laughter.

"I suppose I have!" he chortled "How very rude of me. It's usually polite to ask the same of the owner before moving in the pet!"

I grinned like a Cheshire cat but at the same time butterflies suddenly fluttered to life in my stomach which had now thankfully loosened off since we left the city centre.

"I, I'm sorry, are you asking me to move in?" I stammered as Logical gave me a swift warning kick.

Carter slid his arm out from behind me and clasped both of my hands in his.

"My dear Kira, I've shared a lot with you tonight and before the night is through there is more to come" I felt my whole body flush as I thought of our earlier romp before reaching the club "But it's not safe for either of us to be on our own at the moment. I promise I will explain everything to you once we have arrived at our destination."

His eyes were still dark pools again with no hint of light in them. His face was stoic and completely serious. I knew I couldn't make a joke of the situation but for some reason I couldn't hold onto the laughter building inside of me and it erupted forth like an explosion. Startled Carter leaned back slightly as I folded in two with my giggle fit. He watched in complete puzzlement and fascination while I laughed my way through my minor break down, this was all getting too much. This was an extreme storyline for a novel, never mind real life.

Finally the giggles subsided and I straightened myself back out on the seat. I apologised to Carter and looked out of the window, squinting to see if I could determine our destination. There was an occasional street light but no other markers to show me where we were. After several more moments of silence and watching, Carters hands still tightly clasping mine, we slowed down and turned into a dark road end marked only by a single lantern and a large pile of white stones. The road was bumpy and crunched slightly so I guessed we were driving down a gravelled track. I could now see the light from a house at the end of the track. They grew larger as we got closer to the house. Sam pressed a button on the dash board and I saw slight movement. Large metallic gates began to open. They are only visible due to the light catching the frames.

Carter tugged slightly on my hands to bring my attention back to him as the car slowed to pull up outside the house.

"I need to tell you something before we go in. I don't live alone in this house and as soon as they heard about the issues I've had cropping up at the moment they came over. I was planning on introducing you but it's come up sooner rather than later. I hope you don't mind."

I looked blankly at him for a moment totally unsure on what he meant. Did he mean other staff or family? Do vampires really have families? I had seen the pictures in his city penthouse.

Before I could think any more the door beside me swung open and a silver haired man, he looked to be in his mid-20's, stuck his head in beside me smiling.

"Привет, красавица." he said, looking me up and down.

Carter let out a low growl, causing the man to shrink back slightly.

"Caleb, speak English please? I'm fairly certain that Russian is not one of Ms Jansent's languages"
Caleb bowed by way of an apology.

"My apologies Ms Jansent" his voice was soft and there was an unmistakable hint of a European accent despite the Scottish twang behind it.

"What did you say to me?" I asked curiously.

Carter interrupted as he gently guided me out of his side of the car. As he pulled me to his side he whispered in my ear.

"He said "hello beautiful". My brother is a charmer".

There was slight distain to his tone.

Caleb had now joined us and we walked together towards the front door. It wasn't until I looked up I realised the sheer size of the place.

"This isn't a house, it's a castle!" I gasped.

"Ellon Castle." corrected Caleb before getting an elbow in the ribs from his brother.

"милый." called a voice from the now open front door.

Standing in the light from a rather grand looking entranceway was an older looking woman. She looked to be in her 50's with elegantly tied up white blonde hair. She was about my height and was built like a shot putter. Her dark eyes twinkled with excitement as she inspected me as we all walked towards the front door.

"In English mother" called Caleb as we walked "She can't speak Russian."

She embraced me as we reached the front door. She was wearing a strong perfume that reminded me slightly of an aunt I hadn't seen since childhood.

"Yet!" she smiled at me "You will learn with time."

Carter protectively wrapped his arm around my waist, his mother glowered slightly as he pulled me tight to his hip.

"I don't bite" she pouted, I noticed the same accent in her voice although it was thicker and more pronounced.

Caleb began to laugh at his mother's comment as Carter exchanged air kisses with her.

"We came as soon as we heard about your problem." she continued as we entered the castle.
"We can discuss it in the morning mother." Carter cut her off as he glanced from me to her,
indicating I wasn't in the loop on what was actually going on.

She nodded politely and patted me lightly on the shoulder.
"We can discuss in the morning" She conceded "Come Caleb, we have unpacking to do."
Caleb took his mother's comment as a command and began to follow her off down the hallway. He shot back a parting glance and gave Carter a thumbs up as they headed off down the hallway to the right.
As they rounded another corner and vanished from sight Carter's body sagged and he sighed deeply as if he'd been holding his composure completely for his family's sake.
He tightened his grip around my waist.
His expression was once again serious.

"We have a lot of talking to do tonight" he sounded solemn "But before we get to that…"

He bent down towards me and softly our lips met. His skin was once again searing on mine and the all too familiar static electricity was there. I could feel my entire body thrumming with the pulse of the energy between us.

"I believe we have some unfinished business from earlier to conclude Ms Jansent."

"My non-disclosure?" I asked cheekily biting my bottom lip.

"I have to ensure your absolute secrecy with this delicate matter so we must retire to my office."

"Which is where?" I tilted my head to one side quizzically now unsure of where the conversation was leading.

"My bedroom." he said with a maddening smile playing on his enticing lips "I do all of my best thinking and my best work in there."

"I don't doubt that Mr Brams. I don't doubt that at all. You are truly a very talented man." I smiled.
Carter then released my wrist and clasped my hand as he tugged me along the corridor to the left.

Chapter 10

I had thought his bedroom in the city apartment had been gorgeous, this room was something else. The room was an upper floor turret room. The 3 large curved windows were dressed with satin and silk curtains which billowed with the cool breeze drifting through the slightly ajar window to my right.

A large oak four poster dominated the centre of the room. It too was adorned with silk drapes descending like delicate webs from the four sturdy posts. The sheets on the bed were a deep crimson and a small giggle escaped me before I could suppress it. Carter raised his eyebrow at me.

"The colour of the sheets. Possibly to cover up spillage?" I managed, still giggling.

Carter's expression shifted. His eyes seemed to almost smoulder and the wicked smile playing on his lips was more enticing than anything I'd ever dreamed of. This man definitely had a way of winning me over just by looking at me. I could feel myself giving in to all the dark thoughts I'd had over the course of the evening at the club. The wanton desire to be held captive by this man was now finally becoming reality and despite all I knew there was no fear in my resolve to try living out my book fantasies for once, instead of relying on B.O.B to relieve my evening cravings.

"Perhaps," he growled seductively "we should test that theory of yours."

Before I had time to think or formulate a witty answer I found myself flung into the centre of the massive four poster. I wiggled my feet free of my shoes and tossed them onto the floor as Carter lay down beside me on the sea of crimson. Effortlessly he loosened his tie and let it drop onto the floor beside my shoes. Unbuttoning only the top two buttons on his shirt he began to plant butterfly kisses across my cheek, down my neck and across my shoulder all the while boring into me with those dark pools of caramel. A familiar shiver ran through me as he nipped tenderly at the soft flesh between my shoulder and neck. Gently he wrapped his arm around my waist and pulled my shoulders onto his lap as the intensity of his nips and kisses intensified. I closed my eyes loosing myself in the sensations and vivid colours dancing behind my eyelids. His skin was so warm on mine as he worked his free hand across my opposite shoulder sliding the strap down my arm until he could cup my breast. Gently he massaged and teased at my nipple which was already taught with arousal. This man only had to look at me and I was practically soaking with anticipation. I'd never met anyone who seemed to read my mind so perfectly and anticipate my every desire. I felt his breath on my skin as he moved his attention away from the now highly sensitized skin on my shoulder as he slid the other strap down exposing my chest completely. Swiftly manoeuvring on the bed he positioned himself by my side as he laid me down against the coolness of the sheets. Tenderly he began to lick, nip and suckle at my breasts until I squirmed a little, digging my toes into the sheets of the bed. My skin felt like it was on fire. I was melting into a deliciously horny puddle on the four poster. I opened my eyes and watched him for a moment, the bobbing of his head as he moved between my breasts and the flick of his hair as the braid danced from side to side matching his movements. I raised my hand to stroke his head but his hand immediately shot up and gripped my wrist before I could touch him. He looked up at me, his deep caramel pools tinged with amber. His lips were full, wet and glistened in the dim light of the bedroom.

"No Mon Chéri, trust me, it will be more pleasurable, if you refrain from touching me for now." There was an instructional tone to the way he spoke, like I wasn't being advised but more told.

I raised both of my hands and placed them obediently above my head.
Carter smiled appreciatively and returned to tormenting my now almost electrified breasts.
Subconsciously I let out a loud moan as Carters nips and sucks got harder. The sound startled me as at first I didn't realise the sound had come from my mouth. I bucked slightly on the bed as his next nip sent a spark straight from my nipple to my groin. I was now starting to feel slightly restless and my hands were wringing knots in the sheets behind my head. Carter stopped and moved to straddle my hips. He stretched up and began to unfasten more buttons. Slowly and seductively he was teasing me

with the sight of him. Empowered with the surging blood I could hear pulsing through my ears I decided it was my turn. Tensing muscles I didn't even realise I possessed, I pulled myself upright in one swift and unfaltering movement. Carter only had a moment to look startled as I reached up and tore open the white shirt sending a cascade of peal buttons scattering across the room. I yanked the shirt over his shoulders with a strength I'd never possessed before trapping them behind him as I ran my fingers roughly through his chest hair. He purred beneath my hands as I dragged my nails further down across his stomach to the start of his happy trail. I playfully tugged at the top of his trousers before raking my nails back up his torso towards his nipples which were now very erect. From where I sat on the bed I was too short to complete the teasing action I wanted and return the licking and sucking blissful torture I had endured, so I tenderly tugged on them, twisting them very slightly, just enough to illicit a moan from Carter's lips. As he opened his eyes and stared at me with fire like a spurned wild animal, I knew the tables were about to turn again and my brief rein was over. A second later and I heard the audible tearing of a white shirt and Carter's hands were once again free.

"You are quite the fighter Kira, but I cannot be overpowered unless I want to be."

He drew himself to a standing position off the bed and drew me up towards him. The dress, now pulled down to my waist, fell effortlessly to the floor and I stood out of it. I bent down to remove it from the floor and sit it somewhere when Carter seized his advantage and whirled me around to face the bed before I could blink. I gripped onto the edge of the bed to stop myself from face planting and as I did I heard the sound of more fabric hitting the floor behind me. I could feel my heart hammering in my chest and waited for the next searing touch but it didn't come, I waited a moment longer and still nothing. I felt a light shiver across my skin as the breeze from the window had now become more of a cold draft on my skin. I risked a glance across my shoulder but Carter was gone.

Straightening and turning around he was nowhere to be seen in the room. His shirt lay in tatters and his suit trousers on top of it. Looking further around the room I spied his shoes next to the door I assumed led to the bathroom. The door was closed but I couldn't hear any sound from inside. Gingerly I padded over to the door and knocked softly.

"Carter?" I said barely louder than a whisper "Are you ok?"

I heard nothing for a moment and then the door opened. He stood there completely naked, his previously bound locks were now free and cascaded down over his shoulders.

"I thought perhaps if we continued this in the shower, we could kill two birds with one stone." he smiled raising one eyebrow as if seeking my approval.

He moved back slightly to let me see further into the room. The entire room was in darkness and lit by hundreds of small candles and a single oil lamp sitting on the windowsill. I looked around for a bath or shower but only found a sink and a chaise-lounge. I now raised an eyebrow in confusion. Carter clapped his hands sharply twice and the ceiling began a shower of water and just as quickly he clapped the water off again. I stood in awe, my mouth slightly open. I had no words for how decadent and opulent this wet room was.

"This room is amazing!" I exhaled, still taking it all in as I stepped inside.

Carter quietly closed the door behind me and fiddled with a small control panel beside it.
Beethoven's moonlight sonata began to softly play as Carter took my hand and led me over to the chaise lounge. Gently he coaxed me to sit and I was amazed to find it warm and soft to touch, almost like skin. I shot him a slightly worried look.

"It has a specialized silicone covering on it. I heated it a little for you." he smiled.

I made myself comfortable in a position on my side propped up by one elbow, leaving one hand free should I need it. Carter was about to clap his hands and begin the rains when he noticed I was still wearing my panties.

"It would be an awful shame to get those wet." he said grinning wickedly at me.

"Perhaps you should help me then." I blushed.

Moments later I was completely naked and bundled in Carters arms as we both sat on the chaise lounge.
Perched on his lap he leaned in and kissed me deeply on the lips. I wiggled slightly on his lap and then felt content

with myself when I could feel the heat of his erection throbbing against me.

Breaking the kiss for only a moment he clapped twice and warm water started to fill the room like a storm in a rain forest. Warm and gentle the water soothed my over sensitive skin and eased the slight aches and pains I had been hiding after a night of dancing and socialising.

We remained like that for what felt like hours. Bodies intertwined, kissing deeply and simply caressing each other's skin as the gentle rain fell around us and Beethoven continued to play through his softer pieces and the candles flickered softly from their rainproof vantage points scattered about the room. Finally Carter broke contact as he reached behind the chaise lounge and produced a small dark purple bottle. Tipping some of the contents onto his hand he began to massage the now slightly foaming dark coloured liquid into my skin. Taking his cue I took some of the liquid into my hands and reciprocated. Once our torsos were sufficiently soaped up we both stood and continued to massage and clean each other. I gently cupped Carter's balls with one hand while I soaped up his shaft with the other, he let a low hiss escape his lips as a sign of approval. I continued to foam him up until I could feel the veins throbbing down either side of his now fiercely erect cock. As I released him from my grasp, he returned the favour by nudging my legs apart and caressing my hot and eager sex with his soap covered hand. My clit was firm and sensitive as he brushed past it causing me to squeak slightly as he then inserted two fingers deep into my folds. Using the flat of his palm to rub soap into the rest of my nethers, his two fingers worked and twisted inside of me building the all too familiar beginnings of a wave. The heel of his hand was rhythmically rubbing my now almost unbearable sensitive clit as I tightened around his fingers. Suddenly he withdrew his hand and the wave decreased its intensity and my entire body felt like it was throbbing. Without his arm supporting me I realised my legs had gone to jelly with arousal. Carter gently held me by the waist as he lay down on the chaise lounge. Taking his lead I climbed the chaise and straddled him eager to rebuild my wave of pleasure and let it wash over us both. I kept myself raised on my knees for a moment enthralled with the pleasure of the warm rain running through my hair and down my back and beyond the generous curve of my buttocks. Slowly I let myself lower down onto Carter's awaiting shaft, teasing the head slightly with my folds before I let him fully enter me. As I reached the root of him I moaned low in my throat at the fullness inside of me. As I opened my eyes I looked at Carter who was staring at me intently, his lips slightly parted as I began to buck slowly on top of him. The soft glow from the candles only intensified the flecks of gold swimming in those caramel pools. His expression was soft and loving as he watched me tenderly moving in time with the music. Carefully and slowly he began to thrust upwards on my down strokes intensifying everything. A gasp escaped my lips as his thrusts became more forceful and the delicious fullness began to stretch me helping to build the wave. I threw my head back, rejoicing in the sensation of my wet hair slapping against my back as Carter continued to increase his pace. The track once again transitioned into a new piece with a faster tempo. He was growling now, low and deep, the sound rumbling in his throat as he claimed a piece of me with each thrust. I couldn't stop the moans and gasps that were escaping me now, as the feeling intensified and the wave kept getting higher and higher. His hands were everywhere now, fingers digging into my thighs, across my belly and up to my breasts. Cupping them gently, he thumbed my nipples until the moans became muffled screams and the wave almost reached its peak. A few more thrusts and the wave came crashing down over me drawing a long and seductive moan from my lips. I rode out the orgasm now completely unable to silence the vulgar and guttural sounds emanating from my mouth. With one final thrust Carter's voice joined mine as we both growled in sexual satisfaction as the last droplets of the wave descended and we were both spent laying on the chaise lounge. I altered position until I was lying on top of Carter as he lazily played with my wet hair, winding it between his fingers. Slowly the blood coursing through my ears began to slow and my breathing returned to its regular pattern.

I broke the silence first.

"With a bargaining chip like that Mr Brams, I can guarantee my silence to the rest of the world."
Carter laughed beneath me, the echoes of it reverberating through me.

"It's a deal then Ms Jansent. Our secret, our great sex."

Once we had regained some semblance of humanity again we returned to the bed wrapped in the warmest, fluffiest towels I'd ever had the pleasure to wrap around my skin. As we lay on top of the crimson sheets facing each other Carter traced a line from my shoulder to my neck, across my jaw and then up my cheek to my eyes. His own eyes held a trace of sadness. I opened my mouth to speak but he broke the silence between us this time.

"And now Mon Chéri, we have to discuss the situation we now find ourselves in."

"I have a confession to make." I mumbled as I wrung my hands together.

Carter sat up slightly looking at me strangely. Was he worried about what I was going to say?
"There's been some stuff going on in my life I didn't tell you about. Our relationship is so new and I didn't want to drag you down with my baggage" I could feel the tears welling in the corners of my eyes as I bit back the urge to sob at the thought of what I was about to tell him.

Silently he regarded me wearily as I told him about the shape at the window, the visit to the police station and the texts I'd been receiving. The whole time Carter said nothing and remained painfully far away from me. I wanted his understanding and just a touch to reassure me that he wasn't going to view me as damaged goods.

"When I was a university student, there was this guy," I tried to explain but the tears began to flow and the bitter taste in my mouth felt like it was closing my throat.

Carter stopped me then. He cupped my cheek with his hand and tiled my face to look at him. Softly he kissed me, his hot searing flesh gently skimming over mine. The reassuring gesture I had so desperately wanted now tipped me over the edge and I began to sob uncontrollably. Sitting up and pulling me onto his lap Carter held me softly, stroking my hair until there were no more tears to fall and I was exhausted from the relief of releasing the tears I'd waited years to shed.

"He beat me and raped me." I finally managed as I looked up into Carters eyes.

Carter stroked the last few tears from me eyes and I thought for a moment I saw tears in his eyes too.

"Small wonder you accepted a vampire so readily Mon Chéri, when you've seen the evil beast in humanity and gone toe to toe with him."

"I'm afraid he's back and I don't know what to do. I'm terrified of him." I said in a small voice I barely recognised as my own. Carter pulled me closer so more of my torso was across his lap as he looked lovingly down at me. He tucked a strand of hair behind my ear and kissed my forehead.

"He can't hurt you this time. You are stronger and you are not alone Mon Chéri." Carter slated flatly. The certainty in his tone soothed me as he continued talking.

"I also have enemies and they seem set to make my life uncomfortable too. I fear that as our relationship is now gaining social media attention that it won't be too long before you start to feel the pain of their efforts." A wrinkle or worry creased his brow as he spoke and his eyes seemed to darken. I felt the familiar knot in my stomach from earlier slowly returning as I shivered at the thoughts forming in my mind.

"What do you mean social media attention?" I asked suddenly.

Carter reached under the frame of the four poster and pulled out a small laptop. With one swift movement he flipped it open and woke it from sleep mode. As the screen flashed to life I was greeted by several windows all with different stories and pictures but the one thing they all had in common were the photographs of Carter and I together. One was outside the restaurant, one was on the bridge as we'd stood talking and one was from this evening at the club. I was oddly upset by the images, I didn't remember seeing anyone taking pictures of us at all. All the pieces went on at length to discuss Carter's previous "lady friends" and about their unexplained ends but not one of them knew who I was, at least not yet.

"I had no idea I could be that interesting." I managed a small giggle.

Carter glowered at me slightly as he closed the laptop over and replaced it under the bed.

"You don't seem too worried."

"A man who tried to kill and impregnate me is walking the streets of Aberdeen again and you think I should be worried about what a few hacks type up in an online rag?" I snapped. "I think our priorities might be slightly misaligned Mr Brams."

I was afraid and I was angry that a man like Davey could be on the streets again so soon after what he'd tried to do, but I instantly felt guilty for snapping at Carter. I could see the sting I'd caused reflected in those big dark pools. He was only trying to protect me and had my best interests at heart.

"I'm sorry. I just don't see how an online blog can be anywhere near as dangerous to us as Davey being free is to me." I tried poorly to explain.

Carter smiled wistfully as he once again stroked my cheek. The back of his hand was cooler than his palm and the steady warmth trailed along my cheek and vanished into my hair as he plunged me into a deep embrace until the knot in my stomach began to unravel and the dark feelings in my heart began to flee from the light. I felt lighter and my heartbeat increased slightly as Carter moved his lips from mine towards my neck and that special sweet spot between my neck and my shoulder where the slightest touch causes a spark to shoot through my veins. I closed my eyes and let my body sag a little as I enjoyed his trails of kisses and the building anticipation as I waited for the inevitable jolt. As his kisses got closer they got firmer becoming more like a series of urgent nips. I tugged at the sheet to keep myself grounded as he finally hit the spot. I let out an audible squeal as a sign of approval and that was the precise moment I felt fangs. Logical was screaming in my ears to stop while Dreamy was watching on with keen excitement. For a brief moment I felt like someone had poured ice into me veins and a spike of terror stabbed through me but as I felt Carters warm skin on mine, his hands gently kneading the flesh of my shoulders on then the tops of my arms as reassurance the ice melted and the fear subsided. Maybe I was wrong, maybe I was stronger than I used to be and with Carter by my side I could face the demons from my past.

My ears began to ring slightly and I started to feel a little woozy as Carter released me from his embrace. Turning his head to conceal his face from me I knew he was licking my blood from his lips and savouring the taste. Gingerly I touched the spot he'd bitten expecting it to be painful but there was nothing.

Carter turned back to face me, a ring of deep red now surrounded his pupils which were heavily dilated.

"Our bite has a natural anaesthetic to it. There will be no pain and there will be no bruises."

"Awww." I teased "I was kinda looking forward to nervously hiding a hickey."

I tried to sit up but the room began to spin slightly and I lay back down on the bed. Butterflies fluttered in my chest as I placed my hand over it.

"I might have overdone it a little Mon Chéri but you tasted so good I couldn't help it. I learned a little more about you too."

"That I'm a hopeless romantic who's attracted to the undead?" I quipped, surprised at the speed with which I had formed such a witty retort.

"I have a confession to make." Carter said bowing his head a little.

Uh oh, Logical was pacing in circles and cursing me out loud, *what did he mean?*

"When you open yourself to me like that, it's all too easy to peek past your barriers."

I screwed up my face a little in complete confusion.

"I read you." he stated bluntly.

Once again I tried to sit up to look him in the eye and this time the room didn't spin quite as quickly and I was able to prop myself up on my elbows levelling my gaze at him.

"And what did you learn?" I asked, my tone flat.

"You are what I've been looking for all these years." he smiled. A light shone in his eyes that looked almost like tears forming. "I have been searching for years for another person who could understand me, who wants the same things from life as I do. Someone who doesn't care what I am, man or monster and who wants me for me, not the status or the money."

"You got all of that from my blood?"

"It's more than your blood when a vampire drinks from you and you give willingly. You drop your guard and we can see your whole being. Everything that makes you a whole."

I blushed slightly at the thought of being completely naked and laid bare to him, soul and all. Then a small thought occurred to me.

"Did you see everything inside of me?" I asked, almost embarrassed.

He nodded and Logical and Dreamy sat bolt upright and suddenly took notice.

"Your inner voices are very loud, I'm amazed you manage to hold your tongue as often as you do, but they mean well." he laughed.

I instantly relaxed. Logical and Dreamy were my muses and my inner guides. I had learned to trust them and balance my life between their guidance, which at times were almost polar opposites. I had never told anyone about them, convinced I'd sound crazy. I had come to the conclusion that Logical and Dreamy had come into existence after my night with Davey. It was my brains way of protecting itself from any other possible events that could shatter me. For some reason meeting a real vampire hadn't factored into that equation hence my complete lack of concern for my safety.

We removed the towels and deposited them into the basket just inside the wet room door and then returned to the four poster. Once we were snuggled together under the sea of crimson Carter produced a remote from under his pillow and switched off the lights. He pressed another button and a small flap in the wall opened revealing a large flat screen TV.

"Very impressive." I yawned as Carter flicked through the channels to find something to put on.

"Shhhhh." he whispered into my hair as I nuzzled into his chest feeling the tendrils of sleep beginning to cocoon me "I can give you the grand tour in the morning while we discuss our battle plan."

My heavy eyelids fell closed as the familiar tones of a cartoon theme tune from my childhood played quietly in the background as my dreams took hold and led me from this world to another.

Chapter 11

When I opened my eyes I was standing in a forest, the wind was whipping the branches above my head yet I felt nothing. I looked down at myself and found I was completely naked. Instantly embarrassed I tried my best to cover my modesty with flailing arms. A dark laugh echoed from between the trees and Carter emerged and began to walk towards me a large black wolf was by his side. His eyes were alight with golden fire as he proudly stepped towards me, completely unashamed of his nakedness. His long dark hair fell wild and free from his shoulders. He looked like a cover image from one of my romance novels at home. His seductive smile only grew with each confident step he took towards me until he was only a few paces away from me. The electricity crackled between us as the wind began to howl louder and the trees around us began to creek heavily under the strain. He said nothing as he stood before me, looking down at me with those deep pools of caramel set aflame with passion and lust. He reached out his hand for me and with no control of my own will I offered him my wrist. Gently kissing his way from my wrist he tenderly but eagerly worked his way up my arm and towards that sweet spot on my neck. I couldn't draw my eyes away from him as he wound a strong arm tightly around my waist pulling me

*close until I could feel the heat of his straining cock
against the bare flesh of my ass. I heard his voice hiss
seductively in my ear before the sweet bliss of his bite
electrified my whole body and I bucked and moaned as a
powerful orgasm shook me to the core.*
*Everything faded to black but the words he'd spoken kept
echoing through my head.*
"Now you're mine"

I woke with a start as something cold touched my leg. My
eyes fluttered open to reveal the room just as I had
remembered it last night, the whites and ivories of the
curtains and the walls with the contrasting dark wood of
the bed frame and assorted dressers. Carter was perched
on the end of the bed towel drying his hair. Cold droplets
of water dropped onto my bare foot which had escaped
from its cotton cocoon as I'd slept. I shivered slightly as
the memory of the dream awakened the feelings deep
within me. I pulled the covers up around myself as I
watched him finish drying his hair and then move onto
the other towel, snuggly hugging his hips. Water droplets
slid down his skin and fell silently onto the carpet as I bit
down slightly on my bottom lip to stop Dreamy's
suggestions running away with me. As if I'd said my
thoughts out loud he turned and looked up at me through
the dark mop that was covering his face. That wolfish grin
was once again there sending a heat right through me.

"You slept well." he offhandedly commented as he began
to unravel the Egyptian cotton swathe covering him. His
grin seemed to grow into a full blown smile as he watched
my face as he removed the towel and climbed over the
foot of the bed and up the covers towards me like a big
cat stalking its prey. His eyes never left mine as he stalked

up the bed towards me. Unwillingly a small squeak of excitement escaped me the moment before he pounced trapping me under the covers. One hand grabbed both wrists and pinned them above my head as he stole a kiss.
"What were you dreaming about?" he enquired as he stole more kisses, each one deeper than the last.
"About you." I admitted shyly, averting my gaze from his, no longer able to take the heat.
"I had guessed that." he smiled as he rose up on his knees and let me move.
The shocked expression on my face was all the evidence he needed.
"You talk in your sleep my dear." he laughed as he got off the bed and pulled the covers back, fully exposing my nakedness. Instinctually I covered myself as best I could.
"Mon Chéri, why do you do that?" he asked sounding disappointed.
I blushed all over.
"I don't know. I always feel embarrassed naked. It's gotten better since *that* happened. I dunno, I guess I don't like myself very much." I replied meekly.

Carter's face fell slightly as he reached for my hand and pulled me up off the bed. He pointed my shoulders in the direction of the shower room before kissing my shoulder and tapping me on the buttock to send me on my way.
"I think you are beautiful Mon Chéri" he whispered as I paced off into the wet room "I will meet you downstairs for breakfast once you are washed and dressed. I'm certain after those dreams last night you'll want a shower."
I could feel his smile behind me as I closed the shower room door.

After what felt like an age underneath the rainforest of a shower I finally felt awake and invigorated after the previous evening's events and dreams. I emerged from the bedroom in jeans and a floaty style Pelham top and made my way downstairs. My prized trainers padded softly on the carpeted stairs as I descended. At the bottom of the stairs I realised I had no idea where the other rooms in the castle were located but I could smell newly cooked bacon and freshly brewed coffee so I let my nose guide me and never one to let me down it led me to the kitchen. Carter stood at the stove in the large stone hearth at the far end of the kitchen and his mother and brother were seated at the table also watching him cook. "God his ass looks divine in those tight jeans." sighed Dreamy. I smiled as the thought lingered as I walked into the kitchen. I already knew that all three were aware of my presence before I'd even entered the room but I was grateful when they turned and bid me good morning almost in unison. Caleb got up out of his seat and pulled out a seat for me beside him. Carter took the plates over to the table and sat next to his mother, across the table from me. He nodded his appreciation at my outfit after looking me up and down as I took my seat at the table. Carter's mother had only a tall glass of red wine, she had already declined the array of food that Carter had cooked. Caleb eagerly dug in grabbing a tong full of bacon, two fried eggs and some toast.

Carter kindly loaded my plate for me with a few rashers of bacon, an egg and two slices of toast that he's freshly buttered. He passed me the plate while adding "You can have more if you wish."

I shook my head as I tucked into the bacon. Caleb and I were almost in a race to see who could finish their breakfast the quickest. As the last of the food vanished and we placed our cutlery on the plates we laughed at each other.

"I beat you, admit it?" smirked Caleb.

I downed the last of my tea as I looked over at his place setting.

"I believe coffee classes as part of breakfast doesn't it?" I smirked back raising an eyebrow.
Carter erupted into laughter as Caleb looked dejectedly into his still half full mug of coffee.

The whole time his mother had said nothing and merely sipped at her glass and watched us.
I glanced over to her and noticed the contents of her glass was congealing on the sides. It wasn't red wine after all. I felt that familiar knot beginning to form in my stomach as she self-consciously downed the remainder of the liquid as she caught me staring at her. I was about to utter my apologies when there was suddenly a loud battering at the front door. The sound echoed through the stone hallways all the way to the kitchen. Caleb sprang to his feet as did Carter. Someone opened the front door and the battering stopped but it was replaced by another more subtle sound, there was a pattering on the carpets and a skittering sound almost like...
My thoughts were abandoned as the largest dog I had ever seen came barrelling into the kitchen. I drew to an immediate halt in front of Carter who crouched down and stroked the beast. He removed a note from the creature's leather collar and stood to full height again. He turned his back on the creature and began to unfurl the note as Caleb returned to his seat at the table. I looked over to the large dog and I could swear it winked at me.

"Carter, I think that dog just…"

Carter raised his finger to his lips to silent me but was too late. The dogs form became fuzzy and out of focus as it curled into a ball and was consumed by what I can only describe as a haze of black smoke which spiralled into a tall funnel and then dissipated as suddenly as it had appeared. A woman of about my height stood totally naked in front of me. She slammed her hands onto the table in front of me as she angrily spat at me through clenched teeth.

"Watch who you call a dog, Bitch!"

Carter slammed his fist on the table as he let go of the note. It slid across the table and Caleb instantly began reading.

"Nina, do not call my girlfriend a bitch and she meant no disrespect she didn't know."

Nina bowed her head slightly and muttered an apology. I bounced forward in my seat with excitement.

"You're a werewolf!" I squealed with delight. Nina raised her head and smiled knowingly at me.

"She's new!" she commented to Carter as she grabbed the apron from the counter behind her and covered her nakedness slightly.

Nina was roughly my height but was a lot thinner than me. Her hour glass figure was not completely hidden by Carter's apron which was about 4 sizes too massive for her. Her breasts were perky and her shoulder length hair glistened in the sunlight streaming through the window. She was stunning to look at. I immediately looked to see Carter's response to her naked form. As I looked over to him his eyes were on me and my reaction to Nina. A bemused smile played on his lips.

"Allow me to introduce you" He began waving his arms in a formal manner "Nina, this is Kira my girlfriend. Kira this is pack alpha Nina from the Moray pack. She and her husband keep an eye on events in parts of Grampian I am not readily able to travel to."

"'Sup." Nina nodded as she grabbed the last rasher of bacon from the tray on the table giving everyone a flash of her amazing breasts. Caleb almost choked on his remaining coffee as he winced at Carter's unseen kick under the table. I felt the scuff of his shoe as it passed my crossed ankles beneath the table.

"She's married." Carter growled at Caleb.

"Happily." beamed Nina as she downed a glass of orange juice and nodded towards Carter's mother at the other end of the table.

"Nina." she acknowledged as she rose from the table "I need to visit the powder room."

As she left the room Nina pulled out a heavy kitchen chair, turned it backwards and sat down, legs akimbo behind the large solid back of the chair. Caleb looked slightly disappointed.

"Is she up to speed?" She asked Carter with a sense of

urgency.

"No, but I can fill her in as we go." Carter stated flatly before adding "How is Wilf doing?"
Nina looked slightly startled at his question.
"He and the kids are both fine thanks. Shall we?" she motioned towards the paper Carter had removed from Caleb's grasp. He laid it down on the table and used the coffee mugs to hold the four corners down. It was a letter.

Over the course of the next half an hour my world was turned upsides down. There were plans afoot to overthrow the current status quo, the balance between human and supernatural was being threatened. Somehow I fitted into this but I wasn't currently sure how. Nina and Carter quickly went over plans to secure Moray and draft in others to help with the rest of Grampian. A rival group of supernaturals were poised to take over from Carter and use the humans as cattle rather than live in blissful ignorance as they currently did with Carter's overseeing. If something wasn't done and their spurring forces discovered soon then people we cared about would be hurt if not killed. Carter walked Nina to the door, whispering quietly with her all the way. As they left the kitchen she shot me back a parting look. The fear in her eyes was more than apparent. The knot was now slowly growing in my stomach. Caleb left to find his mother as Carter returned to the kitchen carrying the apron. I raised an eyebrow as he placed it across the back of a chair.

"Left the way she came," he stated "in a flurry of haste and fur."

He sat down and clasped my hands in his as he looked

deeply into my eyes.
"Are you ok?"

"I'm not sure I am taking all this in. Where do I fit into this anyway?"

"Well, except for being someone I care about and potentially a target because of that, someone is gunning for you too."

Panic rose in my throat as I uttered the word "Who?" I knew the answer before Carter even parted his lips.

"Davey Grigor"

I felt like someone had knocked the air out of my. I bent forward as I tried to control my breathing but it wasn't much use. I was hyperventilating as all the memories fell on me, wave after wave. Everything I'd tried so hard to hide from the world was now spilling out of my mind and consuming everything. Logical and Dreamy were helpless as a sea of black consumed them both. I could hear the blood pumping through my ears like a deafening roar. My breathing was now completely out of control and my hands began to feel numb. Carter gripped my hands tighter and began to say something but it was no good. He moved from his chair just in time to catch me as I passed out and fell from the chair.

When I came to again I was screaming and scratching. Caleb looked completely dismayed as he gingerly touched at the scratches I had planted all over his face and hands. I sat bolt upright and looked about me. I was in a sitting room on a large very comfortable sofa. Caleb was in front of me and his mother was off to one side looking wistfully at me. Carter came through the door with a damp cloth in his hands. I took a deep breath and realised I must have been holding it. As Carter neared the sofa I raised my arms to him and he caught me in a tight embrace. Softly he stroked my forehead with the damp cloth which was wonderfully cold across my skin which felt like it was on fire. My back was damp with sweat and I felt more than a little nauseous.

"It's ok Mon Chéri. You had a panic attack, but I won't let anything happen to you. We will find him and stop him before he can do anything to you."
I gripped his arms tighter as I felt the tears forming at the corners of my eyes.

"I'm afraid Carter." I sobbed slightly.

"I know darling." he whispered as he held me tighter "I know."

Chapter 12

The next several days went by in a blur. Scott was safe with his new "friend" as they'd decided to take a trip down to London for a week to see how their "friendship" evolved. I wasn't sure if Scott had been trying to convince me or himself that he was more than just a little into this new guy. I played along with his calls and texts and reassured him that Carter was taking good care of me, which he was. I was never alone for any prolonged period of time. I went with Caleb to the coffee shop to check in with Sophie and Dean only to discover that Dean had been promoted. He proudly showed me his new store badge as he and Sophie talked to me at our usual table. Caleb sat quietly pretending to read a sci-fi magazine he'd grabbed from the train station on our way to the Coffee House. Later on Carter met me at our favourite restaurant and we had a brief dinner with Carter informing his good friend to take care and that matters were afoot but he'd take care of it.

We went back to the harbour view apartment just long enough to clear out the wardrobes and collect a few of Carter's personal effects. There wasn't much as this was merely where he stayed when he had a lot of business on in town. I discovered the castle was his main residence. We stopped briefly by the club on our way back to the castle to deliver the apartment keys off with the bouncer. I don't think I'd actually heard his real name until Carter used it just before we left. I knew him as Griff. He gripped the bouncer in a tight man hug as I stood next to the car and watched.

"Take care old friend and let me know if anything comes up."
The bouncer nodded and tipped an imaginary cap in my direction.

"I mean it Griff." warned Carter as he climbed into the car "Don't chance anything alone with this."

Griff nodded and smiled. I was sure I saw a flash of fang as I climbed back into the backseat to join Carter.

As Sam began to pull away I looked at Carter questioningly.
"Werewolf." he stated flatly not even looking "One of Nina's stationed in the city."

"How many more that I don't know about?" I sighed as I looked out of the window.

"Many." sighed Carter "And now you have entered this world you won't be able to leave it. What has been seen cannot be unseen, as they say."

I turned to face him, his deep brown eyes were heavily tinged with sadness.
"Why so sad?" I asked as I gently stroked his cheek, enjoying the reassuring surge of heat into my fingertips.

"Because you will forever be trapped knowing all the

darkness this city hides and I can't take that pain away from you."

I smiled sadly.
"There was plenty darkness known to me before I met you. I just chose to bottle it up inside of me. Maybe it's time to face my demons and then I can accept this new world you've shown me?"

Carter smiled slightly.
"Perhaps."

We drove in relative silence back to the castle which now had a guard positioned at the gatehouse and new heavy duty gates had been placed at the road end. Security had been heightened but to the untrained eye, it merely looked like some maintenance on an old property. We now had a rather large gentleman with a German shepherd hybrid who patrolled around the castle almost 24/7. I was later to find out that Katie wasn't actually a German shepherd but rather his daughter, but I digress.

As we entered the castle Caleb and his mother were waiting inside for us. Malakai ran up to meet me and immediately began to rub himself in and out of my legs. I lifted him up and snuggled his head under my chin. I placed him back down by my feet and as I looked up all three vampires were watching me as if I'd committed a cardinal sin.

"What?" I asked flatly

Carter laughed as he guided me towards the stairs and our bedroom. Carter had told me to call it ours as I'd be staying with him until everything had been settled.

"Cats don't normally tolerate vampires but Malakai has shown us all nothing by affection since he came here. It's just slightly unsettling as it's so different"

I couldn't contain my laughter at the irony of his statement.
"You think that's weird!?" I squawked in disbelief "With everything else that's going on?"

Carter joined me in laughter and as we reached the bedroom we collapsed on the bed laughing.
Carter lifted a pillow from behind his head and playfully whipped me in the face with it.

"Oh you do not want to play this game." I warned "I'm really good at it."

Carter struck me again in the face with the pillow and I lost it. I launched into a full scale pillow offensive, grabbing one pillow in each hand and alternating left and right with each blow. Carter may have had the luck of supernatural speed and strength but I doubted he had the same sheer determination to win this game. We ended up on opposite sides of the bed launching small attacks from our sides and colliding somewhere in no-man's land in the centre of the bed. Carter kept managing glancing blows but each time I took advantage of the opening and struck him in the chin with what I liked to call the pillow uppercut. After a while I was running out of air from giggling so much and my face was beginning to hurt from the perpetual grim plastered on it. Carter must have noticed my flagging performance as he took the corner of a pillow and waved it in lieu of a white flag.

"Truce." he called out from his side of the bed."

I agreed to a ceasefire and we placed the pillows back on the bed and began to settle down for an evening movie in bed.
Carter had just turned out the lights when my phone vibrated in my pocket. Feeling sure it was Scott I flicked on the screen and unlocked it. The moment I saw the message my blood turned to ice and I dropped the phone on the bed as if it had bitten me. Carter quickly snatched it up and read the message.
It will take more than a pillow fort to stop what I'm going to do to you.

Sam sat on the edge of the bed trying to calm me down while Carter's mother handed me a cup of tea.

"They will find him, if he is out there my darling." she soothed.
Sam nodded in agreement.

Caleb and Carter had taken off outside once they were sure I wasn't alone in search of Davey as they were convinced he still had to be somewhere on the property. You couldn't send a message from that close and take off that fast, even if you were a vampire. Where did that thought come from? No one had mentioned anything about Davey being a vampire and yet somehow the thought in my head made sense. I guess once your eyes have been opened to further possibilities they start to filter into your everyday thinking. I had remembered several moments where I'd wondered if the everyday people bustling past me on busy streets were all that they seemed or if they hid a supernatural secret.

I was disrupted from my musings by a sudden howl from outside and a shiver of ice rose in me and my heart skipped a beat. I could feel the cold moisture on my skin as Sam headed out of the room and into the hallway. Carter's mother remained by my side. She still looked at me like I was a curiosity. I had come to understand that although Carter's reputation with women in public it was all a front and he never got too involved. Finding me in his car and now in his home as if we'd been dating was an oddity to her. It was somewhat a novelty to me too. Our relationship was somewhat of a whirlwind at the moment and I was still on the rise within the dervish and not ready to stop the climb. I felt every fibre of my being come to life when I'm with Carter. A sensation I thought I'd never feel with another human being, a connection I thought had been robbed from me with that fateful night with Davey. Carter had somehow bridged those broken gaps and fixed me. I was loving unconditionally and without fear. Thinking about Davey's damage made me shudder as the remembrance of the pain was now more of a dull throb rather than the acute stab it used to be.

I can almost feel the glassy expression my eyes must have as my mind probes delicately into those thoughts from the past. That night and all the ones that followed once I woke up. Knowing I'd been damaged but not being able to remember the worst of it. Freezing anytime someone had gotten too close. Ending relationships over any stupid reason not to get close. They were all coping mechanisms to keep myself safe, or so I'd thought. Avoidance was the best way not to have to confront the memories and deal with them. Then all this drama from nowhere with work sideswiped me and left me open. Open enough to let myself make a connection and not over analyse it. Open enough to give myself to someone else, scars and all. Open enough to find someone broken like me and let him fix me and now he was out there in the night for me chasing my demons away. I stood up without thinking, my feet moving on their own. The teacup tumbled from the bed but Carter's mother used her cat like reflexes and speed to catch it before even a drop was spilled. It was like an invisible string was in my chest pulling me forward and I was helpless to stop it. I walked slowly towards the window and looked out. I could see torchlight beams flickering between the trees surrounding the castle, I could hear voices calling to each other, echoing between the trees. I strained my ears and closed my eyes. I listened with all the concentration I had until I heard it. Carter and Caleb. They were further out in the forest surrounding the grounds. They were constantly checking back and forth with each other, but their voices weren't carrying, there was no echo like the voices below me. Logical was dumbstruck as she had no explanation for how I was hearing them, or how I even knew to try and listen for them.

"How am I doing this?" I thought to myself "Maybe its stress playing tricks?"

"Kira?" Carter and Caleb's voices echoed inside my head in reply.

Then the world went black.

I re-entered the world into brilliant sunlight cascading through the turret windows in Carter's bedroom, as a gentle autumn breeze caused the sheer material of the curtains to billow inwards towards me. They moved so softly and purposefully, like dancers out on the floor. I was captivated by their swaying motions in the breeze until another motion caught my eye and drew my attention away from the curtains. Carter gently lifted his hand to my cheek and stroked softly. The surge of electricity ran instantly from my cheek straight down towards my toes igniting every nerve ending on the way. The heat of his hand also pulsed a surge of heat through me causing my cheeks to flush and my stomach to flutter a little. He said nothing for a while. Just watched me and gently caressed my cheek, then the back of my hand the then my forearm. Every touch sent another spark through me, jolting my senses into a heightened state. For a few moments I just soaked in the perfection of the scene. I couldn't remember the last time I'd felt quite this serene and at peace with myself. Carter's warmth filled me with every caress of his skin and as I looked into his deep brown eyes I felt truly safe and loved.

"How are you feeling?" he asked finally, his voice sounded husky like he was losing it slightly.

"Ok, I think." I said quietly. My own voice seemed hoarse and strained.

"You gave us all quite a scare. Caleb almost ran straight into a tree when he heard your voice." He chuckled slightly as the mental image replayed for him.

I smiled slightly as the memory slowly surfaced.

"I really did that?"

"Yes, though we're not currently sure on the how. I've never met a human who could do that."

"Is Caleb ok?" I asked, suddenly realising the damage I could have caused.

Smiling Carter nodded his head and held out his hand to me.

"Are you ready to re-join the rest of us?" he asked as I grasped his hand. The jolt of warming static made me moan out loud slightly. Carter raised an eyebrow as he pulled me to my feet next to him.

"Where are the others?" I asked looking around the room.

Carter laughed softly as he wrapped am arm around my back and pushed gently in the small of it, urging me towards the door.

"They are all still awake." he whispered as we walked through the doorway and into a blinding light.

I blinked as my eyes adjusted to the true light of day shining in through the windows. There was no gentle breeze billowing the curtains. They were nestled tightly in their tie-backs and the windows were closed as a mighty gale blew and blustered outside sending leaves and twigs flying past the window. Carter sat beside me on the bed holding my hand tightly between his. His eyes were tightly closed like he was concentrating. His mother and brother were stood at the foot of the bed watching in concern. I tried to sit up but couldn't find the strength to pull myself up. I panicked slightly at the feeling like a weight on my chest prevented any movement. I tugged slightly on the hands surrounding my own. Carter's eyes flickered slowly open and a smile spread across his face as he looked at me. His mother and brother's postures both changed at the foot of the bed too as they looked to relax somewhat.

I tried once again to sit up but again I couldn't move anything from the neck down. I glanced over to the brown eyes that were intently watching me, my panic abundantly clear. Gently and with all the tenderness of a man caring for an injured puppy Carter propped me up on my pillow and adjusted the duvet. He brushed my tussled hair from my face and softly stroked my cheek.

"Better Mon Chéri?" he asked in an almost whisper.

I opened my mouth to speak but nothing came out. I nodded my head slightly.

Caleb stepped forward from the foot of the bed towards me, he looked like he was about to explode if he didn't say something.

"It's only temporary." he burst out "You used a lot of psychic energy to form the connection to both of us and it's left you a little burned out. You should be back to normal in a few hours."

His explanation now out, he beamed with pride at himself. Carter's mother now stepped forward towards me and held out her hand. Carter placed my hand in hers as I was completely unable to do it myself. This paralysis, no matter how temporary was very unsettling. Having said that, everything over the past day or so had been down right disturbing. What the hell was going on!

Carter's mother's hand was as cold as ice. Like the vampires you read about in novels she was colder than the grave to touch and her skin was as smooth as marble.

She muttered something to me in Russian until both Caleb and Carter shot her a dirty look.

"All will be well child. As Caleb said it will take time. Your system has had a large shock and needs time to recover. I have never seen anything like it. You didn't just reach Carter with your thought, you reached Caleb and you reached me. It was like tugging on a spider web, connecting us all for that moment and we all felt your fear and panic. Whoever is hunting you is wanting that. Wanting to feast on your fear, the taste it will be on you. Fear taints the meat as they say. It can be tasted in your blood and to some of our kind it is as powerful as a drug. Now we know you have this gift we must train it. Protect you and gain control of it." She placed her other hand over mine. Completely enclosing them in her own.

The cold feeling began to seep into my wrists and I swear I could feel it like a cold frost creeping up my arms through my veins. As the frost began to pass through me I could feel my heart pounding harder in retaliation, forcing my blood to pump faster, trying to beat the chill passing through me. I could feel my head starting to lighten as my breaths became quicker and I could feel a slight shiver starting in my arms and spreading like the frost. A wave of nausea began to bubble up from my stomach as the frost began to feel all consuming. I shot a glance to Carter, fear forming tears in the corner of my eyes. He instantly growled and shot a warning look at his Mother. She dismissed his challenge with an equally warning stare. Caleb shifted uncomfortably at the foot of the bed. The frost had now numbed my hand arm, my other arm was started to feel numb and I could feel the shiver more forcefully shaking my system. As the cold seeped into my chest I could feel a tightness on my lungs, it was getting harder to breath. Was she trying to kill me?

Logical and Dreamy were nowhere to be found and I was starting to go into full blown panic mode. I wanted to kick my legs, flail my arms, anything to fight this feeling off but I couldn't move at all and I couldn't speak.

The frost was now everywhere, I could feel the ice in my veins and although I couldn't move them anyway, my limbs felt like lead. My breaths were becoming staggered and ragged as I tried to control them. In through nose, out through mouth, gently, slowly, calmly. Nothing was working, my body was panicking on its own and my breathing couldn't be tamed. I began to feel dizzy with the lack of air my stifled lungs were getting and the edges of my vision were beginning to fade to black. She was killing me!

Suddenly I felt Carter's hand grip my shoulder and the blackness subsided a little as a jolt of warmth and electricity jolted through me. For a moment I caught my breath as the warmth only slightly fended off the frost. It was enough, it was what I needed. I closed my eyes and with everything I had I pulled from deep within myself every ounce of survival instinct I had. I thought about what Davey had done to me, about Scott's compassion and care ever since, I thought about my firing at work and Carter's immense kindness. I thought about his touch, the electricity that stirred me to life, about his kiss, about his touch and all that it did to me. My eyes flicked open and my mouth was wide as the loudest and fiercest scream I had ever heard erupted from somewhere deep inside of me.

"Nooooooooooooooooooooo!"

It felt like it went on forever. I screamed until I had no

breath left in my lungs and then I dragged back in as much air as I could. I realised as I inhaled deeply that my chest felt lighter and warmer. The fuzzy feeling in my head was clearing and I was beginning to feel warmer. Carter's hand was still tightly gripping my shoulder as he stared at his mother with complete confusion. Caleb had fallen to his knees and was looking at me with complete bewilderment. Finally I looked at Carter's mother, her hands still wrapped over mine. I scowled at her and tightly pursed my lips together. I inhaled deeply through my nose and once again screamed.

This time no sound came out of my mouth, but Carter's mother dropped my hand and fell to a sit on the edge of the bed. Caleb rose to her side to steady her.

"What happened?" I asked, startled by the sound of my own voice as it came effortlessly from my lips.

"You passed." smiled Caleb as he helped his mother over to a chair to the side of the room.

I looked back to Carter. Fear and confusion wrinkling my brow.

"I don't understand." I could feel the tears forming once again.

"Mother would never have harmed you, but she had to push you and see what you would do. Each vampire has a "gift" if you will. Mother has an icy touch, it can work both as a blessing and a curse. It can kill a person by freezing their heart. She would have stopped in another minute or so but you stopped her first. You fought back and I've never seen anyone fight my mother back like that before. Especially not...." He hesitated.

"A human?" I finished. He nodded.

"That scream was something else. Both of them. I've never heard a voice so strong and full of power."

"But I didn't scream the second time. No sound came out."

Caleb chucked from the chair as he rubbed his mother's shoulders. Her head was down and she was rubbing her temples like she had a headache.

"Not outwardly Mon Chéri, inwardly, telepathically. We all heard it but as you aimed it at mother, she's bearing the brunt of it."

"Telepathically? Like when I spoke to you in the woods?" This was confusing the heck out of me now.

Carter nodded and pulled me closer to him. His warmth spread out from my shoulder, down my numb arms and into my frozen fingers. They twitched in response to the instant thaw.

I searched inside myself for the place I'd found before, it felt like a locked room and I had to work hard to pry the door open. I held tightly onto the handle in my mind's eye.

"Like this? Can you hear me? Only you?" I said inwardly.

Like a faint echo in my head I heard another voice.

"Yes. I can hear you and I find it amazing. I've never met a girl like you." A wide, Cheshire cat grin was spread across his face. His deep brown eyes practically sparkled.

I looked over to Caleb who was still tending to his mother and hadn't moved.

Once again the echo was there.

"He didn't hear you. You are focusing on me. You are controlling it."

Carter gently kissed my forehead and whispered in my ear.

"Don't push it though. You've already done a lot more than you should have for someone so new to this skill. You'll exhaust yourself. Close your eyes for now Mon Chéri. Get your strength back. Once you're rested you'll be able to get up and have something to eat. You'll need to refuel after all that. Mother is making her signature dish."

At his request I could feel my body betraying me, my eyelids were getting heavy again. As I began to drift back into a deep sleep I wasn't sure I wanted to try anything else that his mother was offering after what she'd just done, all in the name of making me a guinea pig! I missed Logical's witty sarcasm and Dreamy's reassurance as a soft darkness enfolded around me like a warm blanket. Where had they gone?

When I awoke it was several hours later and it was already starting to get dark. The winds had subsided a little and I was alone. I twitched my fingers and they responded. I was pleasantly surprised that my body now seemed to be behaving. I wriggled my toes beneath the duvet and almost erupted in elation as the cover moved at the foot of the bed. I pulled one leg up and then the other and slowly pushed myself into an upright seated position. I laid my head back on the solid wooden headboard. The cool feel of the wood sent a small shiver up my spine. I let out a small gasp, which startled me. I then had a small laugh at how silly I was being.

Logical was suddenly there, chastising me for not listening to her in the first place and getting into all of this, while Dreamy was wistfully recounting all of the perfect romantic moments that Carter and I had already shared due to my complete disregard to her warnings. I suddenly felt like myself again. My inner voices were back in place and gave me balance.

Looking past both of them I dug down into myself and looked for the door. I was just about to grasp the handle when I heard the door of the bedroom opening. My eyes were instantly open as Carter entered the room carrying a large tray. He walked over and placed it on the dresser next to the bed.

Perching on the edge of the bed he surveyed me and took my temperature with his wrist.

"You seem to be back to normal then. Are you hungry? You've been through a lot today."

I nodded eagerly and Carter lifted a tray from the floor under the bed and unrolled a napkin containing a silver fork and knife.

"Mothers speciality." he smiled as he took the cover off of both the plates on the tray. "Venison Stew."

The stew smelled amazing, my stomach growled in response to the delicious aroma teasing my nostrils. I was struck with how empty my stomach felt, when did I last eat? It felt like I'd been in and out of this world so many times I'd completely lost track of time.

"What day is it?" I asked as I began to stuff my face with tender chunks of venison and vegetables.

Carter laughed as he wiped some gravy from the corner

of my mouth before it could travel down my chin.

"Does it matter Mon Chéri?" he asked "Time doesn't really have relevance when your safety is at stake."

I shuddered as I thought about Davey and the cruel things he was capable of.
"Has he become a vampire?" I asked with urgency "He should still be in prison."

Carter solemnly hung his head and let out a long sigh, tenderly he gripped my free hand.
"Caleb and I couldn't find any trace of him in the grounds or surrounding woods, but from everything he seems to be doing right now, supernatural involvement does seem the likeliest reason. I'm sorry. It seems one of your demons has truly come to be just that. Caleb is patrolling now along with the others. Mother is contacting some of her people and we have a guest to stay with us right now. Nina has sent us her beta for a short while."

I recoiled slightly at the name, remembering the brazenness and bravado the female werewolf had shown in Carter's presence. She was too familiar and my brow creased as I stressed over how she was connected to Carter. I remembered him saying one of his top men, his cousin, was married to her, but that didn't stop the uneasy feeling in my stomach marring the warming sensation of the stew.
Sensing my unease Carter's hand grew tighter around mine.

"Mon Chéri, seriously, after all we're going through right now, you're worried about Nina? I'm sure she'd find that a novelty. She's got an attitude because she's a female

Alpha, do you know how rare those are? She's a mother and a wife also. Bravado is a mask she wears to keep herself strong. Wilf and I had many talks about her before she became Alpha and I'm still in awe of her transformation. Besides, she liked you, that's why she sent Pete."

I raised a curious eyebrow at his words.

"You'll meet him once you've eaten. We have somewhere to be tonight and we'll need him with us. If you're up for it? I know you've been through a lot since yesterday."

My head tilts slightly to the side as I continue to eat, even more intrigued than before. I can feel my unease settle over Nina a little. A mother and a wife would surely not want another man in her bed? I have no idea what an Alpha does but if it's anything like a Dominant then she looks like she could take on just about anyone.
I finish eating and Carter encourages me to take a quick shower while he prepares our evening outfits. I tried to insist that I could arrange my own evening wear but he insisted it was to be a surprise and so I resigned myself to a hot shower and carried my towels off towards the rainforest shower room. I sat on the edge of the chaise lounge as the first patters of hot water dripped off my skin and the heat brought the nerve endings to life. I closed my eyes and imagined the rainforest as I soaped myself up. In my mind's eye I could hear birds squawking and millions of leaves rustling as the rain pelted off of them in a tropical downpour. I let the heat and mist envelope all of my senses as the mango and papaya body scrub made me think of all the fruit bearing trees and the animals that rely on them. I was relishing the heat and

moisture restoring my humanity as the eerie musk of the past few days events washed from my skin when I heard a yell. My eyes opened and I felt myself gripping onto the edge of the chaise lounge. I was frozen in place as my heart thumped in my chest like it was trying to break free of its fleshy binding. I tried to hone my hearing in on what I'd just heard but everything was silent except for the pattering of the water from the shower. I closed my eyes for a moment and concentrated.

"Carter?"

In a moment the door burst open and Carter took a few large strides to reach me on the chaise lounge. He gently stroked my cheek with his hand as the water drenched his jeans and t-shirt causing them to cling deliciously to his form. He smiled down at me as the water dripped off of him.

"You are getting better at that Mon Chéri. I was outside and I heard you over another conversation, but you mustn't wear yourself out. We'll have a busy night ahead of us. What was it you needed?"
I looked up sheepishly through my eyelashes at him.

"I heard a yell." I admitted shyly "I wasn't sure what it was."

Carter erupted into laughter as I felt myself slip into a deeper shade of beetroot.

"I'm not laughing at you my darling. That sound is what happens when a vampire and a werewolf decide to have a cock fight and arm wrestle each other."

I sat there transfixed on Carter's totally drenched form as he sat beside me on the chaise lounge and put an arm around my shoulder.

"It will take a little adapting to get used to this world my love." He whispers sweetly in my ear.

"Come and get dried and dressed. It's time you met our body guard for the evening's festivities."

Chapter 13

Standing in front of the hearth I could feel the shivers of fear subsiding as I stood in my gorgeous evening gown in the main living room in the castle. The dress was a mint green and perfectly complemented my brown hair and pale, milky skin. I was standing, my backside slowly toasting as I surveyed the other occupants of the room. Carter looked perfect as always, sipping at a cognac as he stood there in yet another amazing pin striped suit. Caleb sat on the sofa next to his mother wearing a faded Superman t-shirt and torn jeans. He actually looked quite hot in a messy, grunge kind of way. His messy hair just pulled out of his face by his fingers. Carter's mother, was wearing her smart skirt and navy blue blouse. It made me feel uncomfortable. Her formal wear made me wonder how many of us were going out this evening. Leaning against the wall opposite me was a young man with dirty blonde hair wearing a short sleeved shirt and smart black baggies with more pockets than sense. Around his waist I could just make out the presence of a knife clipped into his belt underneath a stunning midnight blue waistcoat. I could see a stunning tribal tattooed sleeve down his left arm. I couldn't seem to take my eyes off of the symbols etched into the flesh of his arm. The more I looked at them the more they seemed to spell out words. It was like they were alive and moving, making many words. Carter interrupted my rampaging train of thought as he placed the glass down on a side table and walked towards me in front of the fire, joining me at my side and turning to look at the assembled party.

"Kira, I'd like for you to meet Pete. He will be our personal security tonight. Stand up and say hello Pete."

Pete stood straight from his leaning position against the wall. He was easily about 6' 6" or more. His cool blue eyes felt like they were boring holes into me. The same air of bravado surrounds him as it did Nina. It must be a pack thing, I conclude in my head, with Logical nodding her agreement with my theory.

"Hi." He said quietly "Nina has entrusted me to be your guard for the evening. I know it's not ideal but I'm kinda hoping your guy turns up tonight. I've been spoiling for a fight for weeks with everything going on in our neck of the woods and it'd be a shame to waste all this pent up rage while in the big city."

The words "big city" drip sarcastically from his tongue as his mouth curled in a dark sneer.
I straightened up, squaring up my shoulders.

"Pete, is it? He's not MY guy. He's a living nightmare I'd rather forget is real. But by all means if he shows up, you rip his fucking throat out!"

Carter griped my shoulder as I cussed with as much venom as I could humanly muster. Carter's mother sharply inhaled at the sound of my expletive as Caleb slyly smiled and Pete positively erupted into maniacal laughter.

"Nina was right" he chortled as he resumed his leaning stance on the wall. "You have a hell of a lot of spunk for a human. I can feel the rage radiating off of you. I dunno what this guy did to you, but I can guarantee, I won't think twice before unleashing my rage."

Carter let out an angry interrupting cough.

"Of course, I'll leave enough for you and your man here to deal with." he finished dipping his head towards Carter courteously.

Carter now had a sly grin forming on the corner of his lips and a glint in his eye that I'd never seen before. I shuddered slightly as he lets go of my shoulder.
Blood lust Logical confirms my suspicions in the back of my mind.
Pete looked up at me as I silently nodded to Logical's confirmation.

"Crowded in that noggin of yours isn't it?" he quipped.

Startled I look to Carter.

"Werewolves can evidently hear you speaking to your muses." he shrugged.

"Can you all hear them?" I gasped, suddenly horrified that my mind is now on loud speaker for the supernatural world.

Caleb, Carter's mother, Pete and even Sam standing in the door way nodded in unison.

"It is a skill you will have to work on my darling." soothed Carter as he once again touched my shoulder. "You need to control your emotions and then the voices will be silent to us. You are too open and as a result, almost like a…"

"Loud speaker." I finished shyly.

Everyone in the room nodded.
It was at this point that Dreamy decided to break her silence.

"They can hear me? Really, truly? I can have others to talk to instead of this logical, stifling cow! Oh my goodness! What should I say, where should I start. First of all Carter has a truly…."

"Amazing skill at kissing." I sounded in my head whilst blushing all over. At least it was less embarrassing than what she was going to say.
There was obviously a time delay on this think and broadcast network as I had time to cut her off.
Unfortunately everyone in the room was looking rather startled so I assume they all heard her. Carter was wearing the perfect Cheshire cat grin and I wondered for a moment it he could perceive where Dreamy was going with her little speech.

"I think we should head to the car to our first engagement of the evening." he purred softly in my ear.

A short car journey and we were on the fringes of the city. It was a cooler evening in Aberdeen and a gale was beginning to blow in from the North Sea. As we decanted from the car to walk into the casino for the evenings charity event, the freezing wind whipped around my bare

P a g e | **233**

legs, feeling like claws of ice tearing at my ankles. Luckily I counted on it being colder tonight and I'd chosen to wear a woollen dress that came down to my calves, coupled with some cute fur lined boots with kitten heels. Carter was bringing out a dress sense in me I didn't even know I had. My hair was loosely tied back and I had a stylish yet simple black silk scarf around my neck. We rushed inside into the warmth of the heating inside the casino.

The bright lights dazzled me as we were met with a wall of photographers and journalists eager to see all the wealthy and well known who have braved the cold weather to donate to charity. After posing and prancing for the press we were led through to the main hall where everyone had gathered. Waiters in penguin suits were all dotted around the room with trays of drinks ensuring that the evening was "well oiled" to encourage big spending. I could see several women attached to older, rich looking gentlemen in expensive suits and I couldn't help but feel intimidated. Carter softly tugged my arm forcing me to look up at him. He shot me an inquisitive glance to ensure I was ok.

"Just feeling a little out of my depth." I sounded in my head carefully. I don't want to let anyone else overhear this conversation.

"It's hard for me to feel like I fit in at this kind of event. I mean I'm no gold digger Barbie!" I motioned my head in the direction of one of the bleach blonde, silicon enhanced women who was fake laughing whilst clamped firmly onto her partner for the evening while she threw back another flute of champagne.

The force with which she threw the drink back I am

amazed that she didn't set her "girls" free as the flimsy and thin straps of her dress which sank in a very low v neck that extended from her shoulders down to her diamond pierced navel.

Carter followed my eye line and was also clearly startled by the drinking manoeuvre as he gently gripped my arm tighter, drawing me closer to him.

"It's alright." I heard him say softly in my head. "If you think you're uncomfortable, you really ought to look behind us at Pete."

Trying as subtly as I could I glanced over my shoulder at the tall, muscular form of Pete currently fighting and fidgeting with his 3 piece suit. He tugged at the tie around his neck like a dog who's been put on the leash for the first time. I giggled inwardly at my realisation that this must be exactly what it felt like for him. I guessed werewolves didn't necessary relish the confinement of expensive and tailored formal evening apparel. Of her own free will Dreamy caught a glimpse of the muscles bulging beneath the fabric as Pete once again struggled with the collar and tie.

"It'd probably make him feel better to just burst free of all that stuffy fabric and just stand there in all his naked glory." She chortled.

Carter, who had been leading me along the floor towards a business contact, suddenly stopped dead in his tracks and spun me around until we stood chest to chest. He looked down at me, those little amber flecks sparkling in his eyes as he questioned what he had undoubtedly just heard from Dreamy. I tried to shrug the comment off but as I went to raise my shoulder he suddenly dipped down and bound his lips to mine. For the moment all of time and space stood still and there was only Carter and I and this feeling. Electricity all around me, made me feel alive and empowered as his tongue met mine in an all too familiar dance. I moaned slightly into his mouth as I felt my body sagging into his embrace as our kiss deepened. Then just as suddenly as it had started it stopped and the world began to move again around us. Carter gently bit my lip as he broke our kiss and left me breathless as he gave it a gentle suck before standing to his full height once again. I felt like a child as I suddenly realised the room was staring at us. Awkwardly I tried to back away towards a table loaded with sandwiches. Carter momentarily released my arm sensing my discomfort but the attention was short lived as Pete, still struggling within his tailored prison took a step backwards as he yanked a little too hard on his shirt collar sending the top button flying. He tripped backwards over a light cable that hadn't been taped down and as a result went somersaulting backwards over an empty table. With almost feline grace he adjusted his positioning mid-flight and landed gracefully on his feet on the other side of the table. There was a small round of applause from the room, mostly and most audibly from the enhanced blonde arm candy. Pete stood up and dusted himself off, he then took himself off to the corner of the room to talk to another tall figure. I squinted towards the corner, the figure looked familiar but I couldn't figure out where I recognised the man from. His hair was swept back into a tall, majestic ponytail almost as long as Carters and his beard was expertly groomed and styled into two Norse pleats down either side of his chin. He looked up, suddenly aware of my gaze and my eyes locked with his.

Griff! Carter's nightclub bouncer was also here this evening. I was now filled with a feeling of warmth and love as I realised that Carter truly hadn't taken anything as chance and had arranged a full hidden entourage to keep watch this evening. I linked arms with Carter once again as he escorted me around the room, introducing me to several of his business associates and a few friends. As the evening went on everyone gambled at the tables, bid on a charity auction and took part in several other events staged throughout the evening. Dreamy and Logical remained silent the whole time, watching with fascination as I gracefully began to take to this new lifestyle. I no longer felt self-conscious around these plastic women and their rich benefactors. I was brimming with confidence as each new face I met warmed to my personality and showed nothing but firm affection and respect for Carter. Pete and Griff remained on the outskirts of the whole thing, occasionally patrolling the edge of the room and keeping in contact with each other via a series of subtle movements and gestures. As the evening wound down the final event was revealed, the charity raffle. As the guest announcer took to the stage to announce the draw Carter gently pulled me over to the far side of the room. Griff and Pete shadowing our move.

"We don't have to stay for this." Carter said softly as he strokes an imaginary hair from my face.

I shook my head. "I'm ok, we can stay for this if you like. I'd love to see if I won anything."

I suddenly felt the compulsion to yawn and as I did my entire body shivered and I felt my knees give out from under me.

Carter was instantly there, holding me up and looking down at me with nothing but worry and compassion in his eyes.

"It's been a long night. Our names are on the tickets so if you've won anything we can collect them in the morning. You're exhausted Mon Chéri. Let's go home. I have something I want to show you before you fall asleep on me."

There was a wicked gleam in his eye as he finished his sentence.
My eyelids suddenly feeling heavy, I nodded and we made our way towards the door. Pete motioned in front of us to move as he held the door open with Griff bringing up the rear. We had just reached the foyer when we heard the explosion from the hall behind us. The force threw us all to the ground as several figures ran past and straight out the front door. There was smoke everywhere and pieces of masonry all around us. Griff checked we were ok as we sat in shock on the floor as people limped from the hall crying, bleeding and panicked. Carter motioned to Pete and Griff who both took off towards the hall to help. Carter hauled me to my feet and tugged me urgently towards the doors. Sam was already in the car and waiting at the entrance. Carter threw me unceremoniously into the back seat and screamed at Sam to drive as he darted into the car behind me. We both lay across the backseat, not trying to sit up. Gathering our breath and trying to make sense of what just happened when Carter's phone began to vibrate in his pocket. He answered it, his voice raw and gruff.

"Pete, yes, in the car. Yes, we'll meet at the castle. Tell Griff he will too. The A4 in the College street car park. 3rd floor. Registration plate reads Brams. Keys are in the usual place. Out"

I couldn't contain the fear anymore and tears began to flow uncontrollably down my cheeks. I sobbed deeply into the sleeve of my shrug as I tried to wipe away the flood. Carter sat up and pulled me onto his lap. He held my shoulder with one hand while the other stroked and played with my hair. I looked up at him but his eyes were focused on Sam's driving and the road.

"What happened?" I whispered, trying to swallow back the sick feeling at the back of my throat.
"I'm not sure" Carter said, shaking his head "But we're safe and nothing will harm you now. This has sealed it for me. We need to leave. Tonight. The city is under more of an attack than I'd realised."

"Attack from what?" I asked, feeling the terror rising from the pit of my stomach.

Carter's brow furrowed for a moment as he tried to think of the easiest way to explain it to me when suddenly Sam's voice came over the sound of the engine.

"You remember playing games as a child Kira. The goodies and the baddies? The goodies always won and fought for justice and everything good, but the baddies were powerful and usually quite glamourous?"

I instantly thought back to my days in the playground, re-enacting scenes from my favourite Saturday morning kids' shows.

"Yes." I stated simply.

"Well, the baddies seem to have made their appearance. I'm just not sure why now." He replied, dead pan.

"What do they want? Why are they hurting people?" I asked, desperately trying to find reason.

"That's easy." said Carter from above me. His voice was low and rumbled like thunder through his chest. "They want destruction, anarchy and chaos. They want to expose us to the world and take what they view as rightfully theirs."

"Which is?" I asked quietly looking up towards Carter's chin.

He suddenly looked down at me with more sadness than I think I'd ever seen in anyone's face as he quietly whispered the answer I was afraid of.
"Control".

We sat in silence for the rest of the car journey, Carter gripping firmly and reassuringly to my shoulder as I nodded in and out of consciousness as he played gently with my hair. He wound it in and out from his fingers, pulled it back behind my ears to stroke my cheek then gently letting it fall across my face once again. The soothing motion was what finally lulled me into sleep. When I awoke we were pulling into the driveway of the castle Pete and Griff were awaiting our arrival at the front door. Both were now dressed in jeans and t-shirts. I noted that Pete had a small cut on the side of his face. I raised my hand to touch it as I walked towards him but he caught my wrist and silently shook his head.

"Werewolves heal faster than humans." I heard Carter in my head, which had started to throb a little. "Faster body metabolism."

I smiled shyly at Pete as we entered the castle, he nodded his head, his eyes never meeting mine.

Once we were alone in the sanctuary of the bedroom Carter retrieved a suitcase from the large wardrobe and began to toss clothes into it haphazardly which was so unlike his usual neatness and control. Malakai sat in the cat carrier on the floor beside the bed. He mewed sadly at his captivity.

"What is going on? Where are we going?" I asked, perched nervously on the edge of the huge bed, hugging a corner post. I stroked Malakai gently through the bars.

Carter didn't look at me as he answered, still throwing items into the suitcase beside me.

"Not we, you. And I need to keep you safe. I'm sending you where you'll be safe."

My eyes went wide with shock and horror.
"You're sending me away?" my voice sounded so small and broken.

Carter stopped and looked over at me then as a single tear slid down my cheek.

"No Mon Chéri." He said with conviction and reassurance. "I am making you safe. I need to stay here to manage things in the city. You are a vulnerability. I won't be able to concentrate while I fear for your safety. Tonight has shown me that the city is more infiltrated than I had thought. You need to be safe. I couldn't handle it if…." He let his statement tail off as he continued to fill the case.

All I could do was look down at my hands and fiddle with my fingers as I tried to process all the events of the evening.

"Are you sure this is the best plan?" asked Pete as Carter bundled me into the car with the cat carrier after loading the suitcase into the back.

"Are you seriously asking me that after everything we went through tonight? I need her to be safe. You know she'll be safe there. It's more than Nina's family are worth if she's not." Carter's tone was dark and threatening as he bared his teeth slightly, enforcing his view.

Pete didn't back down against him and stood his ground. "She needs to be near you. I've never seen you the way you are with her. You are happy, centred and complete. Can you control your city without her by your side?" He hissed back through his teeth while still showing compassion towards Carter.

"And if something happens to her while she's in the city? If she's caught out alone? No my friend. This is now up to you and yours. The pack are strong and I know between the pack and Wilf she will be safe"

"Don't I get a say in this?" I almost roared. The volume and intensity of my voice startling myself.
Carter's hands were suddenly on my shoulders, his lips

upon mine in a deep embrace.

His fiery touch ignited every nerve ending as I felt my resolve starting to slip slightly. His tongue teased the soft skin of my lips and gentle nips from his fangs reminded me I was arguing with no ordinary man. As he slowly released me from his embrace I could see the sadness shining in his eyes as if making an apology. He hugged me tightly one last time before helping me fasten the belt over myself, with the carrier balanced on my lap, as Pete climbed into the driver's seat.

As the Porsche roared to life the familiar purr of her engine did little to soothe me as I lowered the passenger window to Carter.

"How long will I have to stay away?" I asked, the fear and tension tying knots in my stomach.

"I don't know my dear. Until I am sure it's safe."

"Are you sure I didn't do anything wrong?" I asked like a small disciplined child.

The sadness in Carter's eye softened slightly as they shone with the love I'd seen so many times before. He held out his hand towards the car and I slipped my hand into his. The electricity crackled between us as the warmth of his skin filled me and created a deep longing within me like I'd never felt before.

"No Mon Chéri. You are perfect. It's me that's flawed. I don't want you to go but that's selfish as I'd be lost if anything happened to you. You have to go and be safe. I will be able to keep my thoughts straight knowing you're safe. Besides, you aren't going too far. I will be able to drive the couple of hours to see you once I've attended to everything here." He kissed my hand gently as he let go and I felt the warmth instantly leaving me as our connection was broken.

With his promise to come and visit me still reassuring me Pete turned the car in the driveway and we started to pull away from the castle. Carter stood at the front door watching until we were out of sight down the driveway. I stopped watching out of the back window once he was out of sight. I slumped down in my seat and pulled out my mobile. A long sigh escaped me as Pete turned on the radio and Unintended by Muse began to play. The gnawing feeling in my belly grew stronger the further away we drove.

Chapter 14

I awoke to the sound of the Porsche's engine abruptly stopping. Sleepily I rubbed my eyes and blinked until my vision cleared. It was now dark outside and street lights were the only light sources. Even the stars seemed to be in solace with me.
Pete got out and opened my door for me before retrieving the suitcase Carter had packed.
I clutched the cat carrier tightly, Malakai was sound asleep inside, and glanced around at my new surroundings. Nothing was familiar. There were no familiar sights or sounds. The night air was eerily quiet, there was little or no traffic and only the occasional hoot of an owl. We were parked in a small cul-de-sac of two storey houses. In front of me stood a block of three attached houses. Only the centre house still had lights on. As Pete nudged me forward I heard the door to the lit house opening. Moments later the familiar form of Nina was standing in front of me along with a tall dark stranger who I guessed must be her husband Wilf.

"Nina." I nodded to her whilst balling my fists slightly. She unsettled me and I still couldn't place why. Carter had no interest in her and she was married for goodness sake.

"Kira, I wish your visit with us was under better circumstances." she replied, a gentle empathy in her voice as she motioned to take the cat carrier from me. Gingerly I handed the carrier over to her.

"I'm Wilf." offered the dark stranger as he offered me his hand.

I gently took his hand as he shook enthusiastically. There was the same burning heat in his skin as there was in Carters, but no spark or sizzle of electricity.

"Before we go into the house there are a couple of rules." warned Nina.

"Not really rules, just things you should be aware of." softened Wilf.

Nina continued on undisrupted by her husband.
"We have two teenaged children. Gabriel and Rosey." she stated very matter of fact.

"They are both mortal and have no idea about any of this world." explained Wilf, motioning between himself and his wife as he mentioned "this world."

I nodded but then stopped myself and opened my mouth to speak.

"Yes they are biologically ours." interrupted Nina before I could voice my thoughts. "Apparently vampires and werewolves cannot agree on a cellular level and so cancel each other out. We'd rather our children were kept out of things as much as possible. They know Carter as he is one of Wilf's oldest friends and they call him uncle. You will now be known as Aunty Kira. You're here to stay with us while Uncle Carter repairs the house."

I felt like I was being briefed on a mission, not welcomed into a home as a temporary safe house. I continued to nod as she spoke. I'd never been called Aunty before so this would be interesting. I'd also not really been around any teenagers since I'd been one. I hoped this situation was only temporary and Carter would join me soon. Pete carried my suitcase as Nina and Wilf lead the way into the house.

Incense sticks were the first thing I noticed as I entered the house, filling it with a smoky yet comforting smell, closely followed by cheering and cursing coming from what I assumed was the living room. As we entered, I noticed we passed a small kitchen just off the main hallway. There was another door to my right at the end of the hallway. The left side of the hallway was the staircase to upstairs.
Pete vanished upstairs to deposit the case. Nina and Wilf stood on either side of me as they summoned their children. A tall blonde haired boy in baggy skater style clothes emerged first followed by his slightly darker haired little sister who was wearing skinny jeans and a baggy jumper. They each held a console pad in their hands.

"This is Aunty Kira. She'll be staying with us for a while." Nina announced.

Gabriel nodded and waved slightly as he returned to the living room. Rosey came a little closer and looked me up and down before speaking.

"Do you like Xbox?" she asked quizzically, tilting her head to the side as she spoke. Her voice was soft and almost musical.

"Yeah." I answered calmly "What kind of games do you like?"

Rosey smiled and briefly glanced over her shoulder towards the living room door.

"Anything I can beat him at." she whispered to me.

I smiled. I think this was going to work out alright after all. At least until I could get a handle on my inner thoughts and then help Carter.
Dreamy and Logical were both silently awake, watching and absorbing everything that was going on around me. Every now and again Logical would dig at me about how she'd told me "none of this was a good idea". Normally she was elbowed sharply in the ribs by Dreamy and the two of them fell silent once again.

My room was obviously a guest room. It was a pale beige colour with minimalist white furniture. The double bed had a warm looking fleecy throw embellished with flowers across it and on the far side of the room an old white wicker chair sat in front of a double wardrobe. Pete had placed the suitcase down on the bed and taken the liberty to undo the padlock so I could easily open it. I closed the door and flicked the light switch behind me as I entered the room and opened my suitcase to unpack. As I lifted the lid a letter fell out and landed on the floor at my feet. Eagerly I tore it open and freed the letter inside which I knew was from Carter. I sat next to the suitcase and slowly began to read.

"Mon Chéri,

    although we've only known each other for a short time, saying goodbye to you tonight is one of the most painful things I've ever had to do. You must understand that I've been around for quite a while and met a great many people but none of them can do to me the things that you can. The caress of your skin upon mine ignites a fire in both my heart and my loins that has never been this strong before. Your touch is electric to me and awakens every part of my being. Since meeting you I have felt truly alive for the first time in a very long while. While it tears me apart not to be there next to you I know you will be safe within the pack. Nina and Pete will in time introduce you to the others. Wilf, as my cousin, is in charge of tracking your day to day whereabouts. He will never be visible to you but be assured he is always watching out for you. Nothing will harm you so long as I draw breath. Life in that small town will be quiet and relatively peaceful, possibly boring for a girl so used to city life but it has its own secrets which I am sure you will enjoy uncovering during your stay.

 Both Pete and Nina are business owners so you will never be too bored as they are both more than happy to let you "help out" should you so wish.

 I will join you as soon as I possibly can my angel, but things here are deeper rooted than I had thought. It may take some time to ensure the city is safe again from attack.

 Please pass my regards on to Gabriel and Rosey, it has been some time since I last saw them both. I hope that they are making their new Aunty feel welcome.

I shall call you in the morning. Caleb and I are patrolling

tonight in the woods around the castle as some local farmers have reported some dead livestock. The local vet says it looks like they were drained of all blood. It is possible your stalker has been staying close to the boundaries to keep an eye on you. I didn't want to upset you with this information but now I know you are safely away from here I can let you know. We WILL find him and ensure he is never a threat to you.
Until tomorrow's phone call, sleep well and think only of me.
Carter."

I sat the letter on the small bedside table and turned on the lamp. Closing the curtains, I got changed into my pj's and settled into bed for the night. I pulled a dog eared and battered paperback from the suitcase. Carter had truly thought to pack everything I'd need. I propped myself up softly on the pillows and began to read from my last bookmarked page. A feeling of comfort fell over me as I read the familiar sentences and paragraphs of the romance novel. Boy meets girl, trouble ensues, girl almost loses boy and realises how much their relationship means and happily ever after ensues. My eyelids began to feel heavy as I continued to read. One more chapter, I could hear myself say as the book slid from my hands and softly landed on the floor. The last thing I thought of before sleep engulfed me once again was the love shining in Carter's eyes before he sent me away. The tortured feeling of being torn from him was still raw in my belly, but the sight of those warm brown pools with only the light of love for me quelled even the fires of hell that raged within my thoughts.

I awoke the next morning to the smell of bacon and the sound of two teenagers squabbling over who was getting the extra slice of haggis.

I picked meagrely at my full Scottish breakfast as I sipped at my blisteringly hot cup of tea. Nina sure liked her tea hot and strong. I watched in fascinated horror as she gulped down her mug of liquid lava and placed the cup into the sink.
The kids took this as a signal and placed their dishes in the sink and vanished out of sight. Nina stood looking out of the kitchen window, her hands placed either side of her at the sink. I could see her fingers straining as she tightly gripped the metal edge.

"So." she grunted finally "Do you think you're up to working today? I have a stock delivery and could really use the extra hands."

"Sure." I replied quietly, trying to gauge her reaction "Do I need to wear anything in particular?"

Without turning to look at me she simply answered "Jeans and a t-shirt should do it" as she stalked off out of the room. A moment later I heard her feet gently padding up the stairs and knew that was my cue to go and get ready as well. I stood to leave the kitchen when Wilf filled the doorway and blocked my way.

"Sorry." he apologised as he realised he'd almost walked into me "Still getting used to having a guest."

His smile was warm and his eyes were a deep brown. Flecks of wild gold disturbed the melding of autumn browns. He reminded me a little of Carter, they were of similar height but Wilf's hair was short and spiked. The same comfortable feeling I got around Carter seemed to emanate from Wilf, I wasn't sure if it was possibly a vampire thing or a family thing. I didn't get the same feeling from Nina or Pete so it wasn't a supernatural wide thing.

I left the kitchen to the sound of Wilf banging and clattering cupboards searching for something.

After a hot shower and a change of clothes I felt refreshed and ready to tackle whatever the day had in store for me. Side by side I walked the short distance from the house to Nina's pet shop just off the town's high street. Down a small lane we stopped in front of a bright red door adorned with paw prints. As we entered, Nina turned off the alarm and flicked on a few light switches. The place erupted to life with the squeaks and squawks of the animals as they awakened.

Through the course of the morning I was taught briefly a little about each animal and their needs. I was shown where the stock was kept and a few other things I needed to note for working in the shop. By the time lunch rolled around the order had been put away and I was fully capable of handling snakes, lizards and small mammals. Nina went to fetch lunch including a meal for Pete who was in his tattoo shop not far from the pet shop. As I waited for Nina to return I decided a little practice was in order. I chose a small corn snake who was slinking slowly around its tank having just woken up. I focused on the small creature and projected my voice mentally towards it.

"I don't think I can do this. Small town life isn't my thing. I miss him so much." I confessed in my head. Dreamy and Logical remained solemnly silent, leaving me to sulk in my misery alone.

To my surprise a small hushed voice lisped back to me. "There are forces you do not understand. The balance is shifting. You need to trust them."

I stared blankly at the small orange and black creature which was looking directly at me with tiny, unblinking black eyes. I raised my finger to the glass and stroked the tank next to its head.

"Was that you?" I spoke aloud.

I could have sworn that it nodded at me. The shop doorbell tinkled behind me and the spell was broken. The snake slunk back into its hide and I heard the voice no longer.

Nina shoved her way past the door, her arms laden with white polystyrene boxes. The smell of hot food hit my nostrils and my stomach instinctually growled with desire. Nina's keen ears heard that signal and she chuckled to herself.

"You can have yours once you've dropped off Pete's. I'd hurry if I were you. It'll get cold if you take too long." she chided me.

Eager to fill my now ravenous belly I grabbed the box and cup set out for Pete on the counter and made my way across the main street and down the lane towards his tattoo shop.
The door was slightly ajar and the sound of rock music flowed out into the street. Inside I could hear Pete singing along. I tapped the door heavily with my foot before

entering, knowing that with his supernatural hearing
there was no way he'd miss my knock.

Pete was sitting with his feet up on his front counter. A
magazine spread across his lap and a pen and piece of
paper in his hands. He was looking up at it as if entranced
by some sort of puzzle. He chewed at his bottom lip.

He moved to sit up and placed the pen and paper down as
I put his lunch on the counter.

He smiled a broad manly grin at me.

"You know I could smell my lunch when you left the pet
shop's lane right?"

Unsure what to say I simply nodded.

"You didn't need to attack my door to let me know you
were here." He stated flatly.

"Sorry." I bowed my head "I forget how good you all are
with your supernatural senses."

I instantly blushed at what I'd just said and nervously
looked about to ensure no one else had overheard my
statement.

Pete stood from his seat and walked around the counter.
He put his arm around my shoulders and pulled me into a
brotherly hug.

"I'd be careful about your wording in such a small town.
Rumours tend to take flight and evolve around here. But
you're safe for now. It's been a slow morning."

As he let me go my shoulders slumped with relief. The last
thing I wanted to do was riel a werewolf.

"I'd better get back to Nina. I don't want my lunch to get cold." I flustered.

Pete shot me another wide grin, I was sure this wolf grinned more like a cat.

"She's put it in the microwave for you. She's a bit hard to start with but she likes you. Give her time to settle around you. It's not easy being an alpha, a mother and having a new houseguest." He almost laughed as he spoke.

I nodded sheepishly and turned to head out of the shop. I was feeling more and more bewildered as time went on. I had no idea how to fit into this new world I'd found myself in. Everything I thought I knew had just been turned on its head and to make it worse, the man I loved was further from me than I could feel comfortable with. If there really was such a great danger coming then I wanted to be with him.
Pete called after me as I stepped out onto the street to start my return journey.

"Keep the faith sweetheart. Carter will come for you once it's safe. We've got your back until then. Ask Nina about tonight's meeting when you get back."

"That asshole." bellowed Nina when I asked her about the meeting Pete had talked about.

Her expression softened and dissolved as she saw the look of horror on my face. Even in human form her feral aggression had a striking effect. I was stunned into complete silence.

"I'm sorry." she admitted "Pete wants you to meet the pack tonight. I'm not so sure that immersing you into this so fully and so quickly is a great idea. It takes time to adjust."

I was stunned by her sudden compassion towards me. I opened my mouth to speak but she cut me off.

"I've been a bitch to you and I'm sorry. Carter is a close family friend and this has all been so sudden. I only just found out about you and now you're suddenly here in my home and in my world. I've been defensive but I shouldn't have made you feel unwelcome."

"You didn't. I just feel so out of my depth." I tried to explain.

Nina shook her head and pointed towards a snake tank. "You spoke to Eddie. He's young but he understands a lot. He told me you spoke with him."

I could feel my cheeks burning with embarrassment. Grassed on by a snake!
"I...." I couldn't think of anything to say. I'd been well and truly busted.

Nina smiled as she removed my food from the back of the shop. It was still hot. Pete had been right about her keeping it warm for me.

"I'm actually quite impressed to be honest. You've handled all of this better than any of us ever did. I almost had a meltdown the first time I changed. Pete took off for the best part of a month to live in the woods. Wilf became depressed the first time he had to drink human blood. Carter has always had a handle on what he is, but he's never been able to handle his heart. Until now that is."

I looked up at her from my food at the mention of Carter's name.

"We've all known each other for quite a while honey. Don't look so surprised. But you're ability to cope and adjust is amazing. As well as how quickly you've managed to get a handle on those skills of yours. I heard you were even able to take on Big Momma!"

I recoiled at the memory of fighting for my life against Carter's mother. I still felt like I hadn't fully recovered from that. Like there was still an open wound somewhere.
Nina was grinning at me from the other side of the desk. What was it with these wolves and their grins?

"No one has ever gone up against Big Momma like that." She gushed approvingly "She'll have nothing but respect for you now."

I raised an eyebrow.
"You think?"

"I know. She's helped all of us along the road somewhere, but none of us was ever able to best her in the beginning. You have something special inside you. A spark that Carter can see inside of you."
I smiled sadly as I picked at my lunch.

"Not big on eating are ya?" Nina teased "First you barely touch my amazing fry up and now you're pushing your amazing pie around your plate. Don't make me go tell the bakers."

"They aren't werewolves too are they?" I asked suddenly feeling nervous.

Nina erupted into laughter and I found myself joining her at the absurdity of my question.

"Heck no." she answered through the tears rolling down her face "I know this world now feels full of monsters but we really aren't that many. The baker isn't one of us. Just a good friend who makes award winning pies. She'd be annoyed to think it was being wasted."

To satisfy her I took a few hearty mouthfuls of my pie and discovered how hungry I truly was. I kept shovelling in the pie and chips until there was nothing left but an empty container. Nina nodded her approval as she removed the packaging and put it away in the bin.
The afternoon progressed in a swift pace as the radio played away in the background. We stopped for a tea break in the middle of the afternoon and Pete entered with the local paper.

"Afternoon ladies." he beamed as he entered the shop.

Nina threw a rubber bone at him as he approached the counter.

"Don't you have your own shop?" she tried to antagonise him.

The bone glanced off his broad shoulder and squeaked as it hit the door behind him. He laughed as he threw the rolled up newspaper straight at her head. I watched in awe as Nina caught the paper between her two hands mere centimetres away from her nose. She placed it down on the counter in front of her. She was about to speak when a new bulletin came across the radio and we all froze.

"A Large fire is raging at an old castle in Aberdeenshire. It is suspected that several people were trapped inside at the time the blaze began. It has been reported that part of the roof has collapsed into the building and is hindering rescuers attempts to find anyone trapped inside the building. Further updates as we have them." Stated the news reader in a very monotone drawl.

I looked at Nina and Pete who were both looking at me with wide eyes. There were many castles in Aberdeenshire, we all knew that. Somewhere in my heart I knew it wasn't any other castle that was currently engulfed in flames. I felt the tears beginning to well in my eyes and as my knees buckled beneath me I felt both Nina and Pete's supportive arms around me as I fell to the floor.

"I need to call him!" I cried.

Pete handed me his phone, Carter's number already dialling as I held the thing to my ear. After a moment it went straight to answer phone and I felt my world start to fall apart.

"He could be out of signal or helping to fight the blaze." Nina suggested supportively.

I let my head fall to my chest as the tears came in uncontrollable streams and the sobs that escaped me became a long mournful howl. My whole body moved in their arms as the sobbing wracked my body. I kept crying until Pete brought his car around to the end of the lane and they bundled me into the car to go back to Nina's.

Wilf was waiting at the door for us as we arrived back home. Apparently the kids were having a sleep over with friends. I collapsed onto the couch as Wilf went off to make a cup of sugary tea. Nina sat next to me with my hand clamped reassuringly between hers.

"I'm sure he's safe honey." she cooed in my ear, trying to banish the dark thoughts swirling in my mind.

"Wolves have a sense for these things, but in case, I've sent a scout for news. Not my usual style but I had no choice, I needed speed over discretion." she continued as Wilf came back through with a piping hot cup of very sugary tea.

My stomach lurched slightly at the sweet taste mixing with the bitterness at the back of my throat. Wilf merely nodded towards me, bowed and headed back through to the kitchen. It was like he instinctually knew seeing him made me yearn for news of Carter even more. Every nerve inside me was burning with energy, awaiting confirmation one way or another. My fight or flight mechanism poised on a trigger.
Nina moved her arm across my shoulders with a fleece

blanket as I realised I'd began to shiver slightly. Her hand gently massaged my shoulder in a tight soothing embrace, almost sisterly.
I lay my head against hers as she gently nuzzled at my hair.

"And I thought you didn't like me." I thought to myself.

Nina froze for a second before I heard a growling voice reply to me.
"I never disliked you. I have a role and it's hard to let my guard down. Carter is family and I needed to be sure but you've already proven yourself extraordinary on so many levels that I've accepted you to our family. Please don't mistake my wolf's gruffness for dislike. After speaking to the snake this afternoon I realised that you are more one of us than even you truly realise. I'm here for you, we all are. I'm sure Carter is alright and just in hiding after the fire. I'm just awaiting word from Gaius."

I turned and looked at her, her large blue eyes were watering with tears yet to fall and her expression was of concern and sympathy for my pain and worry. I hugged her tightly like I would Scott, if he'd been here right now. Her body was on fire. The heat she gave out was on a parallel with Carter but hers was more all-encompassing. Carters felt like radiating waves but Nina's heat was like a body blanket. I found myself wondering if all werewolves were warm like this. It also dawned on me that her children had never seemed to notice this above average body heat.

"Who is Gaius?" I asked after a moment when I felt my threatening tears subsiding.

"Ah," Nina began uncertainly, worrying her bottom lip "He's a scout we tend to use in emergencies when word needs carried fast and we can't afford the timely luxury of getting one of our own to take it."

I wrinkled my nose at her answer. She was keeping something from me, but I wasn't sure how to get the full answer from her.

Suddenly a loud crash against the window distracted me from my thoughts. It was followed by a series of further loud clatters and crashes in the back garden. Wilf was already at the back door as we stood and walked into the hall. Nina stepped protectively in front of me as we neared the open door as the clattering grew louder.

I peered over her shoulder as a large bird seemed to be floundering on the back patio with what looked like a bucket on its head. Wilf was trying to herd the bird into a corner in order to remove the bucket but the bird had other ideas. It flapped about in panic and crashed into the chairs and pots in the garden. Wilf cursed in a language I didn't understand as the bird bolted and crashed into his shins sending him face first into the ground as the bird ran straight into the fence, buckling it slightly.

Nina cleared her throat and let out a low warning growl. Immediately the bucket turned towards us and the bird began to pace slowly towards us, the bucket dipped slightly as if it was hanging its head beneath. Nina muttered something low and menacing in a language I didn't recognise and the bird stopped. Wilf pounced from behind and removed the bucket. The bird had a head like a crow but was about the size of a golden eagle. Its feathers were almost a dark purple or black in hue. Its eyes were large and black, flecked with silver. It bowed to

Wilf in thanks then turned back towards Nina. It opened its beak to speak until it saw me move behind Nina. It perched on one leg and pointed the one long claw towards me before squawking and flapping its massive wings.

"I wish it would calm down. It's scaring me." I projected to Nina and Wilf. Both of them nodded and then the bird sat down and tilted its head quizzically to one side at me.

Nina stepped forwards and softly patted the birds head.

"Guias, this is Kira. Kira, this is our scout Guias." she stated flatly as an introduction.

The large bird nodded and its form became cloudy. It was like a blurry fog that made it impossible to focus on the form within. I'd seen something similar when I'd seen Nina transforming at the castle. As the fog cleared a young man stood in front of us. His short cropped hair was the same blackish purple hue his feathers had been. He was completely naked and I couldn't help but stare. He must have been in his early 20's but he was very well defined for his youthful age. His torso could have been chiselled from marble it was so perfectly sculpted. His hands reflexively covered his manhood as I felt my eyes trailing south. He had a tribal style tattoo made of bold Celtic knots that ran from half way down his side, across his belly and down the opposite leg to his knee.
I looked up into his dark eyes which held their fleck of silver even in human form.
Wilf clasped his hand firmly onto Guias' shoulder.

"Still need to work on those landings lad." he chortled as

he threw a cotton long coat over him to hide his modesty.

"I know Sir." Guias replied quietly in a very broad accent "But I was in a hurry. I had to tell Miss Nina."
Wilf muttered something about his daughter Rosey as he walked past us and vanished back into the kitchen.

Nina beckoned him forward and into the house as we turned and re-entered the living room.
Her demeanour was colder and harder than it had been the first time I met her. She stood with her arms crossed watching the boy as he took a seat on the armchair opposite me.

"Out with it then boy." She snapped. "After that amazing landing there had better be some news worthy of my ruined herb garden."

Guias seemed to still be getting his breath back when Wilf reappeared with a glass of water.
After several large gulps and a mighty belch that almost had me giggling at its ferocity he finally had enough air to speak.

"The house was empty. No traces, no clues."

Nina's shoulders slumped.

"That's good Miss." Continued Guias "It was like someone had hidden their tracks before the fire. There were no notable belongings, no trace of the occupants who had been there. If they had been caught out by the fire there would have been a trace."

Wilf spoke from behind me in the door way, making me jump slightly.

"Guias is a trainee fireman and dabbles a little in scene investigations." he explained.

"So they knew it was coming?" asked Nina, confused.

Guias nodded.

"Right young storm crow. You'd best be getting back to my daughter before she rumbles us." Wilf stated with a sense of urgency.

Guias took this as his cue and darted upstairs for a moment, only to reappear a few moments later dressed and clutching a pair of car keys. Wilf gave him a manly hand clasp against the shoulder and Nina gave him a slight hug.

"Look after her crow, or you'll learn what an Alpha really does." she warned as he darted out the front door, slamming the door behind him.

"What was that?" I asked quietly, not wanting to stir up any trouble.

Wilf entered the living room and took up Guias' vacant seat as Nina sat back down next to me.

"Guias is seeing our daughter." Nina stated flatly. She was obviously none too impressed.

"Guias isn't like other boys his age. His soul is older than even some of our eldest vampires. His race is almost extinct and so rare that they need protection from a pack. There was an age where the storm crows were one of the most powerful clans in Scotland but over time they became fewer and fewer and isolated themselves to the islands."

"Hence the accent. Orkney?" I butted in.

Wilf nodded. "We took him in for a time one summer while his family were traveling through. His ailing grandmother was seeking a pack to protect him as he grew and learned more of his powers. Nina was training to be beta at the time and was tasked with keeping an eye on him. As the summer went on he and Rosey became good friends. Gabriel took him out fishing and they got on like family. We classed him as a friend of the family to stop any awkward questions but over time, the friendship between Rosey and Guias has become....."

"They are still friends" argued Nina "Just closer than they once were."

"There is time for these stories another day Kira." stated Wilf as he smiled towards Nina.

"Yes, probably the same time we have to confess to our kids at this rate." sighed Nina.

Pete burst through the front door and barrelled into the kitchen.
"Kira, Kira!"

I stood and headed to the kitchen to find Pete slumped in a heap next to the sink completely winded. His broad frame heaved hard as he tried to catch his breath.

"More drills for you Beta!" snorted Nina from beside me. "That sprint was sloppy."

Pete stuck a defiant middle finger up at her as he caught his breath and cleared his throat.
"Kira, he's at the stones. He's waiting for you. He won't move until I bring you and he's injured. We've got to get there now!"

"The pack are meeting tonight, some of the younger ones don't know him yet." said Nina in alarm.

"Wilf, get the keys quick!"

"Too long." muttered Pete "Get on." He motioned for me to get onto his back.

"You'll be seen you idiot!" yelled Nina.

"Back roads." growled Pete as his form vanished in the blurry fog.

"Idiot." snarled Nina as she and Wilf both ran out to the car.

I stood in awe as a blonde wolf with dark tribal patterning in its fur stood before me. It nodded its head towards its back. As I climbed on, painfully worried my weight would hurt him he stood to his full wolf height and slowly padded towards the door. Sniffing the evening air he looked left and right before bolting down the front path and jumping the low wall. I clutched desperately to the chain around its neck so I wouldn't fall off. The street lights were on and the night was drawing in. In the dim half-light anyone not paying attention would possibly only see a large dog darting past in the park. We were quickly out of sight of houses and people as we darted past a park, up a dark road and then we were in the trees. Thick and rich with pines the forest smelled of earth and recent rain. Pete's paws thudded into the mud and leaves as we dashed through between trees and bushes. I held tightly onto the chain, making sure it wasn't digging into him but also ensuring my safety. His top coat of fur was slightly hard and coarse but the softer fur underneath was where my fingers were currently woven.

Distant streetlights flickered and vanished between the trees and I could hear water trickling nearby. We were headed towards water. As we climbed and descended over a steep hill covered in ivy and some dying underbrush, my skin crackled with electricity and a dull hum thrummed through my body. I felt myself stiffen and clutch the chain tighter, making Pete yelp slightly as I nipped him. Silently in my head I apologised but explained the feelings I was having, I knew we must be close. As we slowed to a walking pace I could hear a car engine cut out not far away over my right shoulder. I slid from Pete's back as he led me over to a massive standing stone located near a tall pine tree with a hollow in the trunk. There were a couple of wolves looking bewildered as we walked closer. One snarled but Pete quickly barked and put him back in his place. They were flanking the hollow in the tree and even without a wolf's keen senses I knew what was hiding inside. As I got closer I could almost hear the crackle of electricity in the air as my heartbeat grew louder in my ears. I could feel the blood in my veins racing and my eyes slowly adjusted to the darkness inside the tree as I knelt down to climb inside the hollow space.

"Carter?" I whispered into the dark. I could feel the presence of someone else inside the hollow with me but my eyes wouldn't adjust. I heard Nina and Wilf arriving at the tree as the younger wolves howled quietly to her.

I turned back towards the entrance to the hollow as something from the darkness grabbed my wrist and pulled me backwards. I lost my footing and landed on my ass. I felt the waves of searing heat traveling up my arm and I knew immediately it was him.

"You're alive." I whispered as the tears I'd been holding all day finally came.
I felt his arms circling my waist as he pulled me onto his lap. I strained in the darkness, willing my eyes to adjust when my eyes looked right up into his. Those deep brown pools were filled with longing and relief. He kissed me and immediately the tense feelings inside me melted. I was complete once again now my other half was here. The aching chasm I'd had inside of me was finally reunited with its counter.
I moaned slightly as I felt Carter's warmth bleeding into me with each kiss and caress. I could have stayed hidden in that hollow forever but the yelps and whines from outside were giving me cause for concern.
Slowly we both emerged from the hollow and in the dull light of evening I could finally see Carter and his battle wounds. A trail of blood snaked down the side of his face from his hairline from an unseen cut. His clothes were torn and underneath the tears were matching cuts, grazes and bruises. He looked like he'd survived an explosion, in

places the ends of his hair were shorter and singed. Tenderly I cupped his face in my hands and kissed down the length of his nose.

"What happened to you?" I whispered. "You look like hell."

Surprisingly Carter threw back his head and laughed. "Mon Chéri, you have no idea how close you are. I just had to see you. I know it's selfish and placed you in more danger but I had to see you. To know you are ok."

Pete snorted slightly from behind us as Nina and Wilf stood forward. Nina had her arms crossed and a snarl plastered on her lips.

"Of course she's ok." she snapped "You charged us with her care and she's family. I'm actually offended Carter."

She turned on her heel and walked over to the wolves who were still blankly staring in disbelief. She knelt down and began whispering to them.
Wilf stepped forward and embraced Carter in a brotherly hug. He whispered something into his ear and tossed him the car keys as he walked back over to Nina. She stood to hug him and he kissed her deeply. She then fired a look that could kill towards Carter.

"You'd better take that woman there home, get cleaned up and then make up for abandoning and worrying her, no matter how well your intentions. You're just lucky you're family."

She was enveloped in the blurry fog until only her wolf

form was left padding the ground anxiously. Pete padded over to her, still in wolf form. She nodded to him and after a small snarl all of the wolves vanished into the trees. Wilf gave a slight wave as he ran off into the woods behind them at a slower pace.

Carter put his arm around my shoulders as we walked back towards Nina's car.

He half smiled as he looked down at me.

"It's a glamour." he answered, his smile spreading and becoming wider. "It's a fae magic, gifted to the wolves many moons ago."

"What is?" I asked, completely unaware of what he was talking about.

We continued walking to the car and sat for a moment on the bonnet as Carter continued his explanation.

"The blurry fog, as you aptly named it. It's a form of magic to obscure the change from mortal eyes. The change is violent, physically graphic and emotionally distressing to humans. The fae granted the magic to the wolves to stop humans being traumatised any time they accidentally or intentionally saw a wolf change. Although I have it on good authority that other shifters can use it too. Those fae are too generous sometimes."

"How did you?" I began.

"Your inside voice is particularly loud today Mon Chéri." he beamed.

I thought for a moment and then opened my mouth to

speak but Carter raised his fingers to my lips.
His smile was now a pure Cheshire cat grin as he delighted in my realisation.

"Yes, they are all real. Not just vampires and werewolves. Dragons, mermaids, fae and unicorns. They hide in the obvious and fool the minds of men. We have existed for a long time Mon Chéri. We have our tricks and we are very good at staying secret. But we can discuss all of this later. I believe I was ordered to get clean and to make things up to you."

I smiled and nodded at the thought of being in his arms once again but also as my mind swirled with all the thoughts and possibilities that this new knowledge brought. I had always had a sense of magic even as a child. I always felt like there was more and even as I grew and was taught the ways of science and man I felt there was a piece missing. Some had tried to fill those gaps with religion but it had always felt false. Finally the world I had entered was feeling more familiar and made more sense than my regular human one ever had.
I gazed peacefully out of the window on the short car ride back to the house. Every now and again I was sure I saw a glimmer of fur between the trees. The wolves were patrolling for the night, which was now more important that Carter was here. I felt safer knowing that all these forces existed and were in our corner.

Chapter 15

Once Carter had a hot shower, I made him a piping hot cup of tea and we sat on the couch snuggled together at one end. Carter sipped at his tea and told me everything that had happened.

I sat and listened tentatively as he explained how they'd discovered the plot to burn the castle and how he'd gone along with it, sending his mother and brother to safety and making sure no one knew he was at the castle alone. Playing cat and mouse with those who were trying to kill him. He'd ensured the safety of all but two of his men who had sadly burned in the fire as they'd been caught by the flames while trying to escape. Carter had used an old tunnel in the grounds that was untraceable after the fire as it collapsed in on itself effectively erasing it from existence completely. The woods had been riddled with vampires hunting for him after the blaze was underway but he'd managed to escape. The only issue he'd encountered had been a single vampire guarding a remote dirt track off the estate land. They fought and thankfully Carter had won, but not before he'd suffered slightly. He'd then made his way to Forres through the old roads and paths no longer travelled by men. Guided by a few friendly souls he managed to get to the tree where he'd signalled Pete. It turns out Pete had been patrolling with the hope of hearing of Carter but never thinking he'd actually be the one to find him.

"I've never seen a wolf move so swiftly. You were back with me within what felt like mere moments."

"I've never been so scared and yet so exhilarated at the same time." I admitted shyly. "Riding a giant wolf through the woods at full tilt in the dark seems to have an adrenaline charge to it."

"More thrilling than making love to a vampire?" Carter pouted playfully as he sat his empty cup on the carpet.

"I don't think I've encountered anything more thrilling than making love to a vampire." I admitted

"But then the only vampire I'd ever want would be you." Carter lowered his head and chastely kissed me on the cheek. I felt the pulse of electricity jolt between us and as Carters hands moved to gently hold my hips I knew we couldn't stay at Nina and Wilf's place that evening.

Once Nina and Wilf arrived back home we took our leave to spend the night at a local B & B about 2 miles further down the road. It felt more respectful than hooking up under their roof.

The Knockomie Hotel was a large building, it looked like a mansion house or stately home. The large grey building was covered with climbing vines along the front and a warm and welcoming light shone from the front door. As we entered the front hall and reception area we were greeted with warm and cosy wood panelling and a large wooden staircase leading up to the rooms. Once Carter had checked us in, amusingly as Mr and Mrs Wolf we headed upstairs with our two backpacks and closed the rest of the world out as the solid wooden door swung shut and locked behind us.

There was a large four poster bed that dominated the centre of the room and once all our belongings were discarded with careless abandon we continued where we'd left off. As we lay on the bed holding each other I started deep into Carter's eyes. Those deep brown pools of molten brown silk reflected only pure love and every inch of me felt safe as long as I was being held by his strong arms. Gently he butterflied my cheek and neck with kisses and continued down my neck until he reached the "sweet spot" between my neck and shoulder that turned me to complete mush.

"I've missed you so much." he whispered into the flesh of that spot, his warm breath sending tingles right down to the tips of my toes and enflaming every nerve ending.

"I missed you too." I replied as I pulled his body closer to mine until I could feel his torso searing into mine, melding us into one. We lay there for several moments just listening to our breath as we held onto each other. His lips never left my shoulder.

"I can't give you up." he said finally "I thought I could try, to keep you safe. But I'm selfish and I can't be without you. I've felt like part of me was missing. My mother threatened to come and fetch you, and she doesn't normally approve of my seeing human women."

I giggled slightly beneath his touch at the thought of the large Russian woman threatening a fully grown man, a vampire no less.

"I guess it's kind of reassuring she kind of accepts me. I think." I replied.

"It's more than that. She's never seen me like this. I've never been so attached to anyone. She feels it's important that I keep you close and cherish you while I can."

"Sweet and reassuring as that is." I started.

Carter laughed as he sat up. His long hair would need to

be trimmed as the ends were now straggly and singed in places making it uneven.

"Talking about my mother really isn't setting the right sort of mood is it Mon Chéri?" he laughed as he got out of bed and slowly removed his shorts. I felt myself sharply inhale as I marvelled at his body. His body just screamed sex, it was small wonder so many women had thrown themselves at him. He stood erect at the side of the bed as he smiled over at me.

"Your turn."

I rose to my knees and crawled over to him at the edge of the bed. I raised an eyebrow at him.

"Why don't you do the gentlemanly thing and help me?" I teased as one of my bra straps fell from my shoulder.

Carter swallowed hard before he answered. His voice was a low husky growl, like a predator about to lose control at the sight of his prey.

"Because if I do that, I might not be able to stop myself." He leaned forward and flicked the other strap dipping the cups of my bra slightly. I groaned slightly as the fabric slid across my pert nipples.

Softly and swiftly he reached around and unclipped it, letting it fall to the floor off the edge of the bed. I gasped as the fabric covering vanished leaving me bare and exposed to his burning gaze. With a hunters grace he pounced onto me, pushing me backward onto the bed and taking my erect peaks into his mouth, first one side then the other. Nipping, sucking and teasing me until I squirmed beneath him. Propping himself up with one hand he slid the other hand beneath me and there was suddenly a sharp tug and a loud tearing sound as my underwear also hit the floor in one tattered piece. Hungrily his mouth met mine as he kissed me deeply. His tongue forcing its way in to meet mine. He tasted even better than I'd remembered. I moaned and writhed underneath him as he deepened his kiss and firmly fondled my breasts with his spare hand.

"You missed me too then Mon Chéri" he teased as he slid his hand from my tortured breast down to the apex between my thighs "You seem to be very ready for something."

I closed my eyes and exhaled slowly as he trailed his fingertips back up my torso and gently pulled me up into a sitting position.

"Turn around." he whispered gently.

Instantly I complied and kneeled on the bed, my back to him only a few inches or so apart. I could still feel the heat radiating from him but his searing skin wasn't touching mine and a slight shiver ran through me, both in anticipation and from the lack of his heat against me. Agonisingly slowly he slid towards me, millimetre by millimetre, gently blowing on my shoulders causing the shivers to become more frequent. I can feel the anticipation building inside me of as the shivers only intensify the tingling that was now vibrating completely through my body. As I felt his flame burning closer to me, my skin began to almost thrum with electricity. As he pressed his skin to mine I could feel his solid length pressing against my ass as sparks began to fly in the back of my mind. I was about to let out a moan when suddenly his mouth was on the sweet spot and without warning he bit down hard. An explosion of pleasure erupted from within me as he had to grip my waist to stop the tremors that were now wracking my body. My eyes closed and colours continued to explode behind my eyelids as the crescendo of sensation heightened. I could feel his mouth, his tongue working on my shoulder, I could feel his fingers softly raking the skin of my belly as he held me firmly to him. I could feel the throbbing from his hard length pressed against my ass and I could feel my legs turning slowly to jelly as he continued to nip, bite, lick and suck at the sweet spot on my shoulder. Each touch sending a million more fireworks off inside of me. Just as I felt like I couldn't take anymore he released my shoulder from his mouth. Tenderly giving me one last kiss I could feel his breath lingering over that spot. I was about to turn around or say something when I felt his hand slide down my side and between our bodies and then suddenly his probing fingers were inside of me. I blushed slightly at the sound it made as he entered me. I was definitely ready for him and now he knew it. I could feel my muscles tightening around his two fingers begging for something more. Gently he stroked back and forth inside of me, driving me slowly more and more frenzied until an animalistic sound broke free of my throat.

"I can't take it anymore." I admitted shamefully "I need you, need this to reassure me that it's all ok."

My breathing was heavy and my words came out as a desperate whispered rasp but he had heard me. Roughly he pushed me forward and placed his hands on my hips, raising himself up behind me.

"I need this too Mon Chéri but I'm nothing but raw need right now."

"I don't care" I almost begged "I need you, now!"

I had barely uttered the final word when he slammed into me, his searing white heat ploughing straight into my wet and willing core. A roar erupted from deep in his throat, a guttural and feral sound. Echoed by my own needful moan as he thrust harder and harder inside me. I tried to look behind me, imagining the frenzied look on his face but with each forceful thrust, my head was forced to look back in front of me. I closed my eyes and focused on the feelings still spiralling and exploding inside of me. His fingers firmly gripped my hips, pulling me towards him. His nails lightly dug into my padding and I delighted in the feel of the needle like sting each thrust caused as he gripped slightly tighter.

I could imagine his eyes, pupils dilated until almost all of the melted chocolate brown was consumed by lustful black. I could almost see the golden flecks swirling and igniting like embers in a fire.

I could feel the wave of an orgasm building within me as the pressure on my hips also mounted. If I wasn't bleeding I'd be bruised and the thought of him marking me only spurred me on further. Fanning my hands out in front of me on the bed I countered each thrust, pushing back and forcing him deeper. I heard him hiss from behind me as my plan was obviously working. With the added friction of my bucking back at him I felt my wave doubling. The heat between my thighs was now almost scorching but in the most delightful way. If I was going to burn, this was the way I wanted to go. Swept up in the all-encompassing flame of a vampire.

Carter's body collapsed into mine as he whispered into my ear.

"I want to see your face Mon Chéri, Roll over."

At his command I flipped over onto my back and lay on the bed. His eyes were even darker than I had imagined. The golden flecks danced like tiny flames in his eyes, not the smouldering embers I'd envisioned. As he repositioned himself at my damp entrance I could feel his heat radiating into me. My eyes were locked onto his as he once again thrust his engorged length inside of me. My hips bucked wildly as the wave continued to build and the sensation of my skin melting into the duvet began to overtake my senses. My whole body felt like a live wire and every time Carter thrust I was being pushed closer and closer to my limit. Carefully but with deliberate force he grabbed my ankles and raised my feet up to rest on his broad shoulders. Holding me there he began again, only this time far deeper than before and with a frenzied pace. I could feel the length of him throbbing inside of me, racing to build his release before my wave broke. Suddenly without warning he nuzzled then gently bit my ankle causing me to cry out as the sensation only further fuelled the already buzzing sensation across my skin. Softly he licked at the droplets of blood that rose to the surface slowly. After a moment he stopped and let a few droplets trickle down the inside of my leg. My blood felt like molten lava sliding down my skin, setting fire to every nerve ending and sensitive patch of skin on its path. I could feel the crescendo of the wave approaching and at the precise moment the droplets reached the edge of my wetness Carter exploded inside of me. The domino effect caused the wave to crash over me as I screamed out, overwhelmed by the sheer burning bliss that was all around me and inside of me at the same time.

Carter crashed onto the bed beside me and lay his hand across my stomach as my lungs struggled to catch the breath the screaming orgasm had expelled. I placed my hand over his and we lay there for several moments recovering and staring into each other's eyes.

"I missed you." I sighed "I was so worried."

Carter tenderly kissed my forehead as he sat up slowly.

"I missed you too, more than you can know. I needed them to think they had succeeded."

He got up and padded over to the ensuite door.

"Shower my lady?" he gestured, bowing like a servant.

I giggled as I sat up and rolled off the edge of the bed. My legs were like jelly and balancing on them felt alien and difficult.

"Yes please. I think I need a good wash down after that." I teased as I wobbled past him towards the shower.

In the morning we awoke and made love again then after breakfast we headed back to Nina and Wilf's. Rosey and Gabriel were out in the garden when we arrived, sitting on the front grass while Nina hung out the washing. The scene looked to peaceful and normal. I looked up at Carter who was watching the scene with sheer delight. His grip on my hand tightened as I felt a large jolt of electricity pass through us. He wanted this too. A family, but I had no idea how vampires even had family! Was I capable of such a task?

Doubt fogged my mind for a moment until Nina called to us from behind a sheet she was hanging on the line. Gabriel looked over at our approach and nudged his sister with his elbow.

"How does she do that?" he groaned with slight confusion "She always knows where everyone is, all the time!"

As we opened the gate I heard Nina laughing from behind her sheet.

"Parental gift." she answered shortly "Don't you have homework to do?"

Both teenagers groaned and grabbed their tech from the grass before heading back inside with moans and mutterings.

Wilf emerged from the front door moments after his displeased offspring had passed. He shook Carters hand before grinning like a Cheshire cat at Nina, who sharply elbowed him in the ribs.

"What was that for?" he winced.

"Don't be so crass!" she snapped.

Carter began to laugh and I beamed knowing only too well what they were all smiling happily about.

Nina embraced me in a warm hug as we headed towards the house.

As we all sat in the living room, Wilf with his arm around his spouse's shoulders and Carter's arm tight around my waist, everything felt so normal. For this moment we were just two couples sharing each other's company. There was no danger, only a calm that seemed to have settled over everything now that Carter was back with us. Granted, the conversation had a few little hints of the supernatural but it still felt like the most natural thing in the world to just be sat like this. Cups of tea in hand, laughter and boring conversation about Nina's shop and Carter's night club. Guias arrived to take Rosey out for lunch and Gabriel headed out to meet up with some friends while there was some weekend left. We sat like that for a few hours until Carter's mobile began to vibrate in his pocket. After looking at the caller display he stood up, excusing himself for a moment and headed back outside. I looked worriedly over at Wilf and Nina who both shrugged and looked over towards the door. I could see Nina concentrating, trying to hear what was being said until Wilf touched the end of her nose to distract her. She shot him an angry glance but he just shook his head. She looked back over at me, smiling an apology. At least she tried, for that I was grateful.

When Carter re-entered the room the relaxed atmosphere vanished from the room as if the life had just been sucked out of it. Carter replaced his phone in his hoodie pocket and sat back down next to me. He placed his hand on my knee, grasping it reassuringly as he looked over to Wilf and Nina.
"They know who was responsible for both the bomb at the charity event and the fire at the castle." he said

solemnly.

Nina perched on the edge of her sofa cushion and Wilf sat bolt upright. I began worrying at a loose thread on the hem of my t-shirt. Whatever he was about to say, it wasn't good news.

"It's worse than we thought. The mastermind behind the attacks, it was Casavan. He's returned from Russia and he's looking to destroy everything my family has built. He wants to tear the veil completely and take the power that will spill."

Nina balled her hands into fists and Wilf grimaced, showing his fangs, something I'd never seen Carter do.

"That bastard." hissed Wilf.

"The clans will never stand for that." snapped Nina "They will unite and they will go after him."

Carter shook his head.

"He's stronger now than he's ever been. My mother has taken Caleb back home and has warned all our kind to be on guard as he may try to pick us off one by one rather than go for an all-out offensive."

"What can we do?" howled Nina "He can't get away with this Carter? We've never let the veil fall. We can't. Our children!" Tears were forming in the corners of her eyes as Wilf comforted her.

I cleared my throat and they all looked at me in surprise.

"Who is Casavan?" I asked with complete innocence.

Nina stood and started to pace the floor, her movements become more and more animalistic as she paced.

"Who is Casavan?" she laughed angrily "Who is Casavan, she asks!"

Wilf tried to grasp her arm to slow her down but she easily dodged him. Carter stood now and placed his hands on Nina's shoulders, looking straight into her eyes.

"He will not succeed Nina. We can't let him. We've got

centuries of work on this. We must protect it."

Nina calmed slightly and sat back down next to Wilf. Her shoulders sagged in defeat as the anger drained out of her and gave way to fear and despair.

Carter then turned towards me.

"Casavan is an old enemy of all supernaturals. He is an ancient enemy." As he spoke his words became images in my mind's eye. An older looking man, dark hair and a handlebar moustache stood on the ramparts of a castle during a storm, vials of coloured liquids in his hands. He began to shout something in an unknown language. The storm began to rage around him as the cries of a thousand tortured souls cried out in pain and terror. As lightning struck the rampart the vials erupted and exploded all over him. He screamed out and clutched at his skin then he began to burn. The fire quickly consumed him and he was barely visible beneath the searing flames which reached higher and higher into the lightning filled sky. The howling and cries stopped and rain began to fall in heavy sheets. After a few moments the flames were completely extinguished and a smouldering heap of black was all that was left of the man on the ramparts.

Suddenly a brilliant beam of light shot upwards into the sky, completely concealing the corpse and when it cleared the man was stood laughing as if nothing had happened. I knew from the feeling in my gut this man was Casavan. As he raised his hand and lightning struck the land I heard a thousand more voices cry out in pain.

A full body shiver snapped me out of my vision and as my vision returned to the room I was greeted by three very confused faces.

Carter took my hand.

"Are you ok Mon Chéri? You seemed to phase out then then almost black out on us there."

I nodded slowly, licking my lips which were now inexplicably dry.

"I could see him. On a castle, in a storm. There were animals, I think, crying in pain. Then he caught fire but then he was alive again and the animals began to call out in pain again. What was it?"

"Casavan was a mortal man who dabbled with alchemy. He happened upon the existence of supernaturals and felt their blood and essence could be used with alchemy to create a more powerful being. He tortured vampires, werewolves, fae and dragons, all sorts of supernaturals to further his research. He became obsessed and twisted. He sought only power and a way to control it to his will. One night an accident gave him the power he wanted and he became a mage. The vampire blood made him immortal, the fae blood imbued him with magic and the shifters blood gave him strength and rage no human should possess. It was more than he could control and it drove him mad. He was eventually subdued and trapped within a relic which the mermaids hid at depths no human would ever be able to find. It was warded with magic and all knowledge of the place was lost with the sands of time."

I nodded, taking all of this in.

"But how is he back?"

Nina stood again and butted into the conversation.

"Humans have been destroying the earth for centuries, more so recently. The balance of nature has been tipped, it's no longer in balance and deep sea quakes have broken the seal and released Casavan's vessel. He was weak, but he was freed."

Wilf entered his offering to the explanation.

"Think of a kids cartoon. The evil villain has become free after thousands of years to plot his revenge and let his evil brew to new levels. He has built up his strength, found a following and now wants to punish everyone."

"That's crazy. He wants to punish everyone! Where's the power in that?" I gasped.

"He thinks if he tears the veil between supernaturals and humans, the humans will flock to him for defence. He can then enslave or destroy us and will enslave humanity as the price for their protection."

I sat with my mouth open.

"Absolute power corrupts absolutely." stated Wilf.

"How can we stop it?" I asked, completely bewildered.

"We can't." sighed Carter "We need help to stop Casavan. There will need to be a council to form a plan."

"A council!" exclaimed Nina and Wilf together. Carter nodded solemnly.

Suddenly another image flashed into my mind. *A small gathering stood on a hilltop in a ring of standing stones. Each member held a small silver dagger and while muttering the same words they plunge the daggers into their hearts and drop to the earth. As they lay dying their blood seeps into the earth and an ethereal form rises from the centre of the circle. It is a beautiful woman and she's completely naked. She looks down upon the dead and dying beings scattered around her and she begins to cry. A storm instantly erupts around her and lightning strikes the central standing stone, exploding it into a million pieces. As the smoke clears the woman is gone and a small vial lies on the ground glowing where the form once was.*

As I open my eyes, I can feel my cheeks are warm and damp. I've been crying in my sleep. Wait, was I asleep?

Carter is by my side watching me with concern. Wilf is at the foot of the bed looking out the window as Nina enters the room with a glass of water with a bright pink bendy straw in it.

She shrugs as Carter raises an eyebrow at her.

"It was all we had!"

Carefully carter helps me into a sitting position and I sip at the water. As my mind clears slightly I remember my vision.

I glower at Carter and feel my skin bristling all over.

"You are not holding council. There has to be another way."

Carter opened his mouth to speak as Nina and Wilf looked on in complete shock.

"No." I stopped him "They died Carter. The last council died to stop Casavan and all it did was buy you all a reprieve. There must be something else?"

Nina bowed her head and Wilf went to her side.

"There isn't any other way we know." Carter sighed, sagging his shoulders.

"Council must be held, the Goddess must be summoned and we must lock Casavan away again."

I could feel the tears welling up in my eyes. I had only just gotten him back from the jaws of death. Now he was willing to throw himself back into the mouth of hell to stop all of this. I couldn't let it happen, not now I was so close to being happy, happier than I'd ever imagined was possible.

"No." I stated flatly.

"Excuse me?"

"No." I said as I stood up from the bed. "I won't let you. You're not doing this. You're not leaving me and no one else is going to die." My voice was full of sadness tinged with anger.

Carter laughed sarcastically at me, I balled my hands into fists in silent response.

"You can't stop what has been set into motion."

His self-righteous expression burned the final straw and I punched him full force in the jaw sending him flying off of the other side of the bed. Reflexively he immediately stood back up, hissing and bearing his fangs for a moment until the shock of what I'd done wore off.

"You hit me!" he groaned as he rubbed at the spot on his jaw where my fist has connected.

Nina began to giggle and grin, Wilf slunk into the corner of the room trying to fade out of view.

"Maybe she has a point Carter and she seems willing to fight for your ass." Nina gave me a hearty pat on the back. Carter slumped back onto the bed.

"I don't see what choice we have. There is no other known way of stopping Casavan."

We were all wondering what to suggest next when a sound erupted downstairs and a familiar voice called up to us.

Pete stood at the bottom of the stairs along with another young man with ginger hair and blue eyes. His skin was so pale it was almost transparent, then I noticed that he wasn't standing next to Pete, he was hovering slightly.

"Grandmother is awake and she needs to see Nina and Carter." the boy spouted quickly, hardly pausing for breath "She doesn't have much time. She says she knows where the vessel is, but you don't have much time."

With that he turned and darted back out the door. Pete shrugged and vanished back out the door behind the boy.

"What was that all about?" I asked, feeling like somehow my silent prayers were being answered.

Nina patted my shoulder as she flew down the stairs and stopped at the front door.

"Carter." she summoned in a voice I'd never heard her use. It was compelling and slightly frightening at the same time.

"Bloody Alpha voice." muttered Carter as he stepped

forwards almost involuntarily. He grabbed me and pulled me into a passionate embrace. As our lips met I felt like a halo of light had descended around us. This felt right, this felt like the answer. We might just all get our happily ever after in the end.

As he let me go and headed down the stairs I could hear him talking internally to me.

"I won't be long. If grandmother is right then we have a chance and if we have a chance I'm going to take it. I've been alone too long Kira. You have made me so unbelievably happy in such a short space of time. I don't deserve it, but I want to hold onto it. Wait for me."

"Always." I replied and then they were both gone.

Wilf had emerged from his space in the shadows and put a reassuring hand on my shoulder.

"If he's like his grandfather and father before him, he'll be able to stop this." He nodded wisely.

From behind his back he produced a small leather bound book. Its cover was cracked and weathered with age. It had writing in golden font but it was so faded and chipped I couldn't make out what it said.

"You might want to read up a bit before he comes back" offered Wilf "I have a feeling you might need to play a part in this too, so you'd better learn your history."

As he headed downstairs and into the kitchen I gazed down at the book. I turned the first page and began to read.

I woke the next morning with a piece of paper stuck to my face and a puddle of drool underneath me. I was sitting at the small desk in the corner of my room at Nina's. The alarm clock flashed 9.00 at me in neon numbers. I looked around at the many pieces of paper scattered about me and realised I'd spent all night making notes and cross referencing sections of the book. I got up and got dressed, arranging the pages into a pile and stuffing them into my backpack I headed off for the town library after briefly getting directions and chatting to Wilf over a cup of tea.

I spent most of the morning reading and cross referencing terms with other books. All of them were folklore or mythology, there was very little to tie any of the leather book to actual fact or scientific theory. Only snippets of any of it referred to places by name or vague descriptions. I was in my element. I hadn't researched this hard since I'd been at university. I kept on reading, absorbing and researching with relish. Librarians swapped shifts and the patrons within the library changed as each hour wore on.
  As time stretched on, my belly began to grumble and I realised I hadn't eaten before I left the house. Carefully stashing my updated notes back into the backpack I headed out of the library to grab some lunch before I passed out. As I exited the library and headed round the back towards Nina's car, my phone vibrated in my pocket. I slung the bag into the car and closed the door while I read. One message was from Wilf asking what I wanted for dinner. I happily replied he could make whatever he wanted and I would eat it, I was hungry as a wolf. I then put a smiley to let him know I was making a joke. The next message was from an unknown number. A chill ran through me as I hesitantly opened it.
You can't escape your past and now your future belongs to me.
I instantly closed the message and stuffed my phone into my pocket. I took a deep breath and turned to find a café. I felt an icy shiver run up my spine as I walked back through the carpark towards the bustling street. It felt like

I was being watched and that something was behind me. My footsteps sped up as I suddenly felt the panic rising in my chest. A sharp acid taste stung the back of my throat as I quickly shot a glance over my shoulder. Nothing. I turned back around and increased my pace. I turned a corner of the building, the main street was almost in sight when something hit me in the head, hard, and everything went black.

To Be Continued….

Excerpt from Book 2 of the Highland Hunter Series: Hearts Aflame

The wind began to pick up and the sky changed colour by about three shades making the clearing darker and dropping the temperature enough to send a chill through most of us. As we watched a figure began to slowly appear on the stone. Slowly the image of grandmother sitting in the lotus position went from being a barely flickering mirage to being a completely solid form before us. She opened her dark eyes and stretched, yawning as she did so. As yawning is contagious everyone else round the circle began to yawn setting off a massive chain reaction until we had all yawned.

Grandmother laughed, it sounded like happiness and raindrops landing in flower petals.

"I thought I was the one who had been asleep for centuries. What's up with you lot?" She chortled, addressing all of us.

On cue we all bowed before her.

"Stuff and nonsense." she scolded "The times for such formalities are gone my children. No need to bow and beg to your auld gran. Now then, fits happening?"

A small rabbit bound forward and as it climbed the stone to sit next to Grandmother transformed into a small person. His ears were pointed and his nose was bright red, like his cheeks. Silently he whispered into Grandmothers ear, catching her up on the immediate and important matters that she'd slept through. The whole time she chewed at her bottom lip as she listened intently. Occasionally muttering "no!", "well that was a given." and "Oh, really?"

Once the pooka had imparted his knowledge he once again became a rabbit and bounded off towards the trees. Grandmother's expression was solemn but kind. She looked around the assembled crowd.

"Right then my bairns." she sighed sadly "We've got work to be done, or so I hear. Who amongst you knows what needs to be done?"

The crowd began to chatter between themselves as whispers began to fill the air. So many voices all whispering in hushed tones that it was almost deafening. Kira clasped my hand suddenly and pulled us forward. I turned to look at her and realised that she had also clasped hands with Misty. All 3 of us stood forward and the noise from the throng immediately stopped as everyone stared at us.

Grandmother clasped her hands together in delight as her smile beamed at us.

"Ah my bairns. All three of you?"

Kira said nothing, she simply nodded, taking only a second to sideways glance at Misty and I. Looking at each other then back to Grandmother, Misty and I also nodded. Grandmother waved her arms and whistled to gain every ones attention once again.

"Right, you lot. Away hame. Our three volunteers will seek the vessel. Once we have that we can form a plan to get rid of this evil bugger for good. I told grandfather, I said, we need shot of that one before he causes any trouble, but oh no! He said binding him would be punishment enough. Look where that plan took us! But still, I miss the old codger. Oh well, there's plenty time to see him again once we're done with this. Hopefully this time we can avoid the bloodshed and the tears. My heart tears every time I think of the songs of pain they wailed." A pained expression gripped Grandmothers face as the memory of that day replayed in her ancient memory. The crowd slowly dispersed until there were only the 4 of us standing by the stone.

Author links:

Facebook: https://www.facebook.com/TValisAuthor

Facebook group:
https://www.facebook.com/groups/1172438982820141/

Twitter: @TValisbooks

Goodreads:
https://www.goodreads.com/author/show/15395274.T_Valis

Instagram: https://www.instagram.com/t.valis.author/

Amazon: http://www.amazon.co.uk/Tessa-Valis/e/B01I46SF08/ref=ntt_dp_epwbk_0

Made in the USA
Charleston, SC
19 September 2016